Taking on Midnight

by

Jane Drager

Midnight Sky Series, Book 3

Cover Art by *The Wild Rose Press, Inc.*

The Wild Rose Press, Inc.
PO Box 708
Adams Basin, NY 14410-0708
Visit us at www.thewildrosepress.com

Publishing History
First Edition, 2025
Trade Paperback Print ISBN 978-1-5092-6374-5
Digital ISBN 978-1-5092-6375-2

Midnight Sky Series
Published in the United States of America

Dedication

To Betty, fellow author and sister, avid reader and best friend. We might have distance between us, but we will always be close.

Chapter One

With arms crossed over his muscled chest, Logan Greene stood in the shadow of the stairwell while watching the scene on the martial arts mat unfold. Two big bruisers outweighed their instructor by a hundred pounds or more, and combined, they presented a formidable challenge. One of the guys looked as if he snacked on steroids. He also sported a stupid smirk on a face with one too many fight scars. Neither of the men were agents at Monroe Security Solutions, but word got around to the New Jersey police precincts about a good-looking martial arts instructor and the classes she offered. Steroid Guy was about to discover his two hundred and fifty pounds were no match for a three-time black belt expert.

The boss, Robert Monroe, hired Skylar Dawson to train the agents employed in his security firm. Her easy schedule worked well until word spread like wildfire. The demand for her expertise forced Sky to increase her twice-a-week sessions to three days a week. She refused to do any more.

And why would she? She inherited a profitable boardinghouse from her late aunt plus an estate worth a ton of money. In essence, she had no need to leave the comfort of her home. Yet, somehow, Monroe convinced her to teach as a way of staying in shape. Smiling to himself, Logan shook his head. Her shape was fine just the way she was. Whether she agreed to teach or not was of no consequence. Skylar was the love of his life. He just wished the boss would change his mind about her being agent material.

Not that she wasn't a good agent. She proved herself on her last case. Her skill as a bartender had placed her in an Atlantic City lounge where she changed from simple observer to active participant. He was on pins and needles the entire time, but she did well. He preferred working with her more than any other female agent in the firm. She had a brain inside that beautiful head, and her ninja skills were unsurpassed. But she didn't want to be an agent. She'd rather stay here on the mat and teach.

Uh-oh. Steroid Guy must have said something derogatory. Sky's gaze narrowed, and her faint smile slipped. Not a good sign. Bruiser was about to—

Moving like a flash of light, Sky clamped onto the big man's kimono and flipped him over her shoulder.

The man slammed onto the mat with a loud "*oomph*" and shook the entire building.

Logan cringed. Despite the soft mat, any forcible impact had to hurt, but her maneuver always flattened an oversized ego. Otherwise, the man would never learn. So often, guys sauntered in with a huge chip on their shoulder and all because their captain ordered them to learn some martial arts. One simple demonstration of her speed and agility was enough to knock the chip clear across the room and put a little humility into the poor schmucks. Women cops were more compliant. They wanted to learn. Then, they could surprise a jackass like Steroid Guy. Chuckling, Logan headed to the locker room to change into workout gear.

Two years ago, he had misgivings about joining Monroe Security. He left a career as an undercover cop with the New Jersey State Police to become a security agent. His fellow officers told him he'd lost his mind. But, he had to admit he made the best decision of his life. His undercover days were numbered. He understood the odds of survival decreased with each year. On several occasions, he almost lost his life. What good was putting the years in for retirement if he wasn't alive to enjoy himself? So far, working for Monroe challenged every aspect of his cop training. Most jobs involved surveillance and protection services for the ultra-rich, but occasionally—like last year's case—he and Sky went undercover to destroy a murderous enterprise. Monroe paid well, and health benefits exceeded all expectations. The staff, while still small at twelve employees, was fully vetted and the best in their field—like Sky.

Monroe had also worked for the New Jersey State Police. After retiring, he went full-steam ahead into his already-established business. With the need for more space, he had gutted an old warehouse in Newfield, New Jersey, constructed offices on the first floor— along with his personal living quarters, built a firing range in a soundproofed basement, and equipped the second floor with the finest exercise equipment on the market. In the center was Sky's large mat. The far right end contained a small sparring ring, along with a variety of punching bags. Against the walls were a variety of weights and exercise machines. At the opposite end were male and female locker rooms complete with showers, a sitting area with sofa and chairs, and a refrigerator full of cold water bottles. Today, Logan aimed for the weights. This way, he could work out and still watch Sky in action.

Two hours later and fresh from a shower, Logan exited the locker room to see Sky sitting on the sofa and playing with her cell phone.

She looked up and smiled.

His heart thudded against his rib cage. Damn, she was a beautiful woman. Her jet-black hair along with killer, black lashes accented a pair of crystal-blue eyes. Every smile changed those crystals into sparkling gems. She never wore makeup and kept her hair cropped short in a no-muss, no-fuss style. How he fell for a woman so opposite his previous preference for long-haired beauties surprised him, but fall he did. He loved Skylar Dawson, and on their last case together, he told her so. She had yet to express her feelings, and he never mentioned the *L* word again. Deep down, he suspected she loved him but couldn't say the words.

Admittedly, he and Sky had an unusual relationship. Friends with benefits, for sure, but they never dated. She lived in Woodstown, New Jersey—a town about twenty minutes away. He lived in Newfield—five minutes from Monroe Security. Both towns were in the southern part of the state and a far cry from the horrendous traffic up north. When he wasn't on assignment, he stayed with Sky a couple times a week, either at his place or hers. He would love for her to move in with him, but he rented a small, one-room apartment. Sure, with the salary he received, he could spring for a three-bedroom condo, but why would she move? She inherited a nice-sized rancher from her late aunt. She never asked him to move in, and he would in a heartbeat. In a way, her reluctance to take their relationship to the next level bothered him. But he swallowed the hurt—because he loved her. Besides, when they first met, he was the one who gave the no-commitment, career-first speech, but joining Monroe's firm changed his mindset. He wasn't sure she believed him yet. Clearing his throat, he approached the sofa and smiled. "You waiting for me?"

"Of course." Standing, she slipped her phone into a rear pocket. "We're heading to your place."

The comment rushed all his blood south. Sex with this woman was a phenomenal experience. Her martial arts skills kept her body limber, and despite muscles developed from workouts, her body was soft to the touch. Stepping into her space, he wrapped his arms around her, tugged her close, and kissed those luscious lips. He had a hell of a time resisting the urge to get down and dirty on the sofa. Instead, he lifted his head and gazed into her beautiful eyes. "We'll grab takeout along the way. Any preferences?"

Simultaneously, their phones chirped with a text message.

Frowning, Logan pulled his phone from his jeans rear pocket and read. "Monroe wants to see me."

She retrieved her phone and glanced at the screen. "Me, too." While biting her bottom lip, she slipped the device into a side pocket.

The woman never carried a purse. Depending on the season, she wore either cargo pants or shorts for the array of deep pockets. Black, of course. She wore no other color, and he was okay with her choice. She was always sexy as hell. He extended a hand. "Shall we go?"

"Hold on." She clamped onto the front of his T-shirt and tugged him against her, then plastered her lips onto his.

The woman was downright cruel. She knew full well how the feel of her body affected him. Heat and desire shot through his veins faster than water through a hose. The only thing stopping him from plastering her to the wall was Monroe's text message.

She released him and grinned. "Let's go see what the boss wants."

"I can't."

Brows high, she stopped. "Why not?"

"I need a few minutes." He tugged on his belt. Not like it helped much. His jeans were a tad too tight—thanks to her.

She glanced down. "Oh." Sighing, she tsked. "It's a shame to waste it."

Damn woman. He was so tempted, but relieving a hard-on at work would be unacceptable behavior for two Monroe employees. Growling, he grabbed onto her hand and squeezed. "I'll get you for this. Let's go."

****

Skylar couldn't shake the antsy feeling flowing through her body. The last time she and Logan received a simultaneous text, she found herself immersed in a deadly fight for survival. She didn't view herself as agent material and told Monroe, in no uncertain terms, to leave her alone. For the most part, he listened. Somehow, she suspected things were about to change.

As he neared the stairwell to the first floor, Logan released her hand and waved her to proceed.

Mr. Gallant. Always the gentlemen. Because she couldn't stop herself, she slipped her hand behind his neck and drew his lips to meet hers. His longish brown hair was still damp from the shower, and he doused himself with the woodsy cologne that made her knees weak. He was the nicest and kindest man she had ever met—and a great kisser. If she ever had the chance, she'd thank his parents.

Oh, sure. Who was she kidding? The probability of being introduced to his family was about as likely as winning a mega-lottery. She and Logan didn't date. They slept together. He had no reason to take her home to mom and dad. Yes, all right, last year, he said he loved her, but he hadn't mentioned the word since. She was perfectly satisfied with their relationship's uncomplicated status quo.

Usually, his kiss shut down her brain and turned her knees into rubber bands, but not this time. She had way too much on her mind to enjoy him. Releasing his neck, she caught his gaze. "Monroe wants me for another assignment, doesn't he?" As if coming here three times a week wasn't enough. No, the man wanted her full time and as an agent.

Logan rested a hand on her shoulder and squeezed. "I don't have any idea what he wants, Sky, but I must remind you to never reveal your martial arts skills when a client is present. Let Bob mention it first."

She harrumphed. "One of these days, I'll walk in wearing my kimono. No way in hell could he explain that." She never liked all this secret agent stuff. Logan, with his extensive background as an undercover cop, was a natural and could take on the persona of whatever the role required. She'd met him while he impersonated a disabled gardener at the boardinghouse she inherited from her great-aunt. His exaggerated limp fooled everyone, as did his use of the metal crutch. But underneath the scruff, he cleaned up beautifully and made for some nice eye candy. He had a pair of copper-colored eyes that reminded her of fine ale. His light brown hair was long enough for a woman's fingers, and his six-foot-two frame was perfect for her five-foot-eight height. He had muscles like rocks, and making love with him was an experience unlike any man she'd enjoyed.

On the other hand, she hadn't an iota of acting skills. Her last case required the expertise of a bartender, which so happened to be her profession before her inheritance. Really, she should ignore Monroe's text, walk straight out the front door, hop on her motorcycle, and relish the beautiful spring day. It was early April and...*aw, crap.* Come to think of it, her last case occurred in April, exactly one year ago. *Now, I'm suspicious.* Once reaching the first floor, she glanced left toward the front office.

Vittoria Carbone, the office manager, busily stuffed papers into a filing cabinet. Her beehive hairdo gave the illusion of height, but really, the woman couldn't even reach the top drawer. Smiling over her shoulder, she waved.

While Monroe played the father figure to everyone on staff, Vicki fell into the grandmother role. Sky never had a grandparent. As a child, she was uprooted from her Philadelphia home to a small Chicago suburb, and she grew up without a clue as to the relatives on both sides. She found out much later how the family shunned her Irish father because he married a non-Catholic woman, and her mother had no other family. The inheritance from her great-aunt came as a total surprise, but her aunt—like her father—was also shunned by the family.

"Ready, Sky?"

Hell, no, she wasn't ready. Vicki still being in the front office meant Monroe's summons was not a staff meeting. Déjà vu swept through her, and she peered down the hall toward Monroe's open office door. Then, looking over her shoulder, she stared longingly at the front entrance. *So tempting*. She sucked in a calming breath. "Let's get this over with."

Chapter Two

Skylar stepped into Monroe's spacious office and instantly regretted not following through with her earlier idea to run out the front door. Why in the world didn't she listen to her inner voice? She could have been halfway to Logan's place or, better yet, at a fast-food establishment, stuffing her face. Instead, she approached Monroe who stood in front of his desk with a smaller, slightly rounded man alongside. A visitor in Monroe's office meant a client, and she seldom met customers except in passing. She gritted her teeth.

Both men turned their heads as Sky and Logan entered.

Another bad sign.

She liked Monroe. He was the father figure she no longer had. But geez, why was he so determined to turn her into an agent? Well, maybe *determined* wasn't the right word. Nudged would be his style. He said she had the potential to become a great agent. Sure, if she didn't mind dying before her time. She envisioned herself living to a ripe old age, thank you very much.

Logan placed a hand in the small of her back and urged her forward.

Rotating her head, she shot him a glare, but he wasn't looking her way. His focus remained on the occupants in the room. Sighing, she approached the two men.

No matter where in the building Monroe stood, he easily dominated a room. At six-foot-four with a fullback's shape, he towered over everyone. He had no neck, sharp gray eyes that pierced into a person's soul, and gray hair in crew-cut style. He always wore a dark suit jacket with dark trousers and white shirt. The tie he discarded on his first day of early retirement from the New Jersey State Police. Because of his height, he was one of the few men who forced her to crane her neck to meet his gaze.

The man standing next to Monroe had this teddy bear appearance with brown hair and eyes and dressed in a brown suit a size too small for his girth. The guy was probably in his late thirties and, in her mind, resembled a man who sat behind a desk all day, munching on potato chips.

Smiling, Monroe waved them forward. "Midnight, Logan, come in. I want you to meet Donald Brookson."

Oh, bloody hell. Monroe used her undercover name of Midnight Sky. She should turn on her heel and storm out. The damn man was up to something, and guaranteed, she wouldn't like it. After giving her boss a one-eyed glare, she shifted her gaze to the rotund man and forced a smile.

Brookson returned the smile and extended his hand. "Midnight is an unusual name."

She shook his outstretched hand, which, surprisingly, sported some hard calluses. "I had unusual parents." Not really, but the explanation was plausible. The nickname, Midnight Sky, originated in Chicago when she worked late hours in a corner-street bar. For safety reasons, she, along with the drink servers, never gave out their real names. Corner bars weren't known for attracting high-class patrons.

With the formalities of introductions over, Monroe waved her and Logan toward the sofa. "Let's sit."

No, she'd rather be on her way to Logan's place to have glorious sex with the man.

Logan grasped her elbow and nudged her toward the sofa.

Damn him. He knew she was about to bolt. Clenching her teeth, she settled on the plush leather sofa—at a respectable distance from her man, of course.

Barely hiding a smile, Monroe turned both leather wingback chairs in front of his desk to face the sofa.

Being so big, the boss handled the heavy pieces of furniture like they were beach chairs. If he was smart, he could buy two additional wingbacks and keep them near the sofa. The office was certainly big enough.

Before sitting, Brookson unbuttoned his straining suit jacket, then flopped onto the cushion. The air whooshed out.

The poor man had dark circles surrounding a pair of tired eyes, as if he hadn't slept in days. He had tanned skin, which surprised her. Donald Brookson resembled a man who spent all of his time indoors, but his skin color explained the calluses on his hands if he enjoyed gardening or some other outdoor activity. She shot a quick glance at Logan.

As usual, her lover boy couldn't hide his excitement at the prospect of a new case. He leaned slightly forward with his sparkling gaze shifting between the two men. His body language all but screamed at Monroe to get on with the details. She'd seen the look so many times she had to fight not to roll her eyes.

Seriously, though, the setup was a bit too familiar for her liking. The last time she sat across from a client, she got suckered into a case where her ninja training played a crucial role. She'd rather not repeat the experience.

Monroe slipped onto the adjacent wingback and cleared his throat. "I asked you two here to listen to Mr. Brookson's problem. It's a trifle out of the ordinary but perfect for two of my well-suited agents." He shot Sky a pointed look.

How did he know she'd rather put her hands over her ears and start singing? She should do it just to embarrass him.

After a cough that rattled his chest, Donald Brookson shifted his gaze between Logan and Sky. "A year ago, last winter, my wife, Rachael, was attacked by a former family friend, Madeline Harris. To give you some history, Maddie and I grew up together, and we worked summers at my grandparents' lodge in Mount Pocono. I have since inherited the resort, and Maddie was convinced we would marry."

Narrowing his gaze, he waggled a pudgy finger. "I never promised nor initiated any type of romantic interest. I never called her my girlfriend nor had we ever gone on dates—except for a few school dances. Three years ago, I met Rachael. We married with a small ceremony, and things went well until Maddie attacked Rachael. Jealousy was the culprit. Somehow, Maddie's brother convinced her to go for counseling. Maddie signed into a behavior unit affiliated with our nearby hospital and, from what we heard, was doing well. Two weeks ago, Maddie walked out and hasn't been seen since."

A missing person case? *Seriously*? Why in the world would Monroe consider her? Well, okay, she shouldn't jump to conclusions. Obviously, the teddy bear had more to say. She glanced at Monroe, but the damn man kept his gaze on his small notebook. Last Christmas, she'd bought him a digital notepad with the hope of forcing him into the twenty-first century. The gesture flopped. He was a true pen-and-paper man.

Logan raised a hand. "Was Rachael seriously injured?"

"No. Just shaken. The attack was out of the blue and took Rachael off guard." Brookson crossed one leg over the other, but being on the chubby side, his leg slipped off. His foot hit the floor with a thud. Grimacing, he shifted on the seat. "If you're not familiar with the Mount Pocono area, then you don't know how extensive the woods are. My lodge, Chadbury Lodge, is nestled between two state parks. Maddie knows her way through the forests as well as I do. The police can't find her, and Maddie's brother, Wendell, is on the alert. Wendell has worked at the resort for years. He lives in a small bungalow about five miles away." He coughed with another loose rattle.

Hopefully, Brookson wasn't about to give her bubonic plague and force her to die a horrible death. Health aside, the poor guy squirmed on the seat, as if he couldn't find a comfortable spot for his tush. Then, he'd fidget a leg and stop. Maybe the need to hire a private security firm worried him. Monroe's services weren't cheap, and Brookson didn't look like he was rolling in dough—no pun intended.

Brookson sighed. "The police do not consider Maddie a dangerous criminal. We assume Maddie escaped to harm Rachael, but without an actual threat being made, the authorities can't do anything until the assault is done. Our police chief suggested private security and gave me the name of a local outfit, Guardem Guys. Rachael protested, of course. She compromised with the hiring of two men but would only allow one man per twelve-hour shift. They rotate. One man sleeps while the other patrols the outside perimeter of the house. They reside in the gardener's cottage toward the edge of our property." He held up a hand. "I know what you're about to say. One man can't watch both front and back at the same time, but Rachael wouldn't listen to reason."

Yeah, well, maybe Rachael felt capable of handling Madeline this time around—unless Monroe planned to have Sky teach Rachael martial arts. She sure as hell hoped not. Sky kept her expression neutral. "What about cameras?"

Brookson shook his head. "We have no cameras anywhere on the property. Rachael and I discussed this and agreed our guests would not appreciate an intrusion to their privacy."

Logan waved a finger in a circle. "Not even around your own house?"

Grimacing, he rubbed the nape of his neck. "None." Dropping his hand, he met Logan's gaze. "My big problem is Rachael's pregnancy. She's seven months along with our first child."

Geez, he should have mentioned the pregnancy in the beginning. Now, Sky understood the need for protection but not Rachael's reluctance.

Brookson tugged on his shirt collar. "I had a long talk with our police chief. He suggested a covert surveillance firm and recommended Monroe Security. So, here I am." He coughed again with the same death rattle. After clearing his throat, he smirked. "Sorry about this. I quit smoking when Rachel announced her pregnancy."

Still leaning forward, Logan rested his elbows on his knees. "Was the pregnancy the reason for Maddie's sudden disappearance?"

Brookson nodded. "Wendell thinks so. Before she vanished, Maddie commented about stopping the pregnancy."

And the police didn't consider that comment a viable threat? Gasping, Sky placed a palm over her heart. "She wants to kill the baby?"

"So, it seems. Rachael is fully aware of Maddie's intentions and still refuses to allow more security onto the compound. She swears she's not afraid." He tugged on his ear. "The lodge is scheduled to open on June first. We're fully booked. Maddie needs to be found before opening day in six weeks."

Did Monroe expect Sky and Logan to tramp around in the woods in search of Madeline? Was he nuts? Skylar Dawson and nature were perfect strangers, and she'd be the first to admit she didn't know a damn thing about hiking a trail.

After crossing his legs, Monroe shifted his gaze between his two employees. "This is where you two come in. Because of Rachael's resistance, both of you need to stay completely undercover. Logan, you will be a temporary hire to help prepare the cabins and grounds for opening day. You, Midnight, will be Mrs. Brookson's short-term housekeeper. With luck, Madeline will surface before too long."

Sky groaned. Monroe was out of his mind. She wasn't a domestic goddess with her own home and only cleaned when the dust resembled radioactive fallout. How in the world could she tolerate six weeks? Besides, Monroe assumed she would accept the assignment. She hadn't agreed to go…yet.

Brookson gave her a sad smile. "Rachael can't do much cleaning anymore. She's too uncomfortable. She still likes to cook, though. So, you won't have to worry about feeding us."

Thank God. If they depended on Sky's cooking, they would starve to death. Come to think of it, Brookson could stand to lose a few dozen pounds.

While tugging on his suit jacket, Brookson shifted on the cushion. "Our resort housekeeping manager, Mrs. Sanchez, sends a girl over once a week to clean, but I want Rachael protected for more than a few hours. Wendell and I have been driving her to wherever she wants to go, but with opening day approaching, we'll be too busy to continue. You'll take over." He met Sky's gaze. "I'll be forcing you on her, Ms. Sky. Rachael won't think too kindly of having you in our home."

Great. Conflict right off the bat. What else could he say to make her refuse the assignment? Truthfully, she had no idea why she sat here like some bump on a log. Monroe had other more experienced female agents who could easily play housekeeper. She cringed as a thought entered her mind. "Am I expected to sleep there, too?"

Brookson snorted, then coughed. "No. You and your fiancé will use one of the cabins. Mr. Monroe stipulated that I keep you within the compound. Since you're considered temporary, no one will question your accommodations."

Fiancé? She shot her gaze at Logan who merely cocked a brow. She glared at Monroe.

The boss man slowly shook his head.

She didn't like where this conversation was going. Monroe mapped out the entire assignment without asking if she wanted to participate. Fiancé? Housekeeper? *What the hell*? She might explode with all the questions on her tongue.

Brookson cleared his throat. "I should give you a little background on the resort. We have a total of one hundred and forty acres, of which two-thirds are wooded. We're known for our hiking trails along with various water sports on the lake. As I said, we open June first, and our traditional closing date is November first. This pattern was established many years ago by my grandparents." Wincing, he tugged on an ear. "Lately, though, Rachael has been pushing for a year-round resort. I don't know if her pregnancy hormones brought out this argument, but I strongly disagreed with the change. Financially, we make enough to be comfortable. To appease Rachael, I might expand our twenty cabins to twenty-five, but I won't consider the option until after the baby is born." He turned to Monroe. "Did I cover everything?"

"Yes, but if I have additional questions, I'll give you a call." Monroe stood and extended a hand. "I'll let you know our start date. You, of course, should inform me immediately if Madeline is found."

Brookson stood and shook Monroe's hand. "I will."

Slapping the rotund man on the shoulder, Monroe

escorted him to the door. "Remember, not a word of this visit to anyone—not even your wife. Secrecy is our best offense. Explain their presence as you would any seasonal employee."

"I understand." Then, with a brief nod at Sky and Logan, he left the office.

When Monroe returned, he zeroed in on Sky. "Before you say anything, hear me out." He returned to his seat and crossed his legs. "Let me explain why I chose you for this assignment."

Folding her arms across her chest, she huffed. "You're lucky I didn't walk out." After a heavy sigh, she shook her head. "All right, I'm listening. Tell me why you think I'd make a good housekeeper."

Chapter Three

Skylar should get up and walk out. No matter what Monroe said, he couldn't possibly have a good excuse for involving her. *Dear Lord Almighty*. The man cast her in the role of housekeeper. He was out of his mind. Any number of other female agents were available, more skilled, and possibly better with all the domestic stuff. She shot her boss an evil-eyed look, hoping she sent the message of her displeasure. Unfortunately, her attempt to make a point probably resembled something stuck in her eye.

"I'll explain everything." Monroe leaned forward and shifted his gaze between them. "Bear in mind, what I'm about to tell you came from Wendell Harris, Madeline's brother, who, in turn, warned Brookson. This warning is what prompted Donald to seek additional security for his wife." He sat back. "Because time is a factor, I'll be sending you two in before I can confirm all the details of his story." After crossing one leg over the other, he tapped his little notebook on his knee.

"Before the incident with Rachael, Madeline Harris was a yoga instructor who worked at a studio in one of the popular honeymoon resorts in Mount Pocono. After her attack on Rachael and the subsequent publicity, she got fired. According to Wendell, his sister wanted revenge in the worst way. To insure Rachael's safety,

Wendell secured his guns to keep them out of Maddie's hands. Undeterred, Maddie gathered a bunch of martial arts books and studied them religiously. Wendell has no idea what level of skill Maddie obtained, but her yoga limberness combined with martial arts makes her a potential threat to a pregnant Rachel."

Oh, brother. Now, she understood Monroe's request for her presence and the use of her code name. Martial arts videos of Skylar Dawson were all over the Internet. When he deleted one, another would pop up within a few days. But a learn-by-the-book student of martial arts wouldn't have the discipline required to execute some of the intricate moves. Still, Sky had met several such individuals who entered competitions. Some were quite good. "I get it, Bob, but that doesn't mean I'm accepting. I am the world's worst housekeeper." She could have solved her dilemma by getting a few of the female agents on the mat more often. Pamela O'Connor had the potential, but Monroe wouldn't sacrifice his Information Technologist for a mission like housekeeping.

Sitting forward, Logan held up a finger. "Two weeks is a long time to be missing. Maddie's got to have shelter somewhere. A friend, perhaps, or another relative."

Monroe nodded. "According to Brookson, Wendell is her only living relative. As for friends? I asked Donald to talk to Wendell. Maybe he can give us some names, but you're right, Logan. She needs shelter and food."

Sky raised a hand. "What if Maddie took off for parts unknown? You know, figured her revenge on Rachael was a waste of time."

"I won't dismiss the possibility, but until I dig up more facts, I'm sending you two in." He shifted his gaze to Logan. "Your job will allow you to be all over the one hundred and forty acres of property. Your boss is a man by the name of Gabe Rumfeld. He came with the lodge when Brookson inherited, as did head of housekeeping, Barbara Sanchez." He shifted his gaze to Sky. "Your job—"

With a raised palm, she stopped him. "If I go, you mean."

He cocked his head. "Rachael needs you, Sky. We don't know how skilled Madeline is. She could harm Rachael before anyone has a chance to help. Think of the baby."

Sky rolled her eyes. He was laying the guilt on thick. "She has guards."

"True. One guard is always watching the house. I'm sure the two men overlap from time to time, but they need to sleep and eat. Thankfully, Brookson saw fit to keep them close by housing them in the gardener's cottage."

Logan coughed. "Some gardener's cottages can be pretty far from the main house."

"True." Frowning, he tapped his little notebook on his knee. "I sent Pam and Vanessa on a scouting mission. From the satellite views, Chadbury Lodge is isolated and surrounded by woods, but nothing beats a slow drive-by or walk-through. Like I said, time is a factor. With you inside the house, Sky, Rachael will receive the protection she needs." Uncrossing his legs, he dropped his foot to the floor and flipped through his little notebook. "Brookson said he'd email me a map of his compound. With twenty unoccupied cabins, Maddie could hide in any one."

After grabbing a silver pen from his breast pocket, he jotted a quick note, closed his little book, then shifted his gaze from Sky to Logan. "I hate like hell to send you in blind, but I don't have a choice. I've done one other case where I couldn't gather the intel first. Everything turned out okay, but I chewed nails the entire time." He pursed his lips. "The girls should return by Saturday night. We'll meet here on Sunday to discuss their findings. I'll call with a time. Any questions?"

The *girls* were two grown women with extensive experience in their fields. Pamela was their resident IT expert while Vanessa Moore—aka Cracker—was a phenomenal safe cracker and lock picker. Gaze narrowed, Sky leaned forward and drummed her fingers on her knees. "I have one question. What's with the fiancé statement?"

Grinning, he slipped his notebook into his shirt's breast pocket. "Everyone around here knows you two are a couple. You don't have to fake a relationship or pretend to be all lovey-dovey. In order to keep both of you on the premises, what better way than to go in as an engaged couple?" Gaze twinkling, he used the chair's armrests to stand. "I'll make sure you have a nice engagement ring."

"Don't bother." She fell back onto the cushion. "If I agree to go, I can use my late aunt's ring. It's still in her jewelry box."

Her stomach churned. Now, why in thunder had she mentioned her aunt's ring? She sounded like she decided to participate. Besides, trying on another woman's engagement ring might bring her bad luck.

Superstition and all. She heard the saying once…somewhere. *Oh, hell.*

****

At the prospect of working with Sky again, Logan battled with a strange mixture of pleasure and apprehension. On the Atlantic City case, he and Sky worked well together, and she handled tense situations without a problem. She possessed a quick wit and even quicker reflexes. Her biggest problem was self-doubt. Unlike the majority of Monroe's staff, she had no formal police training. Her firearms education proceeded at a snail's pace, primarily because of her aversion toward guns. But over time, she would gain the necessary confidence to feel like an equal by his side—provided she didn't out-and-out refuse to participate. Leaning back against the sofa cushions, Logan lifted his head to make eye contact with his standing boss. "How thoroughly were the woods searched?"

The big man shrugged. "Brookson couldn't answer that question. I doubt the local cops went through a lot of trouble. Brookson has no actual proof of Maddie's intentions, and people make threats against others all the time. I'll make a bet the cops made a few drive-bys and nothing more." Clamping onto the wingback chair, he repositioned the piece to its spot in front of the desk. "I'll give the police chief a call and see what he says. If he recommended us, he might know me or knows someone who used our services. In either case, I want to thank him for the referral." He returned to the second chair and leaned on the back. "I know the area fairly well. A few years ago, I bought myself a fishing cabin over near Bushkill Falls. I have the girls staying there while they do a little recon. If my guess is right, the driving distance is about forty minutes away from Chadbury Lodge, and yes, the woods are very thick. If Maddie knows her way around, she might take shelter in an abandoned cabin or building."

With every assignment, Monroe dug deep for facts to keep his agents safe. He sent personnel to map out an area—like Pam and Cracker. Then, Pam scoured the Internet for discrepancies in a client's story. Both could be done over the weekend, but as far as uncovering long-buried secrets? That part took time and a lot of digging. The uncovered secrets always turned the case onto its head. Right now, he and Sky would go in with general knowledge, and that fact scared him— especially with a still-novice like Sky as a partner.

Sky raised a hand. "Why is Maddie taking two weeks to confront Rachael? What is she waiting for?"

Still leaning onto the wingback, Monroe slipped one hand into his trouser pocket. "I agree, Sky. Something about this case sounds off. Usually, a person on a vendetta doesn't wait around for the victim to surround themselves with protection. I could be sending you two into a trap."

Cringing, Sky bit her lip. "You think Brookson is lying?"

"No, not at all. He's truly worried about his wife." Monroe grabbed the second wingback and placed it in front of the desk. "Nothing would please me more than to have an extra week to gather the facts, but hearsay or not, I can't leave Rachael Brookson unprotected." He faced Sky. "I want you on this case, Sky. Madeline Harris has martial arts training. You are the most qualified to handle her, but I'm not forcing you. If you agree to accompany Logan, be here on Sunday for a briefing. Right now, I'll say early afternoon, but I'll let you know." He strode behind his desk. "Logan, talk to her. And, Sky, have you tried on your aunt's engagement ring?"

She started. "No. Why?"

He raised a brow. "From what Fay told me, your aunt was a small, little thing. Her ring might not pass over your knuckle."

"Oh." She held up her left hand, fingers stretched. "You might be right. I'll let you know."

Logan almost laughed. Sky's knuckles could break through thick wood. No dainty hands on this woman.

"All right, both of you get out of here. I'll text with a time on Sunday." Monroe shifted some papers on the desk.

Standing, Logan turned to Sky and extended a hand. "Come on, beautiful. Let's grab something to eat. Follow me to the Malaga Diner." He could see she teetered on the edge of a decision. Somehow, Logan must convince Sky that no other female agent would do.

****

After hearing Monroe's little speech, Skylar felt her stomach recoil at Logan's suggestion to eat. Earlier, she had acquired a sizable appetite from tossing those two big bruisers around the mat. But now? Their meeting killed any craving for food. She had some serious doubts about accepting another assignment. Monroe wanted her for a protection detail and, of all things, as a housekeeper. *What a joke*! Maybe she should forget the diner, stay on her motorcycle, and shoot straight down to Woodstown for the sanctuary of her cute, little rancher. *Ah, well*. With the hope her appetite returned, she followed Logan to the Malaga Diner in a town called—what else?—Malaga. She'd eaten at the small establishment several times. The food was typical diner fare and certainly better than anything waiting in her refrigerator.

The hostess escorted them to a booth by the windows, which gave them a clear view of the busy intersection of Routes 40 and 47, two popular shore routes. Even though the time of year was April, and shore traffic hadn't started yet, one would never know it from the flow of cars zipping through the traffic lights.

The noon hour had passed two hours ago. Even so, the diner remained busy. Most of the booths by the windows were full, along with several of the tables in the center of the floor. A lot of working men in coveralls sat on the counter stools, and food servers hustled back and forth. Coffee was the predominate aroma, along with pancake syrup. Like many diners in South Jersey, they served breakfast all day long.

After removing her lightweight jacket, Sky perused the multi-page menu. She never understood why so many establishments had menus as thick as a book. Sections for breakfast, lunch, and dinner, children's, vegan, low calorie, light fare, and night fare. *Seriously*? She slapped the book shut. Looking at the menu was a complete waste of time. She knew precisely what she wanted—a bacon, lettuce, and tomato sandwich on toast with french fries and coffee.

The food server arrived with pad and pencil in hand. She was an older woman with a pencil holding up a messy bun. "Hi. I'm Beth. What can I get you two?"

Sky gave her order.

While writing, Beth smiled. "Wow, you're easy. And you, sir?"

"I'll have a double order of chicken Parmesan, coleslaw, house salad, and two sides of pasta. To wash it down, coffee and orange juice." He grinned at the woman. "And don't forget the basket of rolls."

Sky stared. "Didn't you eat today?" Geez, the man probably skipped breakfast.

Beth released a deep chuckle. "He's ordering a hungry man's lunch, honey. I'll be right back with the coffee."

Alone again, Logan patted his stomach. "I'm empty and need a refill."

Oh, good grief. He made himself sound like an automobile. The next thing she'd hear would be a reference to a dipstick. *Ugh.*

Beth returned with a coffee carafe and Logan's juice. Pouring into their uprighted cups, she smiled. "Your food will be ready in no time." Carafe in hand, she moved to the next table.

Sky sipped her coffee—black and strong, just the way she liked it. She lowered her cup to the table. "I suppose this is where you say my participation is critical for the case to succeed."

After sipping, he lowered his cup to the table, then met her gaze. "I have no particulars for argument, Sky. On the surface, this case seems straightforward. We help protect a pregnant woman from a jealous ex-girlfriend who so happens to know martial arts. If anything, you'll run interference and deter Maddie from getting close to Rachael."

"But holy cow, why a housekeeper? You know I open my front door and let Rita loose. She cleans my rancher like a whirlwind." Rita Garrett was a tenant at the manor. She had an obsessive-compulsive disorder for cleaning and kept the manor spotless. Once a month, Sky allowed her free rein inside her rancher.

"A housekeeper is the perfect excuse to put you inside with Rachael. Maddie can watch the one guard on duty and sneak in without him suspecting. If Maddie is good with her martial arts, she could seriously hurt, even kill, Rachael and the baby."

Sky waggled a finger. "Books do not teach the discipline involved to perform the maneuvers effectively. With what I've taught you so far, you could probably handle her."

After unwrapping his napkin-covered utensils, he leaned forward and met her gaze. "But I wouldn't be inside the house."

Oh, drat. He was right.

Beth arrived with a tray full of food and a stand to rest it. She slipped a large plate loaded with a BLT and fries in front of Sky. The remainder she placed in front of Logan, and his order filled the entire table. Last came a basket of rolls. Smiling at Logan, Beth winked. "Enjoy."

Quickly grabbing a roll, Logan slabbed on a hefty amount of butter.

Sky blinked. "Why don't you have some bread with your butter?" *Dear Lord.* He might clog his arteries in one sitting. "You never eat like this at my house." Well, really, she wasn't the world's greatest cook, but she created a few decent meals, just not enough to feed an army.

He stuffed the roll into his mouth, chewed, then swallowed. "I worked with weights while you threw those guys all over the mat. I'm hungry. You, of course, never even broke into a sweat." He dug into his chicken Parmesan.

If he ate like this every day, he'd be as big as a house. He already had muscles that made her drool. After lifting the toast to reposition the lettuce escaping from the sandwich, she smashed the pieces together and bit into her BLT. The flavors burst on her tongue. She loved crispy bacon, and the crunch reactivated her dormant appetite.

Logan downed his orange juice in two gulps, then smacked his lips. "What is different with this case is we're going in as a couple. That aspect, more than anything, eases my mind. We can stay in constant communication without raising suspicion."

Yes, a definite plus. On the Atlantic City case, she had to be careful about what she said and where. She hated all the covert stuff. So, if she could call Logan with a question, she'd feel a lot better. "But what if Maddie doesn't surface? How long do we continue our charade?"

Sitting back, he chewed with his gaze fixed on her face. "I can't answer that, Sky. If Maddie doesn't show before opening day on June first, then Monroe will need to devise another plan. Maddie could easily blend in with the guests who arrive to begin their vacation."

And Rachel would not deliver her baby until mid-June or later. No way in hell would Skylar Dawson play housekeeper for that long. The very notion gave her the heebie-jeebies.

Chapter Four

Skylar slept on her decision—in her own house—alone. She told Logan to let her be. He would only distract her with arguments about how much her martial arts were needed. As a woman with black belts in Jujutsu, Aikido, and Tai Chi, she could handle five big men at one time. Madeline Harris, with her book skills, wouldn't be much of a challenge. But if Sky learned one fact over the years, she should never underestimate an opponent. Truthfully, the housekeeping portion of the job worried her more. Sure, if necessary, she could polish up a storm or scrub a floor until the linoleum sparkled—when the mood hit, of course—but she had no idea how to *act* like a housekeeper. What if Rachael asked her to darn socks or—*God forbid*—iron the laundry clothes? She hadn't ironed in years, and whatever ripped was tossed in the trash. Wouldn't Rachael see her as a fraud?

By morning, after fits of restless sleep, Sky stood at her kitchen window with a cup of coffee in hand and stared at the gazebo in the yard. A few days ago, daffodils broke through the soil and spread their bright-yellow flowers to announce the arrival of spring. If the weather held, crocus would be next week, along with some red flowers whose name eluded her.

One of her tenants, Doreen Hashoff, loved tending the flowerbeds. In another two months, tulips would bloom, and Doreen planted a wide variety of colors.

Sky especially liked the black tulips, with deep purple a close second. She heaved a sigh and turned away from the window.

She hadn't come to a decision yet. All this covert stuff toyed with her confidence. From day one, Monroe wanted her as an agent. Why, she had no clue. Without asking, he'd volunteered her for this job and already introduced her to Brookson as Logan's fiancée. A change now might be awkward and make him look bad. And truthfully, could she let Logan go with another female agent, especially one who pretended to be his fiancée? She trusted Logan, and she also trusted the women on staff, but still…close quarters and all.

During their last case, Logan floored her by confessing his love. To this day, she had yet to tell him how she felt. A whole year had gone by, and he never mentioned the *L* word again. Maybe he hadn't meant it and made the statement because of the danger she faced. Back then, she could have said something to ease his mind. But she stayed silent. In her way of thinking, she was a coward. She faced a martial arts opponent without fear, but as for expressing her feelings for a man who'd become an important part of her life? The words always got stuck in her throat. Turning to the coffeemaker, she poured herself another cup.

What if Madeline's skills were more advanced than expected? No one actually knew her level of expertise, but years of yoga training would give her speed and limberness. She could hurt or even kill Logan. Rachael, of course, would be a sitting duck, and one calculated blow to Rachael's belly would kill the baby. Then, what? Under no circumstances would Sky let anyone get hurt. She *had* to be with Logan to stop Madeline. Faced with little choice, she called Monroe. "Okay, I'm in."

"Excellent. Did you try on the ring?"

First thing this morning, she had taken out the little black box. "It's too small."

"Yeah, I figured. I'll phone a friend of mine and text you with details."

Two years ago, when she first found the ring, she hadn't the vaguest idea what to do with it. Her late aunt was engaged, but not even her best friend, Fay, knew the man's identity. The diamond surrounded by small rubies was pretty, but as far as value? Sky hadn't a clue. Her knowledge of jewelry could fill a postcard and still have a lot of space left over.

Ten minutes later, her cell phone chirped with a text message. Picking it up from the kitchen table, she read.

—Expect Jeff Strausberg from Piscataway to arrive later this afternoon. He will size the ring. I told him to use the patio door.—

Wow. Even on a Saturday, Bob Monroe could make people hop.

By two in the afternoon, a knock sounded on the rear door.

Her late-aunt's rancher suited Sky with its not-too-big, not-too-small size. From the kitchen, she could see past the living room to the door leading onto a patio, where the silhouette of a man stood. After tossing the dishtowel onto the counter, she hurried to open the door. But, because Logan lectured her so many times, she peeked through the curtain first.

A short, middle-aged man fidgeted on the deck,

briefcase in hand. He had dark hair and a shadowed jaw and wore a dark suit and tie. Once the door opened, he studied her with shrewd eyes behind wire-rimmed glasses. "Skylar Dawson? Bob Monroe sent me. I'm Jeff Strausberg from Piscataway Jewelers."

The scope of Monroe's connections amazed her. Who would believe he had a jeweler on call? She forced a smile. "Yes, please, come in." She stepped aside. "I hope you didn't drop everything to come here?"

Entering, he smiled. "If it wasn't important, Bob wouldn't have asked."

"Well, come into the kitchen. The ring is on the table." After closing the door, she led the way, then picked up the ring box and opened the lid.

The man slipped his briefcase onto the table and pursed his lips. Handling the ring like a priceless jewel, he lifted it from the box. After raising his glasses to the top of his head, he reached into his pocket and placed an eyepiece against his right eye. Leaning closer to the window, he peered at the ring. Smiling, he removed the eyepiece. "This is a nice ring, Ms. Dawson."

"I inherited it from my late aunt. Can you tell me anything about it?"

"I can indeed. It's from the 1980s. The oval diamond is real and not synthetic. It's well cut and, judging from its size, is no more than two carats. The four rubies are of an excellent quality. They are the blood-red stones we acquire from South Africa. Years ago, this ring would have had a price tag of about five thousand dollars. Today, the ring would cost closer to twelve thousand. Let me see your finger."

Twelve thousand? She couldn't possibly wear such

expensive jewelry while scrubbing a toilet. Shaking herself, Sky held out her left hand as if she expected the man to kiss it.

He slipped the ring onto her finger until the band jammed at the knuckle. "Yes, this is two sizes too small. I'll cut the band and add a piece of silver to match. Then, you should be good to go." He tapped the watch on her left wrist. "This is also nice. May I?"

Hesitating for a few seconds, she eyed the little man. Her late father gave her the watch as a high school graduation present. She rarely removed it except to shower, but she was curious. She unfastened the clasp and handed it over.

Mr. Strausberg replaced the eyepiece and peered at the diamonds surrounding the watch face. Shaking his head, he smiled. "This is absolutely beautiful. It has a value of around fifteen hundred. If you'd like, I can clean this."

She had no idea what cleaning entailed, but she was about to find out. "I would like that, thank you." She figured the guy had to know what he was doing, right?

The jewelry man accomplished his tasks in record time. The perfectly-sized ring and watch sparkled after a cleaning with a pink solution. Then, he packed his case and left to return to Piscataway—wherever that was.

She stared at the glistening ring on her left hand. The extra piece added to the band could barely be seen, and now, with the diamond on her finger and sparkling, she had to admit the ring was gorgeous. She rarely wore jewelry, mainly because she rarely put on a dress. Rings were out of the question for a martial arts student, but she would keep this on her finger for the duration of the assignment. Until then, she replaced the ring into its little black box and left it on the kitchen table.

On Sunday morning, after a relaxing breakfast of toast and coffee, Sky stood in her bedroom and stared into her closet. She had no idea what to pack. She had never been to Mount Pocono in upstate Pennsylvania, but the area was always included in the nightly TV weather reports. At this time of year in Southern New Jersey, April temperatures hovered in the sixties, but every weather forecast listed Mount Pocono as having temps five to ten degrees lower. Should she take a winter coat?

Over the phone, she'd thrown the question at Logan and got a typical male response of "Pack what you want"—which was of no help whatsoever. She needed a female perspective and knew precisely who to ask. Fay Bartleson, the manor's manager and Sky's business partner, would know. Since Sky had to inform Fay about the assignment, she headed out the rancher's front door and crossed the yard to the manor's patio.

Even with the passage of time, she still marveled at the inheritance her great-aunt bequeathed. The boardinghouse and separate rancher sat on five acres of beautifully manicured grounds in a neighborhood on the outskirts of Woodstown, New Jersey. The income from the tenants kept her comfortable, but her aunt's investments placed Sky in a borderline-rich category. She didn't have to work, but she wasn't one to laze around and watch the world go by. To keep in shape, she accepted Monroe's offer to teach martial arts, not to become some secret agent. For the life of her, she couldn't understand why she let him talk her into this stuff.

After hopping onto the manor's patio, she stepped through the back door and into the large kitchen. She stopped. The room was empty. Breakfast had already been served, but lingering aromas of bacon and eggs filled the air and, of course, coffee. Fay always kept a fresh pot brewing for whoever wanted a cup. Meals were included with room rent, so tenants could eat or drink to their hearts' content. She debated filling a mug with Fay's notorious high-test, but without knowing where her partner was, Sky would rather not wander around the manor with a coffee cup in hand.

A vacuum cleaner whirled to life somewhere down the long hall leading to the front door. Seconds later, Fay entered the kitchen.

The woman had become like a mother to Sky. She was her late-aunt's best friend and housekeeper, and she knew so much more about running a boardinghouse than Sky could ever learn. Because of her knowledge, Fay was a natural for business partner.

Fay spotted Sky and smiled. "Hi, honey. I just chased Joe and Anthony onto the front porch so Rita could clean the living room."

Too-tall Joe Ryan and Anthony Powers were two tenants who loved to debate sports strategy. If a game played somewhere in the world and was televised, the two men sat in the living room and debated. Nothing and no one could get them off the sofa—except Rita Garrett, their OCD resident. Rita wouldn't just pass the sweeper on the floor. She'd do the drapes and upholstery, too. When finished, the room would sparkle and smell like lemon polish. "You can set Rita loose in the rancher sometime next week. I'm going away for a while."

Brown gaze narrowed behind a pair of eyeglasses, Fay arched a brow. "Another case?"

"Yup." She emphasized the *P*.

"You told me you wouldn't do that stuff anymore. Did you change your mind?"

Sky shrugged. "Monroe left me alone for a year, but he said this case requires my special services."

"In what way?" Shaking her head, she pointed to a kitchen chair. "Let's have a cup of coffee. You can fill me in."

When she settled at the large kitchen table with a hot cup in hand, Sky sighed. "I'll be leaving tomorrow morning for Mount Pocono."

"Oh, that might be nice." Fay took the seat on Sky's right. "I've been up in the area several times over the years, most recently at my niece's wedding. That was...oh, five years ago." She sipped her coffee.

"Tell me what it's like. I have no idea what to pack."

Lips pursed, Fay drummed her fingers on the tabletop. "I don't suppose you'll be doing anything fancy?"

Sky shook her head.

"Well, then, sweatshirts and slacks, for sure. The air gets quite cold at night. You should also take munchies and drinks. Most of the resorts are self-contained with restaurants and snack shops, mainly because they're isolated from towns, but they can be fairly expensive. Where are you staying?"

"A place called Chadbury Lodge and Resort."

Fay shook her head. "Never heard of it. It's probably one of the smaller, family-owned resorts.

Most of the larger hotels are geared toward honeymoon couples. They usually stay open all year."

"Not this place. It doesn't officially open until June first."

"Oh." Frowning, she chewed her upper lip. "You definitely need to take food. I'll make several casseroles to get you started. Will Logan be with you?"

"Yes. I wouldn't go alone." Her alone with nature? Never in a million years.

"Too bad you won't be at one of the honeymoon resorts. I hear quite a few have mirrors on the ceiling."

She wouldn't dare tell Fay she and Logan were going as an engaged couple. The woman would have the wedding planned before the case was closed. Although, on their last assignment, Logan's casino suite had a bathroom covered with mirrors. She found that a bit of a turn-on to see his cute butt popping up in the hot tub. She coughed.

Fay patted Sky's arm. "Don't worry, honey. Mount Pocono isn't known specifically as a honeymoon haven. It's become a popular recreational area. There are hiking trails and campgrounds with lakes for fishing and water sports. In winter, the bigger resorts offer ski packages. What role are you playing this time?"

"Well…" Sky shot Fay a glance over her coffee cup. "I'll be a housekeeper."

Fay jerked, blinked, then burst out laughing. After lifting her glasses to wipe the tears from her eyes, she grabbed hold of Sky's hand and squeezed. "Sorry, honey. I couldn't help myself." Releasing her hold, she snickered. "That is so funny."

She harrumphed. "I'm not that bad."

"I hope they don't expect you to cook."

"No, just clean." She considered herself a basic cook. Nothing fancy, minimal spices and herbs. Grilled cheese was a favorite, and she could cook spaghetti with jarred sauce. *See*? She wasn't totally inept.

Fay gasped. "You don't have to wear a maid's dress, do you?"

Holy crap! Wide-eyed, she stared at Fay. Monroe never mentioned if she was required to wear a uniform. Of course, she'd absolutely refuse. Standing, she swallowed the last of her coffee and rinsed the cup in the sink. "I better call Monroe. I am definitely not wearing a maid's outfit. He can send someone else on this job." Gad, she couldn't imagine wearing such a sexist piece of clothing. She shuddered. "If he tells me I can wear what I want, then I'll take your advice and do some food shopping. With luck, the cabin has a refrigerator." She placed the cup into the dishwasher. "I'll let you know."

"I'll start on some casseroles anyway. They freeze well. And we have several coolers in the basement. You should take one or two, just in case. You can always buy ice." She stood. "I'll make four casseroles. Think that's enough?"

The way Logan ate? *No.* "We don't have any idea how long we'll be up there. So, four's a start—provided I go. Thanks, Fay." She hugged the older woman.

Fay squeezed back. "Be careful, honey."

"Always." Maybe Madeline Harris would surface, and she and Logan would be home before the next weekend.

She could only hope.

****

Using his key, Logan opened the side door to the

Monroe Security building, stepped into the employee lunch room, then turned the lock behind him. He'd come early to the meeting with the hope of catching Monroe alone. He wasn't sure why he had so many doubts surfacing with this case. The assignment seemed straightforward enough. Sky's role would be to stick close to Rachael Brookson. His role involved apprehending Madeline Harris. He'd handled protection services many times, usually for some swanky event where he worked as part of a team. The most dangerous jobs involved an outdoor podium where the client was fully exposed. Those, he hated. Too many variables, too large a crowd, and too few agents. This case had simplicity written all over it. Yet, his apprehension wouldn't go away. Moving into the hall, he looked around the darkened offices.

Vicki, the office manager, never worked on a weekend. What phone calls came in, Monroe handled himself. Pam, their IT expert, could usually be found at her desk, but not today. Sometimes, an agent used the exercise equipment to work out an injury, but an empty parking lot was a good indication of no one else around. Monroe parked his car in a huge garage at the back of the property. If he went out for the day, no one would know.

But like any man, Monroe had habits. Every Sunday, he took the time to get the blood flowing through his body. Since he'd built his living quarters onto the rear of the warehouse, he could easily walk through his office access door and head up to the exercise room. Logan listened. *Yup.* The steady thump-thump of someone on the treadmill vibrated the ceiling. He ascended the stairs.

For a man in his mid-fifties, Monroe still had the shoulders of a fullback. He played the position for three years on the Penn State football team and even had the privilege of competing at a Rose Bowl game. Pictures of the win, along with various trophies, filled a display case near the locker rooms. Logan didn't want to disturb his boss on a day off, but he had questions before their two o'clock meeting today with Pam and Vanessa.

Glancing up, Monroe spotted Logan and waved. After another minute, he slowed to a stop, stepped off, and grabbed the towel hanging over the handlebar to wipe his face. "Something on your mind?"

Logan approached. "Don't let me interrupt your workout."

Waving the towel, Monroe snorted. "Five miles is enough. Let me grab a bottle of water."

Logan followed the boss to the refrigerator by the locker rooms. "How do you know I didn't come to work out?"

Monroe opened the refrigerator and glanced over his shoulder. "Want a bottle?"

"No, thanks."

After grabbing one, the big man closed the door and straightened. He faced Logan. "If you came to work out, you wouldn't have stood in the doorway looking like a lost puppy." He unscrewed the cap and took a long drink, then smacked his lips. "What's up?"

Ah, where to begin. "I'm not really sure."

"You obviously have some questions that can't wait until this afternoon."

"I do, and I'd rather not ask them in front of Sky."

"Come on. Let's sit at the table." He draped the

towel around his neck.

Logan pulled out the opposite chair and flopped onto the seat. "I have no idea why I feel so out of sorts. I've been on cases before with limited intel."

"You're worried about Sky's participation?"

He smirked. "Yeah." He sat forward and put his elbows onto the table. "I know she's capable. She did a phenomenal job in Atlantic City, but this case feels wrong."

Meeting his gaze, Monroe raised a brow. "In what way?"

"That's the problem. I don't know. Like you said Friday, if someone is on a vendetta, they don't wait two weeks unless they're planning something elaborate. That statement has been bothering me like crazy."

Monroe took another swig of water. "We can't do much at this point. It's a wait-and-see case and perfect for you and Sky. Neither of you needs to fake your relationship. If you're lucky, you'll find Maddie and be done within the week. If not—" He shrugged. Lifting the bottle to his lips, he drank what remained, then crushed the plastic container. He narrowed his gaze. "Why don't you tell me what's really on your mind?"

The man was astute. Nothing slipped past him. Logan hid a smile. "I hate to put Sky in danger again. She means a lot to me."

Monroe rubbed the towel over his face. "I don't want to put either of you in danger, but what if Madeline developed martial arts skills comparable to Sky's? I'd rather not have you shoot her."

The boss was right. If Sky could kill with a well-placed kick, then so could Maddie. Logan would have no choice but to use his gun. Pursing his lips, he tapped all ten fingers on the table. "And what if Maddie doesn't show?"

"We'll cross that bridge later. Pam and Vanessa confirmed the accuracy of the aerial views taken off the Internet. Brookson's resort is completely surrounded by thick forests. The girls also checked the local motels for Madeline Harris, either under her real name or an alias."

Sitting back, Logan threw his arms wide. "So, where is she?"

Monroe held up a finger. "That, Logan, is precisely why you and Sky are needed. We can't let this woman harm Rachael and the baby." He slapped the table and stood. "You should stay and work off some of your frustration."

No matter how many miles on the treadmill or how many swings at the punching bag, he'd still be frustrated. He loved Sky, and she never said it back. Maybe *that* was his problem.

Chapter Five

On Monday morning, Skylar watched the scenery zip by as Logan maneuvered his black sports car through the heavy freeway traffic. They were on their way to Mount Pocono, Pennsylvania, the vacation mecca for honeymooners, hikers, and Lord only knew what else. In a few hours, Sky would be surrounded by forests and trees and Bigfoot—*oh, my*. The last part she heard on a cable TV show how the big hairy guy liked to live among the trees in isolated regions of the United States and Canada. A surprise encounter with the furry giant would just about make her trip and send her scurrying back to the city, never to venture forth again. She'd quit Monroe Security on the spot.

The weather was perfect, though. Spring was a beautiful time of year for blooming flowers and sprouting tree buds. Nature was coming alive after a long winter rest. Unfortunately, car exhaust filled the air to spoil the enjoyment of sweet-scented foliage.

Last night's weather report listed the Pocono area with nighttime temperatures in the high thirties. *Brrr*. Even so, she'd left the winter coat home, preferring, instead, to layer garments. This way, she'd always have free use of her arms and legs without bulky clothing holding her back.

Seriously, she had to be out of her mind for agreeing to this assignment. Logan, of course, thought they would have fun playing an engaged couple. But, like a typical male, he would find running into Bigfoot amusing, too. Truthfully, the engagement roles required very little playacting. She and Logan enjoyed their time together. Sex was always a phenomenal experience, but deep down, the fiancée part bothered her. She wasn't sure why.

Marriage hadn't been on her radar. She'd never felt this need to satisfy her biological clock like so many women. In fact, she never dated a man longer than two months. If the spark wasn't there, she cut the man loose. Yet, she and Logan had been together for over a year, and their spark was as strong as ever. She glanced at her late aunt's engagement ring on her left hand. Somehow, looking at this ring made their engagement too real.

Logan cleared his throat. "The ring looks good on your finger."

Holding her hand outward, she sighed. "It *is* pretty. Monroe's jeweler said it's worth around twelve thousand." After dropping her hand to her lap, she looked at him and forced a smile. "I've never worn rings, even before I started martial arts."

"If you got married, would you wear one then?"

Would she? She turned her hand to let the diamond sparkle in the sunlight coming through the car windows. "I'd probably wear a band." Placing both hands onto her lap, she covered the diamond ring with her other hand. *Out-of-sight, out-of-mind.* She shook herself and smirked. "For the record, we'll say the ring came from *your* late aunt."

"Okay, makes sense. To add to our record, we've been engaged for four months and are working to save money for the wedding." He shot her a sideward glance. "How's that sound?"

"Like we're any young couple struggling to make ends meet." She shot him a grin.

He nodded toward her hand. "Do you think anyone would notice the age of the ring?"

"So what if they do? Being an heirloom makes the ring more of a curiosity." She shifted her gaze out the window. "Where are we? We've been on the road for two hours. My butt's sore." Even though Logan's seats were cushy-soft, she still itched to walk around. He might be anxious to start, but she'd rather hold off being a housekeeper for a while longer.

Logan glanced in his rearview mirror and shifted lanes. "We're on the Northeast Extension to the Pennsylvania Turnpike."

She frowned. "Not much to look at." Just trees and an occasional warehouse. The biggest break from the mundane scenery was when the turnpike cut through a mountain tunnel. She hated tunnels. They were…too closed in.

"We should be coming to a rest stop soon."

Feeling her spirits lift, she straightened in the seat. "I could use a chance to stretch my legs." She rotated her head to stare at his profile. The guy was handsome, no matter what angle. Strong jaw, straight nose. She could make a long list. "Have you ever been to Mount Pocono?"

"Not since I was twelve. My dad took me and my brother on a fishing trip."

She shuddered. "Ugh, fish. Never liked them."

"I'm not a big fan, either, nor is my sister. She refused to come."

"Smart girl." Logan had an older brother and a younger sister, with both parents still alive and wandering the country in an RV. Sky envied him. Her dad passed over ten years ago, and her mom died from breast cancer four years this June. Without any family to call her own, she latched onto the tenants at the manor. They were her family now. "Have you ever tried skiing?"

He shook his head. "Never had the desire. A lot of the ski resorts have a combination of hills for whatever level a skier might be. For the most part, resorts cut through the trees to create ski trails for cross-country skiing. That's very popular up here. It's nothing like you'll find out west. For higher mountains and bigger challenges, skiers head to Vermont or upstate New York." He glanced her way. "How about you?"

She harrumphed. "I've never been out of Chicago until my aunt's will forced me to move." Even then, she fought tooth and nail not to come. She questioned why the paperwork couldn't be done over the Internet. As it turned out, she was glad she lost the fight. Her inheritance changed her entire life.

After stopping at a service plaza for a restroom break, gas, and something to eat, Logan drove for another hour before exiting the turnpike at the Pocono Mountains tollgate. From there, he activated the car's GPS app and continued north. "I already programmed the lodge's address before we left, Sky. We'll have to keep alert. Chadbury is definitely off the beaten path."

"In other words, lots and lots of trees." She hadn't seen anything that suggested she was in a prime vacation area. The town just off the turnpike had several motels surrounded by fast-food establishments and stores. No hearts floating overhead to suggest a honeymoon haven. Cars and people gave evidence of human life. But Logan quickly drove away from civilization, and she was convinced more than ever she'd run into Bigfoot. Every so often, driveways cut through the multitude of trees. At least, they *looked* like driveways. She couldn't see houses, but two ruts in the dirt meant tire tracks. "Where are all the ski resorts? All I see are clearings with power lines cutting into the hills."

"According to my directions, we're moving away from the major resorts. From Monroe's research, Brookson's grandparents built the lodge as a summer retreat for themselves and the family. As the family grew, they expanded to include cabins, but over the years, family interest waned. So, they expanded into a full-fledged resort with hiking trails and nature walks. The pool and other amenities came later."

"In one-quarter mile, turn right at the next intersection."

The GPS didn't mention a street name. Come to think of it, Sky hadn't seen a street sign anywhere.

Slowing, then glancing both ways, Logan turned right. "As resorts go, Chadbury is small in size with twenty cabins. The place is known for being a quiet place to relax. The isolation makes it dangerous for Rachael. Somehow, we need to find Maddie before opening day."

That left them six weeks. Brookson said they were fully booked for opening day. Once the season started, Maddie could easily blend in with the crowd. They had their assignments—stop Maddie before she reached Rachael. *Easy-peasy.* She sighed.

Twenty minutes later, the GPS instructed Logan to turn left, and he drove through thicker woods.

The entire area put Skylar on edge. Not only did the woods obscure sunlight, but Maddie had far too many places to hide. "There is no way in hell Madeline can live in a forest unless she has survival skills." She looked at Logan. "Does she?"

Frowning, he rested one hand on top of the steering wheel. "By all accounts, Maddie seems like an ordinary woman who earned a living as a yoga instructor. Pam found nothing suggesting she had survival training. If Pam can't find it…" He glanced her way.

"Right. Nobody can." Pam's skills on a computer were legendary. As a Massachusetts Institute of Technology graduate, if information was on the Web, Pamela O'Connor found it. "How come we haven't seen signs for the state parks? Brookson said the lodge was between two of them."

"Brookson was playing with words, Sky. He's near state reserves, not parks."

A mile or so later, a huge wood-carved sign for *Chadbury Lodge and Resort* came into view. As Logan turned onto an asphalt road leading into the resort, he pointed out the side window. "Those must be some of the cabins."

Sky straightened in her seat to see better.

Cute, little log cabins were nestled within the trees. A clearing, large enough to park a car, had loose stones instead of asphalt, and some cabins appeared larger than others.

Signs with arrows directed them to main check-in. Before long, a three-story, barn-like structure emerged, also constructed from logs. Not too far away, on the lodge's left side, a basketball court sat alongside a sand-covered volleyball area. Toward the lodge's rear, a children's playground with all kinds of colorful slides and swings brightened the otherwise drab surroundings. Alongside the playground, a chain-link fence enclosed four tennis courts while a white picket fence protected an in-ground pool. Off in the distance, hidden by tall pine trees, a large metal building could be seen. She wasn't sure what she expected. She'd never been to any type of resort and had nothing for comparison, but everything looked nicely kept. "This compound is huge, Logan."

He clenched his jaw. "I don't like all the trees, either. If Rachael stepped outside unguarded, she'd be a sitting duck." He pointed out the windshield. "Look at the cluster of bushes on the right side of the lodge. Maddie could hide behind them and pounce."

"But the guard follows Rachael whenever she leaves the house, right?"

He stifled a laugh. "According to Brookson, Rachael waits for the guard to come around to the back deck. Then, she runs out the front door."

Sky shook her head. "She's being foolish, as if she doesn't care about Maddie or her baby."

"And that's why we are here. A little covert protection to keep her safe." He turned into the small parking lot in front of the main lodge.

"Do we check in with Donald?"

"No. He said our names are registered with the front desk. We'll call him when we settle in." Guiding the car into a parking slot, he shifted the gear into Park and killed the engine. Turning toward her, he winked. "This is it, Sky. Remember, expect the unexpected."

Yeah, yeah. He drilled the saying into her head from the get-go. Of course, she appreciated the reminder, but her three black belts weren't earned by letting her attention wander. Leaning over the console, she gave him a quick kiss. "Let's get this show on the road." She alighted, stretched, then followed him through automatic double doors.

Since the lodge wasn't officially open, the activity inside the lobby consisted of men with ladders and tool belts. To her left, the registration counter stood unoccupied. Somewhere in the back through an open door, the hum of a printer or fax filled the air. Opposite the front desk, The Chadbury Restaurant entrance with two opened ornate wooden doors showed a man with a buffer machine polishing a pinewood floor. Next to the restaurant was a snack bar, totally dark. An open-area gift shop came next with a young woman stocking shelves.

Across the lobby, toward the far wall, a large sitting area faced a beautiful stone fireplace. And finally, adjacent to the registration desk, a sign pointed to two elevators where a directory on a stand listed game rooms on the second floor. No third floor was listed, even though three floors were obvious from what she saw on the way into the resort.

Logan strolled to the desk and hit a bell.

"Be right there!" A minute later, a young man emerged through the open door.

He was small in size and looked to be in his mid-twenties with medium height, no muscles, trimmed brown hair, and brown eyes. His skin was pale, as if he never stepped outside into the sun. He wore a pullover sweater with blue jeans, but really, she couldn't find anything remarkable about him…except maybe his ears. They were kinda small.

Approaching the registration desk, he smiled. "How can I help you?"

Logan leaned on the counter. "Logan Greene and Midnight Sky are here to work for Mr. Brookson."

The young man broadened his smile. "Hey, welcome. He told me you were coming. For security reasons, I need to see some ID."

He and Sky took out wallets and flashed their driver's licenses.

After a quick glance, he nodded. "Great. Mr. Brookson put you in cabin number eight. It's by the lake and one of our bigger accommodations." He paused and cocked his head. "I hope he explained we're fully booked for opening day, and you'll have to move out—that is, if you're still here?"

"He did." Logan glanced at Sky.

She fought the urge to roll her eyes. Brookson better pray like hell Madeline was found before that time. No one mentioned extending their temporary work beyond opening day. And she sure as hell wouldn't pitch a tent in the woods just to be close by.

The young man reached under the counter and pulled out a colorful paper map of the resort. He slipped it in front of Logan and grabbed a pen. "You're here." He marked an X. "Follow the signs to the lake. Make a right at the docks and drive to the end. Your cabin is this one." He made another X. "Hope you brought food. The snack bar and restaurant aren't open yet. Luckily, your cabin comes equipped with a small kitchen. Not all do."

Sky stepped forward. "We brought supplies, but

where is the closest supermarket?"

With the pen still in his hand, he twirled it between his fingers like a baton. "We have a few mom-and-pop stores around. If you want a supermarket, you'll need to head toward Brodheadsville. That's about thirty minutes west."

Brod...what? Was he for real? She coughed. "Okay, thanks." After living in Chicago her entire life, and then moving to New Jersey, she shopped in stores no more than ten minutes from her house. Here, a quick ride for takeout was out of the question.

"You'll have two keys. I'm John, by the way. I don't have my name tag on yet, but I'm assistant office manager." He handed Logan two card keys.

Logan handed one card to Sky. "Thanks, John. We'll see you around." He took the map and, with a hand on the small of her back, led her out the door.

When she resettled in the car, Sky turned to face him. "How come you're using your real name this time?"

As he started the car, he grinned. "Because I'm not famous like you."

Straightening in the seat, she shook her head. "I'm not famous."

"Sure, you are. Why do you think Pam has such a hard time keeping your videos off the web? She'll take one down, only to see it pop up somewhere else. And since we are dealing with a martial arts student, we have to be careful not to use your real name."

Her martial arts masters had filmed her workouts without her knowledge. Once the videos went live, the downloads occurred all around the world. Because of a growing following, she received countless offers to compete in martial arts tournaments. Why in hell would she want to get beat up for a living? The money she'd make would go toward doctor bills. *No, thank you.* But Monroe better be careful. One of these days, her true identity would surface at the worst possible moment.

Chapter Six

After settling in the car seat and cracking open the window to suck in the fresh mountain air, Sky stared at the cartoonish map in her hands and shook her head. Who in the world designed this? The drawing had to be an eight-year-old's interpretation of the compound. Although, the art wasn't half-bad—better than what she could draw. She smirked. "We have officially entered another dimension."

Glancing over his shoulder, Logan backed the car out of the slot. "Why? Because of all the trees? I know you grew up in a city, but you might enjoy a nature walk or two."

That'll be the day. But she kept the comment to herself. "No, that's not what I mean. Let's just say this resort is geared toward families."

"I'm not surprised." He maneuvered the car toward the parking lot entrance and shot his gaze right and left. "Which way?"

He's gonna laugh his head off. She cleared her throat. "Make a left here on Lodge-Podge Avenue. This is the way we came in. At the stop sign, turn right on Chaddy-Wonker Drive."

Rotating his head to meet her gaze, Logan stared.

"Hey, I'm not making this stuff up. Get going."

"Oh-kay." Shaking his head, he focused his gaze forward and turned left, then right.

"We'll pass Splish-Splash Lane. That goes to the pool and tennis courts. Chaddy-Wonker Drive is the main road and circles the entire complex."

"Nice to know." He released a low chuckle.

"Once we pass the Flipper and Oar Store, we'll be getting close to our cabin."

"The name sounds obvious, but I'll ask anyway. What's the Flipper and Oar Store?"

She held the map closer to her face to see the small print. "*All your swimming and boating needs. Canoe rentals by the hour or day.*" She lowered the map. "The store will be on your left between Chaddy-Wonker Drive and Fishy-Wishy Path. Fishy-Wishy runs parallel to the lake."

Logan burst out laughing. After he released a calming breath, he looked at her and grinned. "What else?"

"A huge playground is on the other side of the main lodge. You can follow Slide and Glide Way to reach it." The names were kinda funny. Since the resort wasn't geared for honeymooners, then logically, the resort catered to fun things for kids.

Around a curve in the road, a row of tall evergreens separated a large house from the rest of the complex. A gate blocked a driveway.

Logan pointed. "This must be Brookson's place."

"Yes, it is. Not much detail on the map, but the small print says *Private Residence*." Watching the passing cabins, she noted the numbers on the doors. "We're coming to the store."

The Fish and Oar Store was slightly larger than some of the cabins. Canoes were stacked alongside the outer side of the building, but other than that, the building was dark. "They have weird names for the hiking trails, too. Our cabin is near Deer Drop Trail." She scanned for their cabin. "We're almost there." She sat forward. "Here, we go. Cabin eight is on the left."

Logan guided the car onto a loose stone parking space in front of a log cabin and killed the engine.

Staring out the front window, Sky gasped. "How cute!"

Built entirely of artificial logs, the cabin stood nestled among pine trees. Flower boxes hung from the two front window sills with what looked to be plastic flowers popping from straw. Evergreen shrubs surrounded a red door with a big number *8* tacked to the wood. She couldn't wait to see inside. She hopped from the car and approached the front door. Glancing over her shoulder, she stopped when Logan didn't follow. "What's the matter?"

While scanning the area, he stood alongside his open car door. "If I'm guessing right, this is not the ideal location for our purposes." Frowning, he shook himself and forced a smile. "Let's see the cabin."

With the use of the card key, she opened the heavy door and stepped into a living room. A sofa and two side chairs faced a stone fireplace and small TV mounted on the wall. The furniture wasn't new, but the upholstery looked clean. Over by the front windows, a round table with four chairs gave a nice view of the outside grounds. In the center of the table, a *Welcome to Chadbury Lodge* folder waited to be read. No wall separated the living room from the kitchen, and the open-air concept fit the cabin perfectly.

Moving over to the kitchen, she opened the overhead cabinets and found a sufficient supply of dishes, glasses, and coffee mugs within reach of the stove and sink. A toaster, coffeemaker, and tiny microwave filled half the space on a laminated counter. What remained left a small area for food preparation. The stove with two burners was half the size of normal. She opened the oven door to see if it would fit Fay's casseroles. The compartment had barely enough space, but if necessary, she could separate the dish into smaller portions or, better yet, use the microwave.

On the opposite wall, a petite refrigerator stood about chest-high and was empty, of course, and it, too, was just big enough for the casserole dishes. Since the appliance was running, she pressed a palm onto the shelves, then turned the temperature gauge two degrees colder. Without a thermometer, she could only guess at the proper temperature. Next to the fridge was a wooden cabinet full of used pots and pans. The kitchen didn't have an area for eating. By process of elimination, the table by the front windows was their only option.

Returning to the living room, she meandered left and took a look at the first of two bedrooms. The room was small in size but had a queen-size bed that nearly touched both walls. The remaining furniture was a bureau with a mirror and lamp. Nothing else. On her way to the second bedroom, she passed the bathroom that doubled as a laundry room with apartment-size, stacked washer and dryer. Someone left a box of laundry detergent. She shook it. Thankfully, the carton was half full. *Lucky me*. She hadn't given a thought about washing clothes. If push came to shove, she'd use a bar of soap until she could drive to a store.

The second bedroom was identical to the first, right

down to the flowered quilt on the bed. Nothing romantic. Still, sex all day while in this cozy cabin would be fun, but she and Logan weren't here to lounge around. They had jobs to do.

Logan walked up behind her and wrapped his arms around her waist. He rested his chin on her shoulder. "Not bad, eh?"

Boy, if he knew where my mind wandered. Smiling, she sighed. "I like it. The entire place has a rustic feel."

Squeezing her tight, he nuzzled her neck. "Do you have a preference for which bedroom?"

Even after all this time together, the man always managed to send a shiver across her skin. She would never tire of the feeling. "The one facing the front would be more advantageous, don't you think? That would be this room."

"Smart girl." Releasing his hold, he squeezed one side of her butt before turning toward the living room. "I'll unload the car."

Her butt tingled from his touch. She almost grabbed his arm to throw him onto the bed, but hey…later. Chuckling, she left the bedroom and returned to the kitchen.

After opening the sliding glass doors, she stepped onto a wooden deck that faced the lake. Even with a bright sun overhead, the air was noticeably brisk. Clean, too, and full of the fresh scent of pine. From where she stood, she could see a boat dock to her left and, farther down, a platform for a flying leap into a roped-off swimming area. To her right, the trees were so thick she barely got a glimpse of the lake, and Fishy-Wishy Path stopped short of their deck. According to the map, cabin eight was in the outermost corner of the property. She stepped back inside.

"Here's the cooler." Muscles bulging, Logan placed the green-and-white chest on the floor by the refrigerator.

Unpacking their supplies took no more than an hour. Even though Logan brought more clothes because of his groundskeeper duties, he finished with his suitcase first in typical male fashion by shoving all his garments into drawers.

Sky, of course, hung her shirts and spaced them accordingly inside the closet. She might have a low-maintenance, all-black wardrobe, but she hated to shop. Taking extra care of her garments kept her out of the stores longer. Finished, she joined Logan in the living room.

He was bent over the round table while staring at the cartoonish map. Straightening, he jammed his fists onto his hips. "I sometimes wonder if Donald Brookson has an IQ above a hundred. Look where we are."

Well, of course, she knew precisely where they were. She scanned the map, then lifted her shoulders and a brow simultaneously. "Your point?"

He waved a hand over the map. "Look where we are in relation to the Brookson house." He pointed. "Their house is in the far left corner of this compound. We are here in the far right corner. The man knows we've come to protect his wife, but instead of giving us a closer cabin, he puts us at the end. He's a moron." He jammed his fingers through his hair. "He should have given us either cabin five or cabin four. Both of those are in close proximity to his house."

Leaning forward, Sky let her gaze wander over the map. "I see what you mean." Straightening, she chewed on her lip. "I'm sure cabins four and five are empty. Maybe we should ask for one of them."

He shook his head. "A change would pique someone's curiosity. We'll make do with this cabin. But I have to say Brookson isn't the sharpest pencil in the box."

Sky agreed. She and Logan had quite a distance to travel in order to reach the house. Without being close by, coming to Rachael's immediate rescue would be downright impossible. She pointed. "Here's the maintenance building. It looks like a big airplane hangar." She pursed her lips. "You have a substantial walk unless you drive yourself to work. I might do better on foot. Whenever I pass the cabins and canoe building, I'll look for Maddie. She could be hiding in any number of the empty buildings."

"Good thinking. We'll both walk. If the map is fairly accurate, Maddie can hide anywhere within the thick trees."

Sky pointed to a square directly behind the Brookson house. "This must be the gardener's cottage where the guards sleep."

He heaved a sigh. "At least, Brookson put them closer to the house." Pointing, he hissed. "Look how near both structures are to the woods and a hiking trail. Not good. If Maddie is trained in martial arts like Brookson said, she could easily take down a guard."

"She might use a weapon."

"That's what I'm afraid of." He rubbed his hands together. "Let's get started. I'll head to the maintenance building. You proceed to Brookson's."

"Eh—what?" She glanced at her wristwatch. "It's almost two in the afternoon. A little late in the day, don't you think? Maybe we can take a leisurely stroll around the complex."

"No, no. We go in and introduce ourselves. This way, we can take a good look at our surroundings and compare notes." Logan glanced at his watch. "I'm to report to Gabe Rumfeld. He should still be working." He headed for the front door. "Ready?"

Hell, no. But like a man, he itched for action, and no way would she win this argument. "Oh, all right, but I should call Mr. Brookson first. He can introduce me to his wife." Slipping her phone from one of her cargo pants pockets, she sighed. "I sure hope he told her to expect me." With her luck? Not a chance.

Chapter Seven

As she strolled along Chaddy-Wonker Drive toward the Brookson house, Skylar looped her arm through Logan's and tugged him close. They rarely took a walk together. She kinda liked the closeness and slow stroll. Maybe their fake engagement had her feeling a little more…romantic. Not so for Logan. From the tension in his arm, the guy was itching to get started. The man loved undercover work. Whatever role Monroe assigned him, he played it like a pro. On the other side of the coin, she was like a stagehand who got thrust into the limelight because the director needed an extra body. Her role as a housekeeper was a big joke. She'd rather be on her exercise mat and tossing burly men over her shoulders.

When she approached the Flipper and Oar Store, Sky released Logan and meandered to one of the windows. She cupped her hands on the glass to peer inside. Fishing rods hung on the walls, along with snorkel masks and flippers. *Gee, what a surprise.* Canoe oars were layered on racks, and blankets filled two shelves. "It doesn't look like the place has been touched since they closed it for the winter."

Logan tugged on the front door. "Still locked. Hold on a minute. Let me go around the building and check all the windows."

While she waited, she moved away from the

building to get a look at the beach area directly behind the store. Fishy-Wishy Path outlined the entire stretch of sand, but right now, a lot of dried leaves and broken twigs created more of a war-zone look than a comfortable place to walk or sunbathe. The boat dock was about a hundred feet to the right with the gentle laps of the lake striking the wooden support beams. Other than the sounds of the water, a deafening silence surrounded her. She grew up with the noise of traffic, trains, and people. Here, nothing. She shook away the unnerving feeling and waited by the canoes for Logan to appear.

A few seconds later, he joined her. "All the windows and a bay door are closed tight. When I get the chance, I'll check all the cabins."

Logan definitely had the better part of the assignment. He could stay outside and breathe fresh air. She'd be stuck inside the Brookson house, sucking in dust and the pungent odor of cleaning fluids. *Ugh*.

When they reached the next cabin, Logan gave her a quick kiss. "This is where I leave you, sweetheart. See you tonight." He turned left to cross the asphalt drive, then disappeared into the trees toward the direction of the maintenance building.

Yup, he broke into a jog. Smiling to herself, she shook her head and continued straight.

Before leaving their cabin, Sky had called Brookson. He was in his office in the main lodge and said to give him fifteen minutes to get home. She almost laughed. Whether he realized or not, he could take all day and maybe take a rocket to the moon and back. She'd wait. Unlike Logan, she wasn't in a big hurry to play housekeeper. Besides, why should she rush this late in the day? More likely, Rachael was preparing dinner. Sky would say hello, introduce herself, and go from there.

With the air nice and crisp, she took a few calming breaths. Monroe needed to hire more female agents. She could easily train anyone to be good enough to take on an opponent like Madeline Harris, but proper technique took time and a lot of practice. Granted, no one could confirm Maddie's level of skill, and her yoga limberness was a distinct advantage. For Sky, those pluses meant nothing. She faced opponents many times without having prior knowledge of their capabilities. As far as Rachael was concerned, at seven months pregnant, the woman could sustain a blow that would kill the baby. Someone had to stay close to protect her. As much as Sky hated to admit it, that someone had to be her.

While walking along Chaddy-Wonker Drive, she let her gaze follow Fishy-Wishy Path until it changed to a dirt trail and disappeared into the forest. If Madeline lived and worked her summers at the resort, then she certainly trekked along every trail. She could use any one of them to come and go without anyone noticing. Not a nice thought.

As a child, Sky hated the idea of summer camp. Some of her friends bragged about the activities, like making beaded necklaces, but she'd rather chew nails than to learn how to pitch a tent or start a campfire. She couldn't imagine staying in the woods and playing with bugs and whatever else crawled out of the ground. Thankfully, her parents hadn't pushed. Her nature education came from books and trips to the Lincoln Park Zoo in Chicago. Even then, she wasn't interested.

Scanning the thick forest, she almost wished she had paid more attention. What animals lurked in these woods? What in the world would she do if one approached? *Lions, tigers, and bears…oh, my*. And let's not forget Bigfoot. Maybe she should test herself on how fast she could climb a tree.

Ten minutes later, she arrived at the Brookson house. The security gate to the driveway was open. She stepped through the opening and followed a brick path that led to the house. The structure was a two-story Colonial built entirely with artificial logs. In front of a two-car garage, a red SUV with silver and gold *Chadbury Lodge* emblems on its doors sat in the driveway. A small, wooden porch accented the front of the house, and she could see part of a large deck on the rear. Situated within its own oasis, the property was completely surrounded by tall evergreen trees to mark the perimeter. Surprisingly, the grounds lacked shade trees. Size-wise, the house looked ordinary—not too big and not too small.

Nearing the front deck, she caught movement to the right. A big, beefy man with arms like boulders hastened toward her. For some reason, the picture of a bulldog flashed through her mind, even though the guy wasn't the least bit bowlegged. His stony glare was a bit unnerving, though, and he had the face of a man looking to tear someone apart. *Hmm*. This confrontation better not come to blows. She'd hate to expose her identity so early in the game.

He held up a hand in a stop gesture. "This is private property."

"Yes, I know." He was casually dressed in a short-sleeve shirt and blue jeans with no jacket, despite the chill in the air. She couldn't see a gun, but he might have one on his ankle, like Logan often wore. The guy even had an underbite. All he needed was a neck collar with spikes to complete his bulldog look. She gave him a closed-mouth smile. "I'm the temporary housekeeper and reporting for duty."

He narrowed his gaze. "No one told me you were coming."

Well, duh. No surprise there. She arched a brow. "Are you a guard or something?"

"That's none of your business. Let me see some ID, please."

She should refuse, but she'd stay on his good side...if he had one. She slipped her right hand into her pants pocket and extracted her wallet. Pulling the license from the first slot, she handed it over.

He raised a bushy eyebrow. "Midnight Sky? What the hell kind of name is that?"

Almost everyone she'd met commented about her name. This guy, though, used a tone that raised the hair on the back of her neck. Lips tight, she furrowed her brows. "Midnight is my name and one you should never forget." She snapped the license from his hand and replaced it into the wallet. "Mr. Brookson is expecting me."

"He pulled in a few minutes ago." The guy scanned her from head to toe. "You don't look like a housekeeper."

If he said one more insulting comment, he might feel a fist in his face. Buddy the Bulldog was getting on her nerves. In a tit-for-tat move, she scanned him just as thoroughly. "I generally don't walk around with a feather duster in my hand. Now, if you'll excuse me,

Mr. Brookson is waiting." She'd like to get this visit over with today, thank you very much.

Frowning, he stepped aside.

She hopped up three steps onto the porch and rang the bell.

Guardem Guy stood on the brick walkway, staring with his arms crossed over his chest.

Yup, a bulldog ready to charge. She waved without expecting him to respond, then faced the door. *Well, this is it.* She rubbed her moist palms on her thighs and waited.

The door swung open.

A petite and very pregnant woman stood on the threshold. Her long, blonde hair was pulled into a high ponytail, and brown eyes changed from sparkling to downright dark as her gaze scanned her visitor.

If Sky had to guess, the woman was expecting someone else on the other side of the door.

"Yes?"

Since Donald hadn't told the guard of her arrival, he probably never mentioned it to his wife, either. *Oh, joy.* Sky cleared her throat. "I'm here to see Mr. Brookson."

Gaze narrowed, she pinched her face. "Who are you?"

She had a strong voice for a little woman. "I'm—"

"Midnight Sky! Come in, come in." Donald came from somewhere in the back of the house and hurried toward the door. His boots thumped loudly on the hardwood floor. "Honey, Midnight is your temporary housekeeper."

Staggering, Rachael gaped. "My—what?"

He wrapped an arm around his wife's small

shoulders and tugged her to his side. "You've got two more months before you deliver our firstborn. I don't want you stressing yourself."

Eyeing Sky, she squinted. "I don't need a housekeeper."

"Sure you do. Didn't you tell me you can't see your feet anymore? Bending and picking up stuff is a chore, too. Ms. Sky will solve that problem. She can also drive you anywhere you want."

"Wendell drives me."

The woman sounded like a whiny child. Sky fully expected her to stamp her feet and throw a tantrum. Since Sky still stood by the open door, which allowed all kinds of bugs to fly into the house, she cleared her throat—loudly.

Neither Rachael nor Donald acknowledged.

Oh, brother.

Donald patted his wife's shoulder. "You know how busy we are this time of year. I can't spare Wendell to go gallivanting everywhere with you. Ms. Sky's fiancé is also here temporarily to help with the grounds. We have a lot of work scheduled before opening day."

Pouting, Rachael crossed her arms on top of her big belly. "This is ridiculous and a horrible waste of money."

"Nonsense. You'll appreciate her help the closer you reach the due date. Come in, Ms. Sky."

Wow, finally. Sky stepped in before anyone changed their minds. "Please, call me Midnight." She shut the door behind her.

Rachael ran a critical eye over her visitor. "That's a dumb name."

Gee, nothing like insulting the hired help. Sky

ignored her and waited for Donald to continue, but the man looked as if he hadn't a clue what to do next. In the meantime, she let her gaze wander around the interior. "Nice place." Was that an okay compliment coming from a new housekeeper? With her luck, Rachael would think Sky cased the joint in order to rob it at the first opportunity. But it was a beautiful home. The front door opened into a large living room that spanned from one side to the other and had beautifully polished pine floors. On the left wall hung a wide-screen TV with cushy recliners facing it, complete with cup holders in the armrests. On the opposite wall, a beautiful stone hearth drew one's gaze. Matching sofa and chairs sat nearby. Along the sofa back was a long table with an ornate bowl. An ugly bowl, in her opinion—battleship gray with painted flowers. The bowl didn't fit in with such a beautiful living room, but it was on full display for a reason.

A staircase with a carpet runner rose to the second floor. The steps separated the living room from a large, formal dining room full of gorgeous walnut furniture, including a huge hutch.

Donald kissed his wife on her forehead. "I've got work to do. Give Midnight a tour. And so you know, she won't cook for us. No one can top your cooking skills." With a wave, he hurried out the front door.

Wonderful. The man couldn't escape fast enough. *The coward.* He left Sky to face an awkward situation alone. This was what Sky called starting off on the wrong foot.

Once the door shut on her husband, Rachael whirled toward Sky with a gaze like fire. "I do not need a housekeeper."

Yeah, Sky figured that out real quick. The house was immaculate. Not a speck of dust anywhere. "Nevertheless, I'm here. In a couple of weeks, you'll be glad of your husband's foresight."

She harrumphed. "He's an ass, and I can't believe he hired you without first talking to me."

"Probably because he knew you'd say no."

"Damn right, I would." After shaking her head, she sighed. "Okay. Come into the kitchen, and we'll discuss some duties. I don't want you here all day."

"That's fine." Brookson never specified hours. What did a housekeeper do when everything was clean and sparkling? She followed Rachael.

The kitchen was huge with lots of counter space and a large round table with four chairs. Through a side archway was the dining room with its beautiful walnut furniture. The kitchen's sliding glass doors opened onto the wooden deck where a grill and table waited. Sky could see the gardener's cottage with Buddy the Bulldog sitting in a chair by the door. The small building stuck out like a sore thumb in the sunlight. It stood about two hundred feet from the back deck, and sunlight hit the white-vinyl siding to create an annoying glare.

"I've never had a housekeeper before." Rachael leaned against the counter and rubbed her forehead. "I don't even know what to tell you to do."

Hell, since she was never a housekeeper, Sky had no idea what to say. She probably should sound like she understood the job. "How about we start with the basics? You know, change bedsheets, wash and dry laundry, that sort of thing. I'm sure you'll be busy with the nursery."

She shrugged. "I suppose. I haven't started it yet. I didn't want to jinx our baby by starting too early. We've had enough trouble conceiving this child."

Rachael considered seven months too early for a nursery? Why would a woman wait until she grew into a big balloon? Feeling a little awkward standing in the middle of the kitchen, Sky shifted on her feet.

With a loud huff, Rachael nodded toward the kitchen table. "Have a seat. For starters, I'll let you do one chore a day. How's that sound?"

Like Sky better clean *very* slowly.

Chapter Eight

Logan entered the massive maintenance building through the open garage doors and looked around. Chadbury Lodge owned some hefty equipment. A front-end loader with backhoe sat near two huge, zero-turn lawnmowers—forty-two-inchers, at a guess. A tractor with a flatbed trailer took up the right wall, and behind it on long wooden planks hung hedge trimmers and chain saws. He felt like a kid in a toy store, because wow, if he wasn't on assignment, he'd have a lot of fun with all this stuff.

On the left wall, two electric carts with attached wagons were plugged into an electrical outlet strip. Judging from the dirt on the cement floor, a third cart was either out for repair or in use on the grounds. Near the carts, an *Office* sign glowed above an open door. Straightening his shoulders, Logan headed for the office and knocked on the aluminum doorframe.

Sitting at a gray, metal desk, an older man glanced up from his writing. "Can I help you?"

The man was perhaps in his fifties with dark hair graying at the temples. His eyes were like two black marbles, and he had the skin of a man who worked outdoors—tanned and leathery. Logan stepped inside. "Gabe Rumfeld?"

"That's me."

"I'm Logan Greene, your temporary employee."

"Ah, yes." He threw his pen onto the desk and leaned back in his chair. "Mr. Brookson said he hired an extra man. Good to see you." He stood and extended his right hand.

Moving forward, Logan gripped a callused hand. The roughness told of a man who worked hard for a living and without the protection of a good pair of leather gloves.

Releasing his grip, Gabe reclaimed his seat. "You got any experience?"

"I was a gardener and overall maintenance man at a boardinghouse. I've also done some carpentry—although, I can't call myself an expert woodworker."

"Fair enough." Sweeping his gaze over Logan, Gabe rocked his chair. "We don't require a rocket scientist to help with the grounds, just a little muscle and a willingness to get dirty. We officially open the resort in six weeks and have a lot of work to do. Winter storms make a mess and always manage to kill a tree or bush. Have a seat." He waved toward the chair resting against the wall.

To be polite, Logan settled on the chair. Like any assignment, he had a role to play, and the interview process was a necessary evil. "How much work is required on the trails?"

"Enough so people won't trip and break a leg." He lifted one booted foot onto his desk. "The property sits on a hundred and forty acres, but the trails go for miles. Chadbury Lodge is surrounded by two state reserves. We'll clear the trails within our boundary. After that, hikers are on their own. Tree and bush trimming goes on all summer, and we have a local woman who comes in to perk up the flower beds." Dropping his foot to the floor and leaning forward, he grabbed a two-way radio sitting in a charging unit on the corner of his desk. He keyed the mike. "Hey, Wendell. Where are you?"

The radio crackled. "By the main building. What's up?"

"Got a new man here. Name's Logan Greene. I'm sending him your way. Give him a tour."

"Will do."

Gabe replaced the radio into the charger. "Wendell's been with us for years. He's the perfect man to show you around. Head to the lodge and look for the guy wearing a Chadbury Lodge T-shirt. And here—" Standing, he walked to the two filing cabinets on the far wall and opened a drawer. Reaching in, he took out a pile of yellow T-shirts. He eyed Logan. "Extra large?"

Puffing out his chest, Logan grinned. "Yes, sir." He stood.

Rummaging through the pile, Gabe extracted two shirts. "Here you go."

Logan took the shirts and suppressed a groan. Bright yellow. *Like wearing a neon sign.*

Once again, Gabe reclaimed his seat. "We have twenty cabins that need thorough inspections to assure everything works. Wendell will show you the checklist we follow so nothing is missed. The main lodge has its own maintenance crew, which is fine with me. We've got enough outside work without worrying about something breaking inside the lodge." He picked up his pen and met Logan's gaze. "Mr. Brookson mentioned he put you in one of the cabins."

Logan threw a thumb over his shoulder. "Cabin number eight. Me and my fiancée. She's doing housekeeping for Mrs. Brookson until the baby is born."

Nodding, Gabe chuckled. "Yeah, that little gal is getting big." He tapped his pen on a calendar desk pad. "Behind this office, we have a locker area. Grab one and put your shirt on here. This way, everyone will know who you are. We start at seven a.m. sharp and try to finish by four—six days a week and off on Sundays. Once the resort opens, we rotate weekends, but by then, Brookson will hire a few college kids to help with the grounds. Questions?"

"None."

"Okay then, go find Wendell."

With a quick salute, Logan exited the office and turned left toward the locker area. After hanging his lightweight jacket and T-shirt on hooks, Logan slipped on his yellow Chadbury shirt, closed the locker, and left the maintenance building. He felt like a daffodil, but at least, the garment wasn't fluorescent orange or some other god-awful color. Even with the crispness in the air, he left his jacket. Ten to one, he'd help Wendell with whatever the man was doing and break into a sweat. Exiting through the open bay doors, he turned right and headed for the lodge, in search of Wendell Harris, Madeline's brother.

As Logan skirted the outer perimeter of the huge playground, he looked around, and his stomach tightened into one big knot. Without question, Chadbury Lodge and Resort was a security nightmare. Nothing was fenced-off, except for the pool and tennis courts. Under the cover of darkness, Maddie could walk in from anywhere or easily hide in one of the cabins. Hell, she could even pitch a tent in the woods. He had far too many variables to consider.

From the get-go, the fact that Maddie revealed her plans to her brother bothered him. She had to know he would report her intentions to Brookson, and Brookson, in turn, would go to the police. What was she waiting for? Someone bent on revenge didn't hold off while security surrounded their target. They didn't tell anyone of their plans, either. As a rule, they struck with surprise on their side. So, why would Maddie leave the comfort of her room at the mental facility to wait somewhere in hiding? Nothing made sense.

Nearing the main lodge, he caught a flash of yellow by the rear corner. He had no idea what Wendell looked like, but the shirt was a dead giveaway. "Wendell?"

The man stopped raking the dried leaves and debris away from the building and stepped away from a bush that had lived through better days. With a sweatband around his wrist, he wiped his brow. "Logan Greene, right?"

"That's me." He shook Wendell's outstretched hand.

Wendell stood about Logan's height with a solid build filling his shirt. He had short brown hair and green eyes that studied Logan with a more wary than friendly look. But nothing about the man raised a red flag. He seemed ordinary enough—not handsome nor plain, the kind of man who blended into a crowd. Of course, a woman might have a different opinion.

Frowning, Wendell leaned on his rake. "So, even though I'm the only guy working the grounds, Gabe wants me to stop what I'm doing to show you around?"

"Sounds like it." Obviously, Wendell was none too pleased about Gabe not getting off his butt, but like any manager, Gabe spent more time at a desk than doing actual physical work. Looking around, Logan placed his hands on his hips. "How about giving me a tour later? Let me help you."

Gaze narrowed, Wendell pursed his lips, then nodded. "I like your idea better." His cell phone rang. After lifting the device from his pocket, he glanced at the screen and then replaced it without answering. He jerked his head toward the electric cart. "I've got an extra rake on my wagon. Take that one and start on the other side of the building. I'm ripping out this dead bush."

"Got it." After grabbing the rake and nearing the corner of the building, Logan glanced over his shoulder to see Wendell turn his back and whip out his cell phone. Since eavesdropping from this distance was impossible, Logan continued around the building.

An hour later, he stood by a pile of debris while wiping the sweat from his brow with a dirty hand. He had a dead bush on this side, too, but he'd need a shovel or ax to break the roots. He turned at the sound of an electric cart.

Wendell pulled up, stopped his cart, and stretched his right arm behind him. After a second, he tossed Logan a water bottle.

Catching the plastic container with one hand, Logan unscrewed the cap and took a long drink of semi-cool water. Afterward, he smacked his lips. "Thanks. I needed this."

Wendell nodded to the wagon attached to his cart. "I always bring a small cooler. I don't know if you looked into the lunch room behind the tractor, but there's a refrigerator filled with water bottles."

"Good to know. Thanks." He pointed the bottle at the pile of debris. "Where do you put this stuff?"

"We'll grab the front-end loader, collect all the piles, and haul them into the woods." He pointed toward the dead bush near Logan's legs. "That thing has seen better days. I'll help you dig it out."

Two men working on a dead bush took no time at all. Wendell stuck the shovel into the ground to break the roots, and Logan yanked until the bush snapped free. On the ride to the maintenance building to pick up the front-end loader, Logan chugged another long swig of water. "You live nearby?"

"Not too far." Wendell stopped the cart and bent down to grab a dead tree branch on the ground, then tossed the limb into the wagon. "During tourist season, we work longer days, especially after a storm." He put the cart in gear and took off across the bumpy grass. He shot Logan a sideward glance. "Frankly, I'm surprised Donny hired you. He usually doesn't increase the staff until opening day. By then, college kids are out of school."

Logan turned his head. "Donny meaning Donald Brookson? He wanted help for his wife. Since I was out of work, I offered to help with the grounds. I wouldn't say the pay is great, but he included free room and board."

Wendell grunted. "He can be a cheap SOB, but sometimes, he surprises us. He gave me one of the resort trucks for personal use. He even keeps it on the resort's insurance."

"Wow, that's generous. How long have you worked here?"

"Since we were both teenagers." He again stopped

the cart and jerked his head toward Logan's right. "Grab that branch, will you?"

Logan leaned over, snatched the small limb, and tossed it into the wagon.

Wendell continued toward the maintenance building. "After we haul the debris to the woods, we'll call it a day. Tomorrow, we'll finish cleaning around the lodge. Then, I'll take you to one of the cabins with the checklist we follow. We like to fix problems before they happen." He glanced at Logan. "You and your fiancée are in cabin number eight, right? I remember hearing Mrs. Sanchez tell her girl to get it ready."

Wendell's knowledge about him and Sky wasn't much of a surprise. Chadbury Lodge was probably like a small town—complete with gossips. "That's unusual, isn't it? I mean, for employees to live on-site?"

"Not really. We've done it before, but with the resort fully booked for opening day, you'll have to find another place to rent. Hotels are out of the question because they are way too expensive. I don't know what you'll do then."

"Yeah, my fiancée is supposed to help Mrs. Brookson with housekeeping until she delivers. If I remember correctly, she's due in two months." He crushed his empty water bottle. "Who's Mrs. Sanchez?" Logan learned early in his undercover career that the best way to obtain information was to play dumb. Even better, he loved it when he caught someone in a lie.

"Barbara Sanchez is head of housekeeping." He swerved to avoid a squirrel. "She has one girl working for her in the off-season—mainly in the lodge tending to the offices. When the resort opens, she'll increase her staff." Tugging his ear with a dirty hand, he chuckled.

"I can't wait to hear what Sanchez says about Brookson hiring a temporary housekeeper."

Shooting him a glance, he frowned. "Why? Is that a problem?"

"It will be. I suggest you give your lady a heads-up." He drove the cart into the open bay doors and pulled into its parking spot. He hopped off. "Always remember to plug the cord into the wall outlet. A full charge lasts all day."

Logan stepped out. "Good to know. And by the way, what's the deal with the guy hanging around the Brookson house? He doesn't look like a man ready to do manual labor."

Wendell narrowed his gaze. "That's a story for another day." He jerked his head toward the opposite wall. "Ever drive a front-end loader?"

Gaze riveted on the big machine, Logan grinned. "No, but I'd like to learn." Truthfully, he couldn't wait.

Chapter Nine

Logan stepped into the cabin, and the aroma of tomato sauce hit his nose. His stomach rumbled.

Sky stood at the small, two-burner stove, stirring a pot. She glanced over her shoulder and smiled. "Hi."

"Hi, yourself." As usual, his heart gave a little thump at the sight of her smile. He loved how her whole face glowed and made her crystal-blue eyes pop. Without realizing, she sent his blood south like flood waters across the plain. Over the past year, he'd walked into similar domestic scenes, usually at her place, either cooking in the kitchen or folding clothes in the laundry room, but lately, he ached for more. What exactly *more* meant, he wasn't sure. Marriage and kids? He wasn't ready, and neither was she. Living together was an option. He already stayed over her place two to three times a week, and she slept in his apartment once or twice a week. Nothing was set in stone, though. Living together would change that. He'd see her every night, except when he went on assignment. Someday, if he ever discovered how she felt, he could move their relationship to the next level—whatever that level might be. Until then…

"You need a shower before dinner?"

Her question jerked him from his thoughts, and he shook himself. "Yeah. I washed up a little before I left the maintenance building, but nothing beats a shower.

How much time do I have?"

"I'm making spaghetti with jarred meat sauce. About twenty minutes." She slipped her stirring spoon onto a small plate and turned with a grin. "I'm saving Fay's casseroles for one of your full work days."

Good ole Fay. She prepared four casseroles with minor reheating instructions. With luck, the dishes would fit in the tiny oven beneath the two burners. At least, the microwave was big enough to heat a platter. Thankfully, the half-sized refrigerator sat on a raised platform so tall people wouldn't break their back reaching for sustenance. The freezer had barely enough room for two ice cube trays and a quart of ice cream, but Fay's casseroles fit into the main compartment, along with their beer and water.

He walked up to Sky and wrapped his arms around her waist. "Care to take a shower with me?" He nuzzled her neck.

Laughing, she pushed on his shoulders. "Take a look at the size of the shower, lover boy. I'm not sure you'll fit, let alone the two of us."

"Darn." He squeezed her torso. She fit perfectly in his arms and always felt so damn good. Ever since he met her, he no longer had this overpowering need to be a loner. She changed him—for the better. Releasing his hold, he patted her beautiful ass and turned toward the living room. "I'll be ready in a few."

"Hold on one second, buster." She grabbed the front of his T-shirt and yanked him against her.

Her gaze flashed with a mischievous glint. The little devil was up to something. He shot her a one-eyed glare. "What?"

"I think you know what." She wrapped her arms

around his neck and plastered her lips onto his.

The rest of his blood pooled south. Wrapping her in an embrace, he urged her mouth to open and swept his tongue inside. Her lips were like a magic potion. But his desire to lift her into his arms and carry her to the bedroom just wouldn't do. Working outdoors with Wendell made him a trifle ripe. He lifted his head and gazed into her beautiful eyes. "You're making it difficult to release you."

With a quick peck on his lips, she broke free and wiggled her nose. "You know how I love a clean man."

He hurried to the shower.

This afternoon, when he had first stepped into the cabin, Logan relieved himself in the bathroom but took no notice of its size. In typical male fashion, he concentrated on unloading the car, then reporting for work. But holy cow! Sky wasn't kidding about the size of the shower stall. If he was a bigger man, he'd never fit into the tight cubicle. Bad enough he thumped his elbows against the wall. Thank God, a shower curtain gave him room to maneuver.

Fifteen minutes later, in fresh clothes, he rejoined her in the kitchen.

She was chuckling while filling plates with pasta.

He frowned. "What's so funny?"

Grinning, she handed him the two plates. "I heard you banging around in the shower. Aren't you glad it isn't the kind with a solid door?"

He harrumphed. "Obviously, Chadbury Lodge is not a five-star resort." Still holding the plates, he scanned the kitchen. "Where are we eating?"

She burst out laughing. "Just like a man. You don't know what's missing until you need it. You'd probably stand by the counter and eat."

"Nothing wrong with that."

Facing him, she patted his chest. "We have one table in this cabin, honey bunch. Out by the front windows."

He sniffed the plate in his right hand. "Smells good." He headed for the living room.

While carrying a bowl of meat sauce and utensils, she followed and placed everything on the table. "What do you want to drink? I made iced tea. It should be cold—unless you want a beer."

"Tea's fine."

She returned a minute later with two tall glasses of iced tea. "I forgot Parmesan cheese."

"No problem." He dumped more meat sauce on his pasta. He hadn't realized how hungry he was until the aroma of the tomato sauce filled the air. He loaded his fork and shoveled it into his mouth.

She joined him at the table. "How was your day?"

Wow. A married couple's question. He liked it. Although, he shouldn't be rude and eat half his meal before she sat down. He swallowed. "I met the boss, Gabe Rumfeld. He sent me to work with Wendell."

She twirled pasta onto her fork. "Did Wendell talk about his sister?"

"Not a word. He did issue a warning for you, though. Watch out for Mrs. Sanchez. She's head of housekeeping."

After swallowing, she arched a brow. "Why? What's the problem?"

"Evidently, Brookson hired a housekeeper without consulting her first." He stuffed another huge wad into his mouth, chewed, and swallowed. "How was your day?"

She shrugged. "Unproductive. Mrs. Brookson had no idea I was coming. She's not happy. She told me the house was clean and sent me home. With nothing else to do, I took a walk along Fishy-Wishy Path, sat on our back deck for a while, then cooked dinner." She pushed her pasta around the plate. "She doesn't want a housekeeper, Logan, and my being there will make for some awkward moments. I hope Brookson reinforces my purpose to his pregnant wife."

Logan chugged several gulps of tea. "He better not reveal our connection to Monroe Security. If he does, he'll spoil everything. Hold on a sec." Rising, he hurried to the refrigerator and grabbed the pitcher of tea. After returning, he refilled his glass and topped off Sky's. He reclaimed his seat. "Did Rachael talk about Madeline?"

"She hardly talked at all. My big chore for today was to empty the dishwasher. She never gave me a tour of the house, and I also got the impression she doesn't want me upstairs."

Sky described a woman unwilling to give up an inch of privacy. He had encountered several male clients with the same attitude, but they understood their life was on the line. Rachael knew of Madeline, but Sky came in as a housekeeper, not a protector. He shook his head. "Hard to imagine a late-stage pregnant woman refusing help around the house. She should be grateful her husband hired you." He ate a smaller forkful and washed the morsel down with a sip of tea. "Maybe tomorrow will be better."

"I hope so. Otherwise, I won't know what to do with myself."

He wiped his mouth with a paper napkin. "Any more pasta?"

Grinning, she jerked her head toward the kitchen. "In the pot. I cooked the whole pound. Help yourself."

He returned with another plateful of pasta, then slathered on an ample portion of meat sauce. "Have you checked out the Wi-Fi like Pam asked?"

While wiping her mouth, she sat back. "Yes. The lodge offers free Internet for all its guests, but the network isn't secure."

"Okay, then. Communication with Monroe via cell phone only. Just make sure your Wi-Fi is turned off. We can't take any chances."

Having obstacles on their first day wasn't a good sign. If Sky couldn't stay in the house with Rachael, she'd have no purpose but to hang around in the cabin. Having another person working on the grounds might help, but she'd need to stay in close proximity to the Brookson house. In either case, he sure hoped Monroe had a Plan B.

When eight o'clock rolled around, Logan lounged on the sofa and waited for Sky. To keep himself occupied, he thumbed through the headlines on his cell phone.

Ten minutes later, Sky flopped next to him with a huff. "I'm ready."

Why women stayed so long in the bathroom must be the world's best-kept secret. Although, he caught a whiff of mint. To confirm, he leaned over and kissed her. Afterward, he licked his lips. "Yup, minty fresh."

She rolled her eyes and pointed toward his phone. "Call the boss. We're a tad late."

"Any whose fault is that?"

Pinching her face, she punched him on the arm.

Chuckling, Logan hit Speed Dial for Monroe's office phone. When the call connected, Logan leaned closer to Sky. "We're on speaker, Bob. What do you have for us?"

"Not a hell of a lot, but for starters, I have some preliminary info on Maddie's institution. As I mentioned, she wasn't in a maximum security facility. In fact, the place has an open-door policy. Some patients stay. Others go home and return for therapy." He sighed. "Patient confidentiality is in full swing, so I couldn't uncover any details about Maddie's mental state. But the administrator, a Gloria Whitman, told me Madeline's yoga classes were popular with the residents. Ms. Whitman offered her a full-time position, but Maddie preferred to work part-time. And get this. Maddie is still working with her yoga students and now has her own apartment."

Logan exchanged a quick glance with Sky. "So, technically, Madeline is not missing."

"Not at all. Ms. Whitman also said she never understood why Maddie stayed at the institution. The monthly price for a room was far beyond what a small apartment would cost."

Sky grunted. "You mean Wendell forced her to stay."

"Sounds like it."

What the hell kind of brother turned away his own sister? If any of Logan's siblings needed shelter, he wouldn't hesitate for a second. "Who paid for her room?"

"I don't know yet, but Pam's digging." A slight pause. "I contacted the police chief who recommended us. His name's Tom Snyder. He knows my former captain at the state police barracks in Newark. Chief Snyder faxed me the detective's report on the Brookson case. As expected, he found no proof of a threat against Rachael. Maddie denied the allegation. Wendell adamantly insisted the threat was real. Even Mrs. Brookson denied hearing a word from Maddie. In a nutshell, the case is one big he-said, she-said scenario."

Sky leaned forward. "How come Donald doesn't know any of this?"

"He should know. The chief mailed a copy of the detective's report to his house."

Logan shook his head. "Mail can be intercepted or lost."

"True, and I'm more than a little annoyed by all these facts." The sound of papers shuffled in the background. "What did you find out about the Wi-Fi?"

After a nod from Logan, Sky leaned against his arm. "It's not secure, Bob."

"Okay, I'll tell Pam. Cell phones from here on. Any news on your end?"

Sky snorted. "Brookson never told his wife about hiring a housekeeper, and she was not happy. She doesn't want me there."

"Hmm. That's troublesome. In the meantime, make a pest of yourself. I'm about to have a long talk with our client."

Logan cleared his throat. "When you talk to Brookson, make sure you emphasize how we need to stay undercover. I don't think the guy's too bright. Instead of putting us in a cabin closer to his house, we're clear across the compound. To change now would raise a few red flags."

"Yeah, that wasn't too smart. What are your plans?"

Sky lowered her head onto Logan's shoulder. "We're going for an evening stroll around the complex."

"That's a good habit to establish. Okay, we'll talk tomorrow night. I've got more digging to do."

The call ended.

Frowning, Logan tossed his phone onto the small coffee table.

Sky lifted her head and squeezed his arm. "What are you thinking?"

"I like the well-thought-out jobs. This case makes me feel like I've got blinders on." After a heavy sigh, he slapped his knees and stood. He extended a hand. "Let's put on our jackets and take our evening stroll."

She slipped her hand into his and smiled. "I'd love to. I want to see for myself just how big this resort is. Should we carry a flashlight?"

Bending, he snatched his phone from the coffee table and waggled it. "I'll use the flashlight app, if necessary. Otherwise, we should familiarize ourselves with the location of buildings in the dark." He raised her hand to his lips and kissed her knuckles. "Now, my darling fiancée, we will show everyone how in love we are."

A cheesy statement, for sure, but only fifty percent true—on his part. If only he could get her to commit…

Chapter Ten

The next morning, as she approached the Brookson house, Skylar didn't have to guess who waited on the rear deck. The woman's dark gaze could cut through steel. And here, Sky had enjoyed a nice, leisurely walk in this beautiful mountain air with its crisp scent and glorious sunshine, only to have her day ruined by Matilda the Hun. But since Sky had to follow orders and use the back door at all times, she couldn't sneak around to the front to avoid the battle-ax. She heaved a sigh. Life was never easy. Squaring her shoulders, she approached the deck with a smile. "Good morning."

The woman jammed her fists onto ample hips. "Don't good morning me, young lady. All housekeeping staff reports for duty at seven sharp every morning."

"And you are?" Sky already knew, but hey, innocence could go a long way.

The woman lifted her chin. "I'm Barbara Sanchez, head of housekeeping."

Well, lah-de-dah.

At a guess, Sanchez was in her late forties. She wore a black dress with black rubber-soled shoes. The way the woman stood like a lion ready to pounce conjured memories of Catholic school and Sister Teresa in third grade. Man, that nun was a witch. Mrs. Sanchez even projected the same severe expression. Her dark hair was pulled into a tight bun and perfect for a nun's habit. She sported a husky build, as if she spent a lifetime moving furniture. The woman could easily go five rounds in a boxing ring. Sky climbed the three steps onto the deck. "I'm not part of your staff, Mrs. Sanchez. Mr. Brookson hired me to help ease his wife's load during her pregnancy. He certainly never mentioned anything about reporting to you." To keep Sanchez from opening her mouth to argue, Sky held up a finger. "Just so you know, Mrs. Brookson demanded I not show my face before ten."

With a pair of dark eyes flashing, she huffed. "An oversight I'll rectify with both Mr. and Mrs. Brookson. I hire and fire housekeeping staff for this resort. Everyone must meet my stringent criteria, or they are out the door. You should be no exception." Face pinched, she scanned Sky from head to toe. "Your attire is totally inappropriate. You should be in one of the resort's uniforms. Pants are unacceptable."

Why, so people could see the color of a maid's underwear while she bent to make a bed? What century was this woman from? *All right, keep cool*. After pinching the bridge of her nose, she dropped her hand and met the woman's steady gaze. "Mrs. Sanchez, if you have objections to my being here, you should take your complaint to Mr. Brookson."

"I most certainly will, young lady." She peered down her nose. "As you are probably aware, Mrs. Brookson keeps an immaculate house. She would only need you for an hour a day—at most. On the other hand, I need all the help I can get to ready the cabins for opening day." She descended the deck steps, turned, and pointed a finger at the back door. "Rachael and I are in agreement. Donald was ridiculous for hiring outside of my staff. My girl, who cleans the offices, comes to the Brookson house once a week to do Mrs. Brookson's bidding. The lady of the house needs nothing more." She started along the brick walkway to the front of the house, then whirled where Sky stood near the deck rail. "I expect to see you in my office at seven tomorrow morning and not a minute later!" She stomped off.

When donkeys fly...bitch. Sky hadn't forced herself out of bed at seven a.m. since high school. After graduation, she worked nights, stocking shelves at the local supermarket. A few years later, she tended bar—also at night. An alarm going off before nine was akin to torture, but she sacrificed occasionally for Logan. Whenever he spent the night and was scheduled to go into the office in the morning, he'd find her joining him for a cup of coffee. Then, she'd kiss him goodbye before stumbling back to bed. With luck, Brookson would show a little backbone and stand up to his wife and formidable head of housekeeping.

Now, for her immediate problem... She stared at the back door.

Sanchez was right. The house was immaculate. Anyone could eat off the floor. A housekeeper wasn't needed—at least, not currently. When Rachael reached eight months, maybe she would appreciate some help—definitely at nine months when she felt ready to deliver a bus. So, what in the world could Sky do to stay by Rachael's side?

Rachael burst through the door with a poncho covering her pregnant belly. She shot Sky a crooked grin. "I see you met Barbara. You might as well report to her now. I won't need you today. I'm heading to the office."

Gee, what a surprise. Sky caught movement in her peripheral vision.

Buddy the Bulldog had jumped to his feet and stood ready to follow.

The man was probably thrilled for something to do besides stare at the back door. Sky frowned. "Where's the office?"

"In the main building." Rachael waddled down the steps.

For a small woman at seven months pregnant, she was surprisingly light on her feet. Sky hurried after her. "I'll walk you."

"That's not necessary." Face pinched, she glanced at Sky. "I suppose I could show you where to find Mrs. Sanchez."

"Mrs. Brookson, I was hired to help you, not Mrs. Sanchez."

Rachael snorted. "Since I'm the one who writes the payroll checks, I should have a say in what you do."

A valid argument. She inwardly sighed. "Yeah, okay, show me where Sanchez is." Not like she had any desire to speak to the woman ever again, but she'd humor Rachael until Brookson had a serious chitchat with his wife.

They walked only a short distance along Chaddy-Wonker Drive until turning onto Splish-Splash Lane. This path would lead to the pool and the rear of the lodge.

A flash of white to Sky's left caught her eye.

Buddy the Bulldog again. Wearing a white shirt and black jeans, he followed roughly a hundred feet behind.

Sky gestured with a thumb over her shoulder. "I saw this man yesterday and a different one last night. Are they guards or something?"

Rachael waved a nonchalant hand. "My husband thinks I'm in some kind of danger from one of his ex-girlfriends." She glanced over her shoulder and frowned. "He's one of two men hired to keep an eye on me."

Sky hid a grin. "I'm surprised you didn't sneak out the front door."

"I tried already and got reprimanded." She harrumphed. "I promised Donny to always use the back. It's totally annoying."

"I can see that." Sky's long strides easily kept pace with Rachael's shorter ones, but geez, the woman could qualify for the Olympics walking event. *Slow down already*. She must be in a big hurry to get to the office. "Does this girlfriend live nearby?"

"Not anymore. She's been in a mental institution for several years now. She escaped a couple weeks ago."

"Oh. Well, that's a bummer." *Hmm*. Maybe she should have acted a little more surprised, but obviously, Donald and Rachael hadn't the whole story about Maddie. Was Wendell purposely hiding facts? But for what purpose? Sky exaggerated a shudder. "No wonder your husband wants to protect you."

"He's being ridiculous and spending money we don't have. I can handle myself."

"But you have a baby to consider." She tilted her head. "How dangerous is this girlfriend?"

Rachael shrugged. "I don't have a clue." She

stopped to pick up a small tree branch, then tossed it into nearby bushes. She continued at the same brisk pace. "Maddie's jealous, you know. She always wanted to marry Donny and live happily ever after in this second-rate resort. Instead, I got stuck here."

Oh, my. The woman wasn't happy. But how the hell did Rachael bend over so nicely? Not even a grunt. Sky hurried after her. "This place isn't so bad."

Rachael shot her a glare. "We're a boring resort and way too far from tourist attractions. I've been pushing Donny to modernize the play area, like put in a climbing wall. A small movie theater would be nice, too. The kids would love it. Something, anything to get this place hopping." She shook her head. "Don't mind me. Pregnancy hormones speaking." Stopping, Rachael faced her. "I'm guessing that's why he hired you. You're an extra body to hang around and watch me. He knows how I protested having bodyguards." While shifting on her feet, Rachael eyed her through narrowed lids. "What agency are you from?"

Oh, boy. Nothing like a direct approach to speed up the heart rate. But Monroe covered all the bases at their meeting with his just-in-case scenario. She plastered on a smile. "I answered a want ad your husband placed, Mrs. Brookson. He hired me to help with your household chores and, at the same time, hired my fiancé to work on the grounds. I can take you shopping or to your doctor appointments. Whatever you need. I'm temporary until the baby comes."

"Well, you can show up all you want, but I don't need you." She waggled her fingers. "Let me see your engagement ring."

Wow, she sure changed the topic quickly enough.

Sky held out her left hand.

Lifting Sky's hand closer to her face, Rachael fingered the ring. "This is one pricey piece of jewelry and way too expensive for a groundskeeper." She frowned. "It's pretty, though." She raised Sky's jacket sleeve to expose the watch on her left wrist. "This is pricey, too." She released Sky's hand.

"The ring is Logan's great-aunt's. I don't know much about the history." Yeah, she could lie like the best of them. "The watch I received from my father before he passed."

"Well, you're wearing some quality diamonds." Whirling, she resumed her fast pace. "Once we reach the lodge, go through the front door and ask John at the desk to direct you to Barbara's office. If Donald insists you stay, then you should be working for her."

Annoyance flashed through Sky's veins. Plan B better be a good one because Plan A sure wasn't working too well. And this was only Sky's second day.

They approached the fenced-in pool area.

On the far side, Logan and another man had their heads inside a large metal cabinet.

Eyes growing wide, Rachael tripped and quickly corrected her footing. "Wow! That ass is a nice distraction, don't you think? Who's the hottie near Wendell?" She dropped her jaw. "Don't tell me he's your fiancé?"

Sky bristled. For Pete's sake, Rachael was a married woman. She shouldn't be ogling another man's ass, especially while she carried her husband's baby. Sky coughed. "He's mine, all right."

"Oh, my, honey." Using a hand, she fanned herself. "You are one lucky gal."

Sky should be flattered, but Rachael hadn't even seen Logan's face. She called him a hottie by the shape of his back and butt. The nerve of the woman. Sky followed Rachael to the rear of the main building. "Where's your office?"

"On the third floor. You can't come in. Authorized personnel only." Reaching into her pants' pocket, she took out a set of keys. "This door stays locked at all times." She slipped a key into the lock and opened the door. She shot Sky a smirk. "You're dismissed for the day." She slammed the door in Sky's face.

Well, that was rude. While staring at the closed door, Sky frowned. What more could she do for a woman who didn't want her around? Stuffing her hands into her jacket pockets, she strolled to the pool area. Logan and Wendell still had their heads bent into the metal cabinet. Since Logan had the instincts of an animal hunted by prey, he looked over his shoulder first.

Straightening, he turned and smiled. "Hi, honey. How's it going?"

"Lousy."

He cocked a brow. "Why?"

"Mrs. Brookson went to the office. I've been dismissed for the day."

Wendell also straightened and turned.

Madeline's brother stood at Logan's height but was not as solidly built as her muscleman. He had average looks with brown hair and green eyes. A protruding bump on his nose would make a great eyeglass stopper—if he wore glasses.

"Honey, this is Wendell Harris. He's showing me around."

"Hi, Wendell." Since both men had hands covered in grease, Sky kept her hands tucked into her jacket pockets. "Midnight Sky. Nice to meet you."

Brows high, Wendell shifted his gaze between Logan and Sky. "Midnight, eh? That's an unusual name." He grabbed an oily rag to wipe his grubby hands.

Sky inwardly rolled her eyes. *Men*! A clean rag would do wonders to remove the grime. "I like to think my name is unique."

"That it is." Gaze bright, he smiled.

The man might not be much to look at, but he had a set of straight, white teeth.

Wendell's cell phone chirped. He unclipped it from his belt and read. "Mrs. Brookson's office chair broke. I better go see."

"I can go." Logan adjusted his tool belt.

Wendell grabbed a few tools and wiped them with a clean rag.

Oh, good grief. Tools got a clean rag, but human hands did not. Men sure had different priorities.

Wendell stuck the tools into his tool pouch. "You're not cleared to enter the offices, Logan. In fact, since you're temporary, you won't be going into the main building at all. Stay here and finish with the filtering system. Then, break for lunch. I'll meet you in the maintenance building around one." Wendell headed for the same door Rachael used. After inserting a key, he disappeared inside.

Sky stared at the door. "At least, Rachael will have Wendell nearby." She nodded over her shoulder. "Even the security guard doesn't have clearance." The poor man stood to the side of the building with his hands in his pockets. Like Sky, he had no idea what to do.

Logan glowered at the guard. "If Madeline gets inside the building without anyone realizing, she'd take care of Rachael in no time. What's more, if the security guard followed Rachael, who's watching the house? Did you see him use his cell phone?"

"My back was to him. So, no."

"Well, I hope he woke his buddy."

"Then, I'm not the only one to think this entire setup is downright ridiculous. We need to tell Monroe."

"I agree. I also question why Rachael called Wendell to fix her chair when Gabe told me the lodge has its own maintenance crew." Placing a hand on his lower back, he arched his spine, then met her gaze. "What are your plans?"

"Truthfully, I haven't a clue. Rachael talked a little about Maddie. She hates having the guards watching all the time, and she suspects I've been added for extra protection." She let her gaze wander over the pool area. The pool's concrete walls had a green film that would take some muscle to clean. "Brookson should have covered the pool over the winter. The walls look disgusting."

Logan followed her gaze. "Wendell claims Donald won't spend a dime unless he has to."

"Well, he hired us, and Monroe Security isn't cheap." Looking around, she chewed on her lower lip. "Rachael called this place a second-rate resort. She sounded like she wasn't too happy living here."

He raised a brow. "Is that so? Trouble in paradise?"

"I'm not sure. She blamed pregnancy hormones." She casually scanned their surroundings. "What should we do?"

"Break for lunch. Tonight, we talk to Monroe."

With luck, the boss had a couple of tricks up his sleeve. Without experience as a reference, Sky needed some tips to protect a woman who didn't want protection.

Chapter Eleven

After lunch, Logan stared at the debris cluttering the beach area. Tree branches and dried leaves covered the sand in layers about four inches deep. High winds over the winter really did a number on the area. He whistled. "This cleanup might take a few days."

Wendell grabbed a rake. "We see the same mess every spring. Can't be helped with all the woods around us. Once we get the junk out, then we smooth the sand. Takes a lot of time."

At least today, Wendell sounded happy to have Logan around. Yesterday? Not so much. "Yeah, I can't imagine one man doing this alone."

Wendell's walkie-talkie crackled. "Yo, Wendell."

Sighing heavily, he unclipped the radio from his belt and keyed the mike. "Yeah, Gabe?"

"Just got a call from the lodge. A tree fell by the resort entrance. It's partially blocking the roadway."

"Okay. Logan and I are on the way." After replacing the radio onto his belt, he met Logan's gaze and shrugged. "We'll do the beach later. Let's go." His cell phone chirped. Removing it from his pocket, he read and frowned. Without a word, he hopped into the cart and turned the ignition.

Logan followed and hung on for dear life as his coworker cut across Chaddy-Wonker Drive and onto the grass toward the playground. The man drove the electric cart like he was on a speedway. How fast could these little put-puts go? Hell, with no doors or seat belts, Logan might find himself doing a flying leap on the next curve.

Ouch! That last rut hurt. Why was Wendell in such a hurry? Was he afraid the tree would take root and grow? And if he was in a hurry, why not stay on the asphalt and make the ride more pleasurable, not to mention, faster? Logan studied the man. His jaw was set, and his eyes blazed like fire. Maybe he didn't like his plans changed. Or maybe the text message soured his mood. Logan gripped the front post supporting the cart's roof. "You don't strike me as a man who beats the clock to get a job done."

Wendell shot him a glare. "What?"

"If you need to be somewhere, you can let me cut the tree." He nodded toward the small steering wheel that Wendell had a death grip on. "You're driving this cart like you want to qualify for the Indy 500."

Blinking at his hands, Wendell released a nervous chuckle. "Oh." He eased up on the speed. "Sorry. I've got a lot on my mind."

Yeah, no shit. "More than the tree, I assume."

"Yeah, more than the tree." He pressed his lips into a thin line.

Was the text from Maddie? How the hell could Logan get Wendell to talk? They were still strangers, and the chances of Wendell confiding in a new coworker bordered on slim. He had to try, though. Now, with the cart's speed at a more normal pace, Logan loosened his grip on the roof post, but not by much. Wendell still drove on the bumpy grass. Logan cleared his throat. "I know we just met, but do you want to talk about it?"

"No."

All right, I took a shot. "Fair enough." He shifted his butt. "So, what was wrong with Mrs. Brookson's chair?"

"Huh? Oh, yeah, the seat lever lost its screw. We looked everywhere and couldn't find it. Luckily, I had a few screws in my pouch that worked." Glancing toward Logan, he grinned. "We don't throw anything away around here. Remember that."

"Got it." Another bump rattled his teeth. Damn good thing he didn't wear dentures. His teeth might fly clear across the yard. "Gabe told me the lodge has its own maintenance crew. How come she called you?"

"Hey, what can I say? She's known me longer than those guys." He waggled both brows.

A legitimate excuse—except for the innuendo behind the brow movement. Did Wendell have an interest in Rachael that went beyond friendship? Hell, it wouldn't be the first time a best friend went after a buddy's wife.

Wendell steered around a small mound of dirt and stopped. "That's a mole hole, Logan. Make a note to fill it and collapse the tunnel before someone breaks a leg. We're about three hundred feet from the west side of the lodge."

Logan grabbed the pad and pencil sitting in a small leather pouch that hung on a dashboard hook. He found it difficult to write even a brief note while bouncing over grass. The least Wendell could do was wait for Logan to finish. All the movement made his handwriting look like a preschooler's attempt to write cursive. Replacing everything to the pouch, he again gripped the roof post. "Are you going to tell me why a guy followed Mrs. Brookson to the lodge, then waited around like a lost puppy?"

Frowning, Wendell shot his coworker a one-eyed stare. "It's a long story."

Turning in the seat and squaring his shoulders, Logan glared. "I don't care how long. My fiancée is working for the lady. I'd like to know why the hell a man is hanging around the house and acting like some sort of bodyguard?"

"All right, all right." Wendell eased the cart off the grass and onto the asphalt drive.

Wow, at last. After releasing the roof post, Logan dropped his hand to his lap and let out a slow breath. "I'm listening."

"Yeah, well." He cleared his throat. "Rachael should have said something to Midnight, but I know she's not keen on the whole housekeeper idea." He glanced right, then left.

Logan followed with his own right-and-left glance. Although, he had no idea why. No one else was on the road or grass. "Go on."

Wendell shrugged one shoulder. "My sister, Maddie, and Donald went to school together. They never dated, but they hung around for most of high school. All three of us spent our summers at this resort and worked for Donny's grandparents, doing odd jobs and such. I'm two years younger than Maddie. Even so, we were like the three musketeers." He released one hand from the steering wheel and flexed his fingers. "Anyway, Maddie somehow believed she and Donny would marry and live happily ever after at the resort. Truthfully, I thought so, too, but Donny thought of

Maddie as nothing more than a friend. Then, the day came when he met Rachael Foxwood. He was totally smitten. Maddie lost it. She tormented Rachael to the point where a restraining order was issued."

Restraining order? Monroe hadn't mentioned anything of the sort. Logan made a mental note to ask him tonight. "That's not good—whoa!"

Wendell braked for a huge deer running across the drive. "Don't worry. Once the tourists come, the deer hide. Where was I?"

Before answering, Logan waited for his heart rate to decrease. That was one big-ass deer. "Maddie's restraining order."

"Oh, yeah." He resumed up the drive. "Despite the order, Maddie disrupted the wedding. I literally carried her out the door. Because of her temper and this obsession with Rachael, I suggested some counseling. We found an institution not too far from here where she could receive decent therapy. A few weeks ago, she walked out of the place and hasn't been seen since."

Well, we know that isn't true. Even Brookson could find Maddie teaching yoga at the institution. All he had to do was ask. Not to give anything away, Logan simply nodded and averted his gaze.

Nearing the main entrance, Wendell braked to a stop in front of a big hunk of tree covering a third of the asphalt drive. Without moving, he simply stared into space. A minute passed before he shook himself. "Prior to Maddie's grand escape, she told me she would get rid of Rachael once and for all. I informed Donny, and he went to the police. We both felt Maddie would make good on her threat."

"Okay, I don't like the sound of that at all." Logan

frowned. "The guy following Rachael is some kind of cop."

"Security, actually. A local outfit." He shot Logan a brief smile. "Donny wanted four men—two per shift, but Rachael protested. She compromised with two men."

"And where's your sister?"

He shrugged. "Nobody knows. I can't say she was happy at the institution, but her counselor told me she was doing well with her therapy." Twisting his mouth to the side, he drummed his fingers on the steering wheel. "One of the orderlies told me she'd been studying books on martial arts. She used one of the moves to escape." Gaze glaring, he slammed a fist onto the wheel. "I'm afraid she'll hurt Rachael this time."

Logan wasn't sure if Wendell was a good actor or really serious about his sister. Why would he make it sound as if Maddie escaped from a maximum security prison? He also never mentioned Maddie's job at the facility. Did he purposely mislead Donald in order to secure protection for Rachael? *Well, hell, that idea makes no sense at all.* Logan shifted on his seat to see Wendell more clearly. "But where is your sister hiding? She needs money for food and shelter. Do you have any other relatives or friends?"

"We have several aunts and uncles in the area. I told all of them to call me if they hear from her. As for friends…" He pursed his lips. "I can't think of a damn one."

Women almost always had a close girlfriend to call. Either Wendell didn't know, or he wasn't divulging the information. Come to think of it, Sky never mentioned a close friend. Since she was born and raised in Chicago, she had to have friends, right? Were any of them close? At the first opportunity, he'd ask her so he wouldn't be as ignorant as Wendell. Logan grunted. "You'd think your sister would contact you to tell you she was okay." He scanned the forest, as if Maddie would pop out from behind the trees. "Maybe she left the area altogether, you know, cut her losses and moved on."

Snorting loudly, Wendell turned in the seat to meet his companion's gaze. "She still needs money. Besides, she won't give up Donny so easily. Every time I visited, I'd be swamped with a ton of questions about dear old Donny. Then, she'd diss Rachael."

Logan tsked. "That's a damn shame. An obsession like that is never healthy." Logan lifted one butt cheek off the small bench seat. Electric carts were built to be lightweight to save on battery drain, but did the manufacturer need to skimp on seat cushions? Hell, how much did foam weigh?

Wendell killed the cart's electric motor. "Rachael's nice. I like her, but she doesn't deserve Maddie's wrath."

"And with Rachael being pregnant, she's more vulnerable. I'll warn Midnight to keep her eyes and ears open—that is, if Rachael lets her stick around. Does Maddie know about the baby?"

"Yeah, I told her on one of my visits. I asked her to move on, but she became more determined." Huffing out a breath, he slapped the steering wheel and stepped from the cart. "Grab a chainsaw. Let's cut this log into manageable pieces."

After slipping on ear protection and safety glasses, Logan pulled the cord on the saw, and the motor roared to life. Between him and Wendell working two chainsaws at once, they created enough noise to wake the dead. But his mind still pondered one question that noise couldn't squelch. Why the hell would Wendell lie?

****

After watching Logan run off like a little boy anxious to play with his toys, Sky gathered their lunch dishes and carried them into the kitchen. He really was cute. During lunch, he gloated about the front-end loader and how he drove it for the first time. He described every detail from turning the ignition to putting the shift in gear. Like she really wanted to know. At least, one of them was having fun on this assignment. She certainly wasn't. But until Monroe told her otherwise, she would follow his instructions and make a pest of herself at the Brookson house. Surely, Rachael could find something for her to do, like vacuum the rugs or scrub the oven. What pregnant woman enjoyed pushing a sweeper around or bending into an oven to breathe in the toxic fumes?

With the dishes done and despite Rachael's orders to the contrary, Sky headed for the Brookson house by taking her usual leisurely stroll along the gravel path beside the lake. The water was like one big mirror and reflected the overhead sky to turn the water blue. Were fish in the water? *Oh, for Pete's sake*. Fishy-Wishy Path said it all. Even the sign on the boat rental building listed fishing rods for rent. *Ugh*. The floating rope marked off the swimming area, but nothing would stop the fish from coming in and nibbling on a swimmer's toes. *Double ugh*. Who wanted to swim with the fishes? *Give me a pool any day with clear water to see my feet*.

She paused where the gravel path ended behind the last cabin. The dirt trail continued into the woods and, from what she could see, skirted the outside perimeter of Brookson's private property. A high fence would do wonders for security. Shaking her head, Sky crossed the grass and approached a break in the evergreens where a gate displayed a red and yellow *No Trespassing* sign.

Well, too bad. I'm trespassing.

The gate wasn't secured. Not like a lock would do any good. Anyone could hop over the barrier or squeeze between the bushes and the support poles. Donald and Rachael probably used the opening as a shortcut to the beach. After closing the gate behind her, Sky headed for the rear deck with thoughts on what to do if Rachael hadn't returned from the office. She'd probably take another stroll, maybe into the woods...not far. She'd rather avoid any wildlife, thank you.

But at the sight of the two security guards sitting on plastic chairs in front of the cottage, she sighed. Rachael was home...*darn*. If both guards were awake, shouldn't one of them watch the front of the house? She hadn't a whole lot of experience guarding people...well, all right, she had no experience whatsoever. But even she could see how Maddie might sneak in from one of the many trails surrounding the house. Hell, the woman could hide anywhere and wait for the perfect moment to make her move.

Sky hopped onto the back deck and knocked on the door. After no response, she knocked again. The woman would be bitchy enough to leave Sky standing here, twiddling her thumbs. Then, what?

Donald answered the door. Giving a closed-lip smile, he waved her in. "You don't have to knock. The door is always unlocked."

Really? Even with a woman out to murder his wife? What the hell kind of brain did this man have in his head? Sky stepped into the kitchen. "Is the front door unlocked, too?"

He shot his brows upward. "Oh, no, that stays locked." He stuffed his hands into his trouser pockets. "Where've you been?"

Face pinched, Rachael stuck her head through the adjacent archway to the dining room. "I told her I don't need her. If I wanted a housekeeper, I'd have talked to Mrs. Sanchez—which is what you should have done." She disappeared into the dining room.

Oh, boy. Donald hadn't won his argument—assuming he confronted Rachael. Would he admit defeat and send Sky on her way?

Frowning, Donald stuffed his hands into his trouser pockets. Change jingled. He shot Sky a sideward glance. "Rachael's being stubborn. I want her to take it easy. This is our first child, and we've been trying for a while." He stared at the archway. "I don't know why she's being so resistant. In a few more weeks, she'll be thankful you're here."

"No, I won't." Again, Rachael stepped through the archway. "And I don't see why Wendell can't drive me around. It's his sister who's after me. He can stop her."

Hmm. Maybe, maybe not.

Donald released a heavy sigh. "We have too much work to do before opening day, darling. We can't afford to let him leave the resort to cart you around. It's either Midnight or one of the security guards."

Rachael threw her hands into the air. "Fine. Have it your way." She disappeared into the dining room.

Every time the woman moved her head, a pair of gorgeous diamond studs reflected the light from the windows. Even though Sky wasn't one to adorn herself with jewels, with the exception of her diamond watch, she could tell the studs were expensive.

Once again, Rachael stuck her head through the archway. "By the way, I called Wendell to check out the water heater. The pilot light went out again."

Donald raised his brows. "That's the second time in a month. Maybe we should buy a new one."

Stepping into the kitchen, she huffed. "You're always spending money we don't have. First, you hire security guys. Then, you turn around and hire a housekeeper. Both expenses are unnecessary. The water heater is only four years old. It's probably more a problem with the gas line." She jerked her chin at Sky. "Midnight can leave when Wendell arrives. I'm going upstairs." She stomped out and thumped her way up the staircase.

Brows furrowed, Donald stared at the kitchen floor.

Since Sky hadn't stepped away from the door, she wasn't sure what to do. Did Logan ever encounter so much resistant from a client? If anything, Rachael should appreciate the protection for the baby's sake. So, why didn't she?

After another minute, Donald faced her and gave a wan smile. "My wife handles the books for the resort. She found the check I wrote to Monroe Security."

Yup. Logan was right. The man wasn't the sharpest pencil in the box. "And?"

"I told her I had Monroe run a security check since you'll spend time in our house."

"Okay, that's plausible." For a woman who handles

the books, she'd figure out the amount paid was far more than a security check. Sky almost told him so, but the man looked a little…depressed? Unsure? "If you're worried, you can tell Monroe about your money problems. He'll work out something."

After releasing a heavy sigh, he shook his head. "That's just it. I don't see money problems, and I don't understand why Rachael said otherwise."

Sky shrugged. "An auditor would help ease your mind."

Catching her gaze, Donald blinked, then blinked again. "That would mean I don't trust my wife."

She held up a finger. "Not necessarily. Rachael's pregnant. As she gets farther along, she'll tire easily. Tell her you want to ease her burden. FYI, Monroe has one of the best on payroll. It wouldn't hurt to call him." Pam, their IT tech, wasn't an auditor, but boy, the woman could dig up the dirt. Give her an opening, and she could hack into anyone's computer. Besides, Monroe probably *did* have an auditor on payroll. "You could handle the books until she delivers the baby."

Snorting, Donald stared out the kitchen windows. "I don't have the time."

Okay, then. Sky sucked in a deep breath and scanned the kitchen. "In the meantime, let me see if I can clean something." Hell, if need be, she'd polish glasses. As a former bartender, she was an expert at making glass shine. After removing her jacket, she draped the garment over a kitchen chair. "By the way, you should keep all your doors locked. You can't depend on the guards seeing everything."

"Rachael refuses." Shrugging, he shot her a sheepish look. "Wendell should be here soon. He always uses the back door." He grabbed his Chadbury Lodge jacket off a kitchen chair. "I need to return to the office."

"Where's the water heater?"

He slipped on his jacket. "In the garage. Wendell knows where it is."

He should. Turning toward the kitchen sink, Sky opened the hot water faucet. As it ran, the water got hotter…just as she assumed.

Chapter Twelve

At the end of a busy day, Logan returned to the cabin with a stomach rumbling like an impending volcanic eruption. The physical labor on this assignment gave him an insatiable appetite. If he wasn't sawing tree limbs and hauling wood, he was yanking out dead bushes or climbing onto rooftops to repair damaged shingles. At this rate, Fay's casseroles would turn into more of a snack. He and Sky wouldn't last the week unless one of them scheduled a trip to a supermarket.

After a refreshing shower, Logan sat at the living room table and took a large sniff of Fay's shepherd's pie casserole. Damn, that woman could cook. And because Sky knew him so well, she supplemented the meal with a grilled cheese sandwich. Otherwise, he'd eat the entire casserole in one sitting. He smiled at his pretend fiancée. "I'm glad you brought a lot of tea bags and sugar."

She took her seat. "I figured we couldn't go wrong with iced tea and pitchers of water. I found several large containers to use." She pointed her fork toward the kitchen. "There's two gallons on ice—one tea, the other water. Don't be shy. The way you're working, you need to keep up your body fluids."

He nodded toward her plate. "Why aren't you having a grilled cheese?"

Smirking, she cocked her head. "I'm not working like you. Fay's casserole is filling enough."

The grilled cheese had a perfectly melted center, and he devoured it in no time flat. After a second helping of the casserole, he slowed his pace and actually chewed his food while savoring the spicy meat under the potatoes. He glanced up. "A question popped up during my conversation with Wendell. I asked if Maddie had any girlfriends who would hide her." Using his fork, he pushed his food around on the plate. "He said he didn't know of any, and his answer got me thinking." He lifted his gaze. "I don't know if you have any girlfriends, either. Do you?"

Not removing her gaze from her food, she forked in a mouthful and chewed. "There's a lot we don't know about each other, Logan." She met his gaze and shrugged. "For some reason, I never formed a close relationship with another female."

"How about men?" He wasn't sure he wanted to hear her answer, but he was damn curious. A man would have to be blind to ignore a beautiful woman like Skylar Dawson.

She shook her head. "I went on dates, of course, but the men frequenting the bar where I worked were never interested in anything long-term." She grabbed the paper napkin and dabbed her mouth. "Truthfully, neither was I—until I met you." She gave him a closed-lip smile. "I can honestly say the people who surrounded me wouldn't give a damn if I suddenly disappeared. Everybody was wrapped in their own little world and trying to survive." With her gaze focused on her tea, she poked at the ice cubes. "After my mom died, I turned into a recluse. I worked, then came home.

When my inheritance forced me to come east, I truly expected to make arrangements to sell everything and return to Chicago. But from the start, Fay became the mother I no longer had. When I joined the tenants at dinnertime, I was treated like part of their family. Then, Monroe offered me a job with his security firm. For the first time in a long while, I felt like I belonged somewhere."

She hadn't mentioned the one factor uppermost on his mind. Hiding a grimace, Logan shifted on his seat. "Was I a consideration for your move?"

After finishing the last on her plate, she gave him a sad smile. "If you remember, you disappeared without a word. So, no, you were never a reason for my move to New Jersey."

Her bluntness hurt, but she was right. He went incommunicado for two months without a word to anyone. His intention was to sever ties to everyone connected to the case and return to his apartment in North Jersey to await his next undercover assignment. But Sky and the manor tenants got to him, too. He liked every damn one of them. He liked Sky even more. In fact, he fell so hopelessly in love, he left the state police and accepted Monroe's offer to work in his firm. The job change allowed him the freedom to pursue a relationship.

Sky locked onto his gaze. "You've turned into my best friend, Logan. I know I can depend on you in a crisis."

Her admission humbled him. He hadn't heard a statement like that from anyone, least of all, a woman. Curling one side of his lips, he winked. "Oh, you can depend on me for more than that, honey. I'm equally sure Fay would send out an army if she didn't know where you were."

Nodding, she lowered her gaze. "Fay, along with Monroe and the tenants, was why I packed up my life in Chicago and relocated. I was tired of being alone."

"And now, you are surrounded by a bunch of people who care...especially me. I would move heaven and earth to keep you safe." Reaching across the table, he took hold of her hand and stroked his thumb along her knuckles. "Yes, I know you can take care of yourself, but don't deny me the privilege, Sky. You know how I feel about you."

Again, their gazes locked. Questions flitted in her beautiful eyes. Was she unsure about his feelings? Did he need to take out a billboard to tell her how much he loved her? Of course, he could ease her mind and tell her again, but he put his heart on his sleeve that night in Atlantic City. She had yet to reciprocate.

After clearing her throat, she lifted her chin and smiled. "What about you, Logan? Do you have close friends?"

Before answering, he released her hand, shoveled in the rest of his food, then washed the mouthful down with the iced tea. He glanced at what was left of the casserole. He could easily wolf down the rest, but hey, cold shepherd's pie would be great for breakfast. He sat back and toyed with his tea glass. "When I became an undercover cop with the state police, I lost touch with a lot of people. I had bar buddies and even a girlfriend."

She arched a brow. "Really?"

"Yeah, really. Carol was her name. She wasn't happy about my switch into undercover work." He shot her a quick glance.

Grinning, she leaned forward. "Let me guess. She was more serious about your relationship, and you hadn't a clue."

With a slight shrug of his shoulders, he chuckled. "Sounds about right. She expected a ring on her finger. Instead, I gave her a boot."

"That's harsh."

"Not really. I did what I had to do to keep her safe."

"And what about your family?"

"Well, that was the rough part. I had to make them understand they couldn't call me to chitchat. I visited between cases, but any emergencies had to come via text and in code." He sat back. "They actually celebrated when I took a job with Monroe."

"But you still do undercover work for him."

"Sure, but Bob won't go after the type of people who will blow off your head without blinking an eye. Besides, Bob pairs his agents—like us. I never had the advantage of a partner with the state police. And I can tell you, I got into some scary situations with no backup."

She could picture him lying in an alley somewhere, bleeding. She shuddered. "I'm glad you left."

"Me, too." He gulped the last of his tea and smacked his lips. "Any dessert?"

She rolled her eyes. "Only cookies. We'll need to coordinate a trip to a supermarket soon. But in the meantime…" She checked her watch. When she caught his gaze, she waggled her eyebrows. "We have time before we call Bob. What do you say about a little dessert in the bedroom?"

He wiped his mouth and stood, nearly knocking

over his chair in his haste. "You read my mind, woman."

****

After a few rounds with her muscleman, Sky forced herself out of bed to straighten the kitchen before their call to Monroe. She should have put the rest of the casserole into the fridge to prevent bacteria growth but too late now. Knowing Logan, he'd eat anything, even if hair sprouted.

As eight o'clock arrived, Skylar joined Logan on the sofa. With luck, Monroe would have news about Maddie's whereabouts, and she and Logan could get the hell out and home. Placing a hand on his arm, she stopped Logan from dialing. "Why doesn't Monroe like to use the camera feature so we can see each other?"

With a finger poised over the phone, Logan smiled. "Security reasons, honey. Pam isn't the only one who can hack into a phone. Besides, you know Bob. He's a bit old school and prefers to use the landline." He hit Speed Dial.

Monroe answered on the first ring. "Tell me something good."

The man was blunt. Sky laughed. "We were hoping you'd do the honors." She sobered and leaned closer to Logan. "Look, Bob. Rachael found the check her husband wrote to Monroe Security. He told her the money was for a background clearance on me, but she's not stupid. The amount alone would raise questions. FYI, she handles all the books for the resort."

"Hmm. He should have used a separate account or even a money transfer." A pause. "What else?"

Sky shifted her butt. "You might want Pam to check on the resort's financials. Donald and Rachael

121

have different opinions about their money situation."

"In what way?"

"She says he's spending money they don't have, and he says otherwise. He looked genuinely concerned."

Logan leaned closer to the phone. "A lot of men let their wives handle the money. He could be oblivious."

"I told him my services weren't cheap, and he hadn't balked at the price." A tapping sounded over the line. "I hate to delve where we don't belong. The situation with Madeline doesn't involve money. As a rule, I don't do credit checks on my clients."

Sky never involved herself with the business side of Monroe Security. As office manager, Vicki had the responsibility of maintaining the books. Sky came in, worked with her class, then left. The invention of direct deposit took the stress out of waiting around on payday.

Logan nudged her arm. "Tell him what you said before I made this call."

"What did she say?"

Well, geez, she only had a suspicion. Sky met his gaze, then nodded. "Something doesn't feel right in that house, Bob. I suspect Rachael is cheating on her husband, but that's not what bothers me. Every time I'm near her, I get such an odd vibe. I can't put my finger on why. It's more than her not wanting a housekeeper."

"In other words, you're saying this case isn't what it seems?"

"Exactly."

"Okay, that's good enough for me. I'll talk to Pam and see what she can uncover. What else?"

Send me home. Please, please, please. Shooting

another glance at Logan, she smirked. "Rachael got Barbara Sanchez, head of housekeeping, involved. Mrs. Sanchez demanded I report to her. She is not happy Mr. Brookson ventured outside her department." She rested her head on Logan's shoulder.

"I'll have another talk with Brookson in the morning. Anything you need to add, Logan?"

Logan wrapped an arm around Sky's shoulders and kissed the top of her head. "Gabe and Wendell said I can work alone now. That gives me ample opportunity to watch out for Maddie."

"Did Wendell talk?"

"Surprisingly, yeah. He told me Rachael has a restraining order on Maddie."

Sky jerked back and stared. He'd never said a word at dinner. Come to think of it, neither had Brookson.

Monroe cleared his throat. "That's interesting. I haven't found anything of the sort. I'll widen my search. What else?"

"Wendell mentioned Maddie has a violent temper. He also described an entirely different institution. He made it sound as if his sister is in maximum security and escaped by incapacitating an orderly."

"Well, we know that isn't true. Why would he lie?"

"I don't know, but I feel like Sky. Something is totally wrong here."

A heavy sigh. "I don't like it either, but Sky, I want you to be persistent. Show up at the house anyway. We'll talk tomorrow night."

The call ended.

When she thought about it, she couldn't put her head on Logan's shoulder if they communicated with the camera feature. *Yay, to Bob's old-fashioned ways*!

Lifting her head, Sky stared at Logan. "Did he sound in a hurry?"

He shrugged. "Not any more than usual."

"But he didn't tell us anything new."

"That usually means he's confirming the information."

Shifting to rest her back against his solid body, Sky draped Logan's arm across her chest. "I don't know how Bob expects me to push my way inside the house. I already feel like an intruder. And I forgot to tell Bob about the back door always being unlocked."

"I'll text him, but I don't know what we can do if Rachael refuses to follow through. She's making it easy for Maddie to walk into the house. All Maddie has to do is study the habits of the two guards and wait until the coast is clear. Does Brookson secure the door at night?"

"I don't know, but I sure hope so."

Giving her a squeeze, Logan lifted his arm and sat forward. "It's time for our perimeter walk. And by the way, the blue pickup truck Wendell drives is his. Donald gave him a resort truck for his own personal use."

"Wow, that's generous." Sliding to the edge of the sofa cushion, Sky yawned. "I'm dog-tired, and I hadn't done a damn thing all day." She stood and stretched. "Let's go." Maybe the night air would help wake her so she could return to the cabin and jump Logan's bones…again. Judging how his gaze followed her stretch and the heat that poured out, he'd be more than willing.

Chapter Thirteen

If not for the intimacy she shared with Logan every night, Skylar would have packed her bags and hitchhiked back to New Jersey. She was wasting her time. Rachael didn't want protection. Maddie denied making threats. So, what the hell was going on here? She and Logan should be back home in her rancher, making love in her own bed. She grabbed him by his yellow T-shirt just before he left for his morning chores and verbalized her complaints.

"Persevere, Sky."

That's all he could say? Hell, at least, he did something with his time. He worked the grounds and searched for Maddie, but if Maddie denied the threats, what was he searching for? Maddie might never show—which was precisely Sky's argument. She had no patience to wait around for something to happen.

By mid-morning, after locking the cabin door behind her, Sky sucked in a long breath and braced for another day of working a job where she wasn't wanted. She could have avoided all this by refusing Monroe from the get-go. Rachael wasn't the least bit afraid of Madeline Harris. Any normal pregnant woman would barricade all doors and windows until the culprit was found. Sighing heavily, Sky took her slow stroll toward the Brookson house.

Glancing skyward, she smiled. Tiny puffs of clouds

floated across the clear, blue sky. They resembled broken pieces of cotton balls meandering in the breeze. The air, so crisp and clean, filled her lungs and made her wonder how she survived living in Chicago for so many years. Looking around, she didn't see any flowers popping from the soil, but trees had lots of diminutive buds ready to burst. She approached the side gate to the Brookson property and let herself in.

Now, the big question. Was Rachael home, or had she skipped out for the day? Sky wouldn't put it past the woman to run and hide somewhere. But at the sight of Buddy the Bulldog looking ready to charge, Rachael had to be inside the house. Sky waved. He glared. *So rude*. She hopped onto the back deck and knocked on the door.

The door flew open.

Rachael glowered. "You again?"

Sky internally rolled her eyes. "As long as your husband pays my salary, yes, me again." She stepped into the kitchen.

Moving aside, Rachael crossed her arms over her belly and smirked. "Mrs. Sanchez wants you in the main lodge today."

Here we go again. Why couldn't her mornings start with a request to do a load of laundry? No, right off the bat, Rachael pushed her out of the house. In truth, she should consider herself lucky to step inside at all. Frowning, she removed her jacket and draped it over one of the table chairs. "I'm not part of Mrs. Sanchez's department. You know that."

Rachael waved a hand in the air as she turned toward the dishwasher and hit the Start button. "FYI, the resort offers babysitting for staff and guests. It's one of our most popular amenities." Turning toward the table, she grabbed the dish towel and folded it. "Because the resort isn't open, the service is basically for staff, and she's had a callout. She wants you to fill in until four o'clock."

More likely, Rachael volunteered Sky as another ploy to get her out of her hair. Bad enough Sky agreed to be a housekeeper, but to be a babysitter? *Get real.* She had absolutely no experience with little children. God forbid she'd need to change a diaper. Sky pushed one of the kitchen chairs under the table. "Your husband told you I'm here for you alone. Yet, you refuse to have me do any chores. Why?"

Turning with a glare, she slammed her perfectly folded dish towel onto the counter. "I can do everything myself." She grabbed the washcloth and wiped the already sparkling tabletop. "I don't know what Donny was thinking when he hired you. I'm not having any problems with this pregnancy."

The sunlight off the deck hit her diamond-studded earrings and created a sparkle. They were a beautiful pair and probably worth some coin. The woman must sleep with them in her ears. "He's worried, Mrs. Brookson."

She harrumphed. "Of course, he's worried. It's our first child, but he doesn't have to pamper me." She tossed the washcloth into the sink. Then, squinting, she faced Sky and jammed her fists onto her hips. "I think he wants someone else around because of Maddie."

The woman was stubborn. Any normal woman with a threat over her head would welcome the added company. Sky resisted the urge to tell her so. "If that is true, Mrs. Brookson, then he hired me under false pretenses."

"You can quit."

"The way you're treating me, I'd say it's coming. But he hired me until you gave birth. I like to honor my contracts. As for Mrs. Sanchez, I don't work for her, and for the record, I do not babysit."

Rachael whipped out her phone. "I'll text her. She won't be happy." Fingers flying across the keyboard, she typed.

This damn woman was a piece of work. Sky should join Logan with the grounds work. She'd, at least, feel useful. She frowned down at the immaculate tabletop. Even the fruit bowl sparkled.

The front doorbell rang.

Rachael looked up from her phone and grinned. "Wendell's here. The upstairs showerhead broke this morning. See? I won't be alone. You can let him in."

Wendell again. The house must be falling apart. And why was Wendell using the front door when Brookson said he always used the back? *Talk about confusion.* Sky headed for the living room and peeked through the door's peephole.

Wendell stood on the front porch with a work pouch on his shoulder. His blue pickup truck with the resort emblem on the door sat in the driveway.

She opened the door.

Rachael hurried into the living room, carrying Sky's jacket. "You can go."

Gee, nothing like being direct. With little choice, Sky took her jacket and slipped her arms into the sleeves.

Wait...what? Instincts alerted, Sky paused. Since the jacket was constructed of a lightweight material, the subtle weight of something in her left pocket bounced against her side. She mentally scanned the contents of her pockets. With the exception of a few tissues, she rarely carried anything in her jacket. She preferred utilizing her cargo pants with its zippered or buttoned compartments.

Sirens sounded in the distance.

Brows rising, Sky shot her gaze from Rachael to Wendell.

With arms folded above her belly, Rachael smirked.

Still blocking the doorway, Wendell nodded with a curl to his upper lip.

Well, what do ya know? The entire scene smelled of a setup, and one glance at Rachael's empty earlobes told her precisely what was in her left jacket pocket. Sky slowly backed up a few steps. Then, quicker than a flash of light, she took a flying leap and collided into the table along the sofa back. Fumbling to right the table, she caught the ugly ornate bowl before it crashed to the floor.

Jumping toward her with a growl, Wendell grabbed onto Sky's arm and yanked her away from the table. "Trying to escape, Midnight?"

Yeah, he was in on it, all right. *Like I had any doubts.* She gave him a wan smile. "Sorry. I'm a little clumsy today."

Two police officers barged through the front door.

Rachael pointed. "Wendell stopped her, officers."

Logan burst through from the kitchen, slightly breathless. "What's going on?"

The two bodyguards hurried in right behind him.

While rubbing her belly, Rachael snorted. "Your

129

fiancée stole my diamond earrings. They were on the kitchen table." Narrowing her gaze, she leveled a finger at Sky. "Besides me, you were the only one in this house. They have to be on you. Those earrings are worth thousands of dollars."

Slapping a palm to her chest, Sky gasped. *See*? She could act. Glaring at Wendell, she yanked her arm from his grip. *Ouch*. The damn man was lucky he still stood on his feet. She rubbed the spot.

One of the officers, Sgt. Adams from his name plate, stepped in front of Sky. "Can I see your purse, ma'am?"

"I don't carry a purse."

Waving a hand, Rachael jerked her head toward Sky. "She always wears those tacky cargo pants, Officer. They have lots of pockets to hide stuff. But I'm guessing the studs are in her jacket pocket."

Tacky? Yeah, that's right. Piss me off.

"Let me have your jacket, ma'am."

Ma'am? How old did she look? Suppressing a snort, she slipped off the jacket and handed it to Sgt. Adams.

He inspected the pockets. "Nothing. I'll need to check your pants pockets, please."

Logan came alongside. "Midnight, what's going on?"

Sky rolled her eyes. "Rachael is suffering from a hormonal imbalance." She shifted her gaze to Sgt. Adams. "I didn't steal anything, Officer. You can check my pockets, but Rachael has a habit of always misplacing her earrings. If she doesn't throw them near the fruit bowl on the kitchen table, then she tosses them out here into this ugly bowl." She nodded toward the slightly askew table by the sofa.

Eyes wide, Rachael gasped. "I do not!"

Sgt. Adams raised a black brow and approached the table by the sofa. Tilting the bowl to check its contents, he shot a glance at Rachael, reached inside, and his fingers came out holding the diamond studs.

Rachael whirled. "You put them there!"

Sky adjusted her T-shirt. "Hardly."

Turning toward the officers, Rachael gaped. "I know she took them. I don't know how they wound up in the bowl."

With a kind smile touching his thick lips, Sgt. Adams handed Sky her jacket. "I can't arrest someone without proof, Mrs. Brookson."

Lips tight, she shifted her gaze between the cops and Sky. "I guess I was wrong." She peered at Sky.

"I guess you were." *Gotcha, bitch.* Then, she shot a glare at Rachael's co-conspirator.

Wendell puffed out his cheeks and released a slow breath while staring at the floor.

What she wouldn't give to make Wendell look like a raccoon. And Rachael...damn her. No matter how tempting, Sky wouldn't hurt a pregnant woman.

Muttering under her breath, Rachael whirled to face the two guards. "What are you doing in my house? Get back to your post—now!"

The guards exchanged a frown, shrugged, and left the way they came in.

Internally seething, but before she said or did something she'd regret, Sky lifted her chin and shot a laser gaze at Rachael. "Since you don't need me today, I'll head back to my cabin." Eyes turning into slits, Sky leaned toward Rachael. "We will discuss this later."

Grabbing onto Logan's arm, she met his wide-eyed stare and, with a nod, motioned for him to follow her out the front door. Once clear of the Brookson house, Sky hissed. "I'm furious."

"I can tell. What the hell happened?"

"That damn woman tried to frame me."

Logan patted the hand gripping his arm. "You need to calm down. You're stopping my circulation."

She opened her mouth, then slapped it shut. Seeing the color of his hand, she winced. *Oh, my God, his fingers are blue*! "Sorry." Loosening her hold, she rubbed his arm to get the blood flowing.

Logan flexed his fingers until they turned pink. "How did you know?"

Releasing several slow breaths to get her blood pressure under control, she stared at nothing in particular. "If it wasn't for Wendell coming to the front door when Donald told me he always used the back, I would not have had any idea anything was amiss. She sent me to let Wendell in, then came out carrying my jacket. Once I slipped it on, I knew something was in my pocket."

"They were tiny earrings, Sky, with hardly any weight. How could you feel them?"

She nudged his arm. "You know how you can feel a penny in your pocket?"

"I never feel a penny. I'm not even sure I'll feel a quarter."

"Well, when you have heightened senses like I do, even a feather can be felt. As soon as I slipped on my jacket, I sensed the change in weight."

Rotating his head, he stared. "I didn't know this about you." He shook himself. "You're right. There's a lot we don't know about each other. But how did the earrings get into the bowl?"

She shrugged one shoulder. "I tripped."

Stopping, he gaped. "On purpose?"

"Of course, on purpose. You know damn well I don't trip." She nudged him to continue along the road.

"Why the hell would she frame you?"

"She wants me out of the house, Logan, and Wendell is her partner-in-crime." Damn, just thinking about them made her blood pressure rise. "I don't know what kind of game they're playing, but she was willing to have me arrested."

Logan's muscles tensed under her fingers. She looked his way just as he twitched his jaw.

"I don't like this, Sky." He squeezed the hand on his arm. "We definitely need to talk to Monroe."

Yeah, maybe Bob would cancel the contract, and she and Logan could go home. *Wishful thinking.* "Where was Donald Brookson during all this? He had to hear the sirens."

"He left the resort about an hour ago."

"Wow, that's good timing—unless they planned their little scheme to coincide with Donald's absence." *Those sneaky, little devils.* If Sky had agreed to babysit, all would be well. But she refused, and Rachael activated their Plan B by texting Wendell, not Mrs. Sanchez. More than ever, Sky was convinced something more serious was going on within the Brookson house.

Chapter Fourteen

After assuring Logan she would be all right, Sky entered the cabin and stood with her back to the closed door. She lied to her lover boy. The anger still churned deep inside, and the thought of smashing something into pieces played on her mind. That infuriating woman! And Wendell... What Sky wouldn't do to get both of them onto her mat. Before her blood pressure squirted out her ears, Sky stomped around the cabin, kicked and swung at the open air, until the boiler within her chest lost some of its steam. Luckily, she hadn't broken anything, but she was tempted. Even worse, she didn't give a damn.

That night, with one of Fay's wonderful chicken-and-mushroom casseroles for dinner, Skylar stared at her portion. The physical exertion of a MA workout only relieved her tension for a short time. A long hot shower didn't help, either. She still seethed over the scene in Rachael's living room, and as hard as she tried, she couldn't hide the pain of such a betrayal.

Logan stretched his long arm across the table and squeezed her hand. "Your lightning speed saved you, Sky. If you hadn't sensed something in your pocket, you'd be in a locked cell."

Snorting, she toyed with the food on her plate. "You're not helping."

After giving her hand a light pat, he slid the

casserole dish closer and spooned on another hefty portion. "We'll talk to Monroe and see what he wants to do. In my opinion, it's ridiculous for you to continue as her housekeeper."

"I agree." After today's stunt, how could she possibly step foot into the Brookson house? She wanted to strangle Rachael, not protect her. If Logan wasn't her partner on this case, she'd be back in her rancher with her feet propped on the sofa. She took a sip of her iced tea. "I don't care what Monroe says. I'm sleeping in tomorrow." *Like until noon.*

He shoveled in a mouthful, chewed, and swallowed. "Talk to Monroe first. He might have a few suggestions." He eyed her plate. "Eat your meal. It's very good."

Everything Fay cooked was good. If Sky ate with the tenants every night, she'd gain a lot of weight. Sighing, Sky nibbled on a small portion, and the taste of charred chicken smothered in mushrooms and white sauce triggered her appetite. She took another bite.

Throughout their relationship, Sky often ate dinner with Logan, either at her place or his, sometimes two to three times a week. She never reflected on how it looked or felt, but here, sitting together for dinner every night in a small cabin, she had a good idea what marriage would be like. For this assignment, she and Logan were actually living as an engaged couple. Should she consider the arrangement a test run? All preliminary evidence pointed to a successful union should they give up their separate residences. But was she ready to relinquish her freedom by allowing a permanent man into her life?

She glanced at the engagement ring on her left

hand. Logan told her more than once how marriage didn't fit into his lifelong plan. But since then, he'd hinted at sharing expenses. He hadn't explained *how* they would share. She assumed he meant living together. He'd certainly planted the seed, because the idea of living alone for the rest of her life held no appeal. Maybe she should seriously consider taking the plunge.

When eight o'clock rolled around, Sky flopped onto the sofa next to Logan for their nightly chat with Monroe.

After a quick kiss, Logan hit the Speed Dial button.

Monroe answered on the first ring. "Okay. Talk to me."

She nudged Logan. "Should I go first?"

"Definitely. You've had the more exciting day." He held the phone closer to her face.

Just thinking about Rachael ignited the anger again. But, at least, the urge to destroy something disappeared. She heaved a sigh. "Look, Bob, Rachael did a number on me today. This morning, she told me to babysit the staff's children in the main lodge. When I said *no*—" Glancing at Logan, she took a deep breath and recounted the earrings setup.

Afterward, Monroe cursed. "What is wrong with that woman?"

Yeah, Sky would like to know, too. "The whole scheme felt prearranged. More likely, she pretended to text Mrs. Sanchez when, in fact, she texted Wendell and told him Plan B was in effect."

"So, when she asked you to answer the door, she used the opportunity to slip the earrings into your pocket. Damn, Sky, that arrest would have complicated the entire case."

Yeah, no shit. Not to mention she'd need a good lawyer.

Logan leaned toward the phone. "Brookson was not at the resort when the police sirens echoed off the trees. In all probability, Rachael knew beforehand when Donald was leaving. The frame-up would have worked if Sky didn't possess her ninja speed."

"And thank God for that." A tapping sounded in the background. "I talked to Brookson earlier about his wife's behavior. After today, though, I can honestly say I'm stumped. I hate to do it, but I might have to pull you out, Sky."

Yes! "I don't know what else to do."

"Since Rachael doesn't want a housekeeper, maybe she'll settle for a driver."

Sky suppressed a groan. "Well, that's swell. I can sit on the front porch all day to wait for her to call me like some dog." Smirking at Logan, she rolled her eyes.

"It's our only alternative, unless Brookson can convince his wife to keep you in the house. Frankly, I don't have a whole lot of faith in the man. Any news on your end, Logan?"

Logan lifted the phone toward his mouth. "None."

"Okay, then. Tomorrow, I guarantee I will have all the information we need. Keep on your toes."

The call ended.

Logan tossed his phone onto the coffee table. Sitting back, he combed all ten fingers through his hair. "I've worked some strange cases, but this beats them all." Meeting her gaze, he extended his arm. "Come here."

He needn't ask twice. Like a magnet, she went

willingly and placed her back against his chest. Then, she grabbed his arm and draped it over her shoulder. This position was her favorite. She loved the feel of his strong arm pressing against her breasts. If possible, she'd sit here forever and forget about what tomorrow might bring. "Somehow, this doesn't feel right."

He jerked his arm. "What, us?"

Geez. He got all tense from her simple comment. Lifting his forearm, she kissed his bare skin. The coarse hairs tickled her upper lip, and as usual, she kissed a hairy rock. She almost giggled. "No, I mean sitting here like this while all the questions about Maddie's intentions go unanswered. Maybe Wendell fabricated the entire story."

"It's a strong possibility. But we should hold off with speculating until we talk to Monroe tomorrow night. Right now, think of the facts we have." He counted on his fingers. "One, Maddie is not missing. She's still teaching her yoga class. Two, Maddie did not escape a maximum security facility nor did she injure an orderly. Three, Wendell lied."

"Wendell should be at the top of the list."

"Yes, something is going on here. But we'll wait for Monroe's update tomorrow. For the time being, we'll continue our perimeter walks around the complex. That's all we can do." He kissed the top of her head.

She toyed with his arm hairs. "This is getting confusing. Wendell probably lied about Maddie's MA skills, too." Rotating her head, she caught his gaze. "Nothing makes sense."

Logan squeezed her hip. "I agree." He kissed her nose. "By the way, Pam sent us a more recent photo of Maddie. Have you seen it?"

She harrumphed. "I was too busy avoiding arrest."

"Reach for my phone, will you?"

Leaving the comfort of his arm, Sky leaned forward to grab his phone from the coffee table. After handing it over, she fell back against him and replaced his arm to her favorite position.

He skimmed through the photos. "Here she is." He handed her the phone.

The woman was very attractive with auburn hair cut in a flyaway style. Her brown eyes twinkled, as if the photographer caught her at a happy moment. "She almost looks like Wendell." She flipped between the photo provided by Brookson to the new one from Pam. "Maddie looks totally different with this new hairstyle. Is this shot from the institution?"

"No, her yoga studio. You'll notice Brookson's photo is at least five years old, perhaps more."

"Judging from her clothing, I'd say more like seven years." She handed him the phone. "I do marvel at what Pam finds over the Internet. Remind me never to get on her bad side." Again, she toyed with his arm hairs. "What does Donald do all day if his wife handles the books?"

After slipping his phone onto the end table near him, he snorted. "I have no idea."

His fingers caressed her left hip. Even after all this time, his touch still created goose bumps. She hoped the sensation never stopped. "Do you ever get the feeling we're wasting our time?"

"I do." He patted her left hip. "Bob said he'll have all the answers tomorrow. Be patient."

Easy for him to say. He wasn't being pushed away by Wendell.

After squeezing her torso, he lifted his arm and stood. Turning, he extended his hand. "Let's go for our walk. When we return, I want to make love to my beautiful fiancée."

Smiling, she took his hand and stood. "Can't we go into the bedroom first?"

He gave her a one-eyed glare.

"All right, all right." Pouting, she tugged on her T-shirt. "Business first, pleasure later." *Darn.*

****

As Logan leaned against the kitchen counter sipping his morning cup of joe, he couldn't fight the feeling of helplessness deep inside his gut. For years, the honed instincts that kept him alive as an undercover cop saved his ass more times than he could count. A tingling scalp? That meant danger. The hairs rising on his forearms? His person of interest just walked through a door. But the one instinct that persisted ever since he arrived at Chadbury Lodge was the damn itchy feeling crawling across his skin. That meant something wasn't right. The whole case bothered him. Why was Rachael so reluctant to have a housekeeper, and why would she connive to have Sky arrested for theft? Why would Wendell lie about his sister's institution and whereabouts? What the hell was the real story here?

Usually, Monroe took a week, sometimes two, to gather his intel and all for the purpose of keeping his agents safe. But he and Sky left New Jersey with the barest of facts. Any wonder why he was swamped with confusion. With luck, tonight's conversation would satisfy this itchy feeling.

With short hair mussed and a gaping yawn, Sky lumbered in and headed straight for the coffee machine.

Her eyes were half-closed, and she passed by him as if he was invisible. While watching her, he smiled into his cup. She wasn't a morning person, but she'd often wake to kiss him goodbye. Her effort always shot an arrow into his heart.

Like he'd done a thousand times, he let his gaze scan her from head to toe and take in the beauty that was Skylar Dawson. She wore an oversized black T-shirt. Her legs and feet were bare, and he loved the look of the toned muscles in her thighs and calves. Her choice of an all-black wardrobe was a bit unusual, but he couldn't complain. Black hair with black clothes made her crystal-blue eyes pop. And her floral scent always smelled so good. Even now, the fragrance permeated the small kitchen and created visions of her floating through a flower field, like some fairy-tale nymph. He'd never tell her, of course. She'd give him a one-eyed glare and demand he have his head examined. But she was as beautiful in the morning as any time of day, and he was damn lucky to share her bed.

She had no idea of her power over him. He loved this woman and, if necessary, would die for her. During their last case, when the danger level increased, he opened his heart and told her how he loved her too much to let the words go unsaid. He shocked her, of course, and she never returned the sentiment. He was okay with her silence. She needed time to process. He wasn't sure how long she'd take, but someday, she might tell him what was in her heart. Until then, he'd wait. After a sip of coffee, he chuckled. "A cold shower would do wonders to help open your eyes."

Lips pursed, she narrowed her gaze. "Not when you keep me awake for half the night." She sniffed her coffee before taking a sip. Catching his gaze, she smiled. "Don't stop, by the way. I love how you keep me awake."

He gave a curt nod. "Anytime." She was a hellion in bed. Her martial arts kept her in shape, and she pushed for fast and furious. On the other hand, he loved slow and leisurely—and to drive her wild with want. "Why are you up? You said you wanted to sleep in."

Moving to his side, she clamped a hand behind his neck and kissed him. Releasing her hold, she smiled. "Call me crazy, but I like my morning kiss."

His ego soared. One of these days, she might actually say she loved him. He stroked a finger down her cheek. "Monroe texted you last night about Rachael agreeing to keep you as a driver. Maybe she'll go out somewhere, and you'll see some of the nearby towns."

She rolled her eyes. "What Rachael says and what she does are two different things. Just because she agreed doesn't mean she'll call me." She scanned the kitchen. "Did you eat?"

"I had some of Fay's leftover casserole. It tastes good cold, too." Gulping the last of his coffee, he placed the mug into the sink, pecked her lips, and grabbed his phone. "I need to get going. See you at lunch?"

She yawned in answer.

God, she was so damn cute. Before he ravished her with kisses, he hurried out the door.

Chapter Fifteen

Forty minutes passed as Logan waited for Gabe Rumfeld. He propped an arm onto the top of a filing cabinet in Gabe's office while fighting off the nervous energy to do something besides stand here and stare at the wall. Every morning, like clockwork, Logan and Wendell met their boss at precisely seven fifteen to receive orders for the day. Granted, he'd only been on the job for four days, but people rarely deviated from a pattern. After shooting another glance at the clock above the door, Logan drummed his fingers on the filing cabinet. "Should we call someone? Maybe Gabe got in an accident."

Slumped in the lone office chair against the wall, Wendell played on his cell phone. Without removing his gaze from the screen, he smirked. "Gabe already called to say he'd be late. Emergency staff meeting." He glanced up. "Department heads only." He resumed his focus on the phone.

Logan clenched his jaw. A heads-up might have been nice. Why the big secret? Hell, he could have raked the entire playground by now. But if Wendell wanted to waste time, then Logan would do the same. He suppressed a yawn. "Does this happen often?"

"No. Usually, staff meetings are scheduled for mid-morning. So, something's up." Meeting his cohort's gaze, he grinned. "Gabe will fill us in."

Hmm. Whatever prevented Gabe from his morning briefing must be important. In Logan's book, any break from routine always raised a red flag. His damn itchy feeling increased.

Ten minutes later, Gabe stormed into the office and marched directly to his desk chair. Cursing profusely, he slammed his clipboard onto the desk.

Whoa. Whatever went on at the meeting gave the older man a beet-red face with veins pulsing at both temples. If he wasn't careful, he'd have a stroke right in front of his staff. What the hell happened to cause such a reaction? The guy was usually so laid-back.

Hands jammed on hips, Gabe shifted a hot glare from Logan to Wendell. "Mr. Brookson has decided to open the resort early."

Oh, shit. Logan's gut tightened. Opening early would change everything. He cleared his throat and put as nonchalant a tone in his voice as possible. "Is that a problem?"

Wendell harrumphed. "Depends on how early." Gaze narrowed, he tucked his phone into his shirt pocket. "What's our new date?"

Gabe rubbed his neck. "May first."

Mouth agape, Wendell sat forward. "Next week? Is he nuts? Did you tell him we'll need more staff?"

"I did. I even showed him the list of chores on my clipboard, none of which can be done in a week. I'm still waiting for delivery of roof shingles for cabins ten and three. Donald just shrugged his damn shoulders."

Logan glanced from one man to the other. Obviously, opening early hadn't been done before. And considering the circumstances that brought Sky and Logan to the resort, Brookson truly had a screw loose.

What prompted such a sudden change? He pushed away from the filing cabinet. "I'm sure some of the other departments put in their two cents."

Cursing softly, Gabe kicked his chair. "Hell, yeah. Mrs. Sanchez is throwing a royal fit. She has one girl who works part-time in the lodge, cleaning offices and such. The majority of her staff will be in college classes until mid-May. She relies on them to clean the cabins." He flopped into the chair. "I use college kids, too. So, I'm in the same pickle."

Wendell shot Gabe a one-eyed glare. "What brought this on?"

Using one hand to rub his forehead, Gabe released a long sigh. "Evidently, the money is going out faster than coming in. Mrs. Brookson suggested an early opening to generate some cash flow."

Well, hell. Sky was right to suggest a financial check on the resort. But why would Brookson agree to an early opening? With the addition of tourists roaming the grounds, he'd need to hire more personnel to protect his wife. Whether Brookson realized it or not, he already had a security nightmare on his hands with all the woods surrounding the resort. Adding tourists to the equation would jeopardize any hope of protecting Rachael—especially for a woman refusing protection.

Gabe scrubbed his hands over his face. "The restaurant isn't ready, either." He dropped his hands to the armrests. "The chef won't be here for another two weeks. There's no food in the pantry and no wait staff. The lifeguards aren't scheduled until June first, but thankfully, the weather will be too cold to open the pool."

"Donny needs an eye-opener." Wendell sat back

and crossed his left leg over his right knee. "Every department uses college kids. Without them, he'll have to hire a slew of people to get this place ready. So, his money outlay will cost more than if he waited for his normal opening day. What do you think, Logan?"

Nice argument, Wendell. Logan nodded. "I agree. He'd have to hire an employment agency or some temp service because advertising won't be fast enough. Also, with the resort's history of opening on a certain date, he'd need to broadcast the new opening day, and that costs money."

Leaning back in his chair, Gabe ran both hands through his thick, dark hair and pulled the strands. "Mrs. Brookson said no hiring of additional personnel until further notice." He eyed both men. "They can't afford it."

Was Rachael tying a noose around her own neck? Considering he and Sky had questions about Maddie's true intentions, he couldn't just dismiss Wendell's story without proof. So, why in hell would Donald agree to an early opening? Didn't he have the guts to say *no*?

Gaze glaring, Gabe leaned forward and slammed an open palm onto his desk. "I refuse to let you two work sunup to sundown. The grounds and cabins won't be ready, and that's too damn bad."

While glancing from one man to the other, Logan crossed his arms over his chest. "Did a department have an unexpected expense over the winter?"

Frowning, Gabe flopped back in his chair. "Not in my area. I can't say about inside the main lodge." He shifted his gaze from one man to the other. "Mrs. Brookson handles the books. She would know what's going on."

Logan tugged on an ear. "She should also consider the possibility of no one booking a cabin. She'd rush everyone to get their jobs done only to have the staff sit around and twiddle their thumbs. Maybe Brookson should hire a general manager."

Slamming his foot to the floor, Wendell straightened in the chair and glared. "You saying the missus is siphoning money?"

Hmm. The man came to the lady's defense pretty darn quick. Siphoning money never entered Logan's mind—until this exact moment. Logan held up his left hand, palm outward. "All I'm saying is Mrs. Brookson might be too busy to keep track of every department. From what Gabe told us, Brookson sounds a little disconnected from reality. A general manager would solve the problem. And let's not forget about the baby due in a couple months. Rachael will be busy with a newborn."

Relaxing, Wendell sighed. "Yeah, you're right." He caught Logan's gaze. "I hate to say this, but your fiancée is collecting a full-time salary, and she doesn't do anything. Rachael wants her fired, but Donny insists she stay." He narrowed his gaze. "I suspect Donny hired her to keep an eye on his wife, like the guards."

Logan waggled a finger. "Midnight was hired to help a pregnant woman who refuses to acknowledge her due date is approaching. I, for one, don't want my fiancée to put her life in danger because of your jealous sister."

Nodding, Wendell recrossed his legs. "All right, but forewarn Midnight. My sister is unstable, and with her martial arts skills, she could do some serious damage. Best to let the guards handle her."

Wendell sounded as if he didn't give a damn about his sister's safety. Logan had a sister, and no way in hell would he want her hurt by some overzealous bodyguard.

Brows high, Gabe swiveled his chair to face Wendell. "Since when is Maddie unstable? I heard she was doing very well with her therapy."

"She was, but she disappeared a couple weeks ago and hasn't been seen since." Wendell tugged on the hem of his pant leg.

Gabe narrowed his gaze. "That doesn't sound like Maddie. Are you sure something didn't happen?"

Wendell shot him a glare. "Yeah, I'm sure. I'm her emergency contact. If anything happened, I'd have heard. Trust me, Gabe. She's jealous of Rachael's pregnancy."

Brows furrowed, Gabe rocked his brows but said nothing else.

Interesting. Another opinion about Maddie's mental state? Since Logan heard two versions about the resort's finances, could two impressions about Maddie exist? If possible, Logan would like to catch Gabe alone to talk about this further. Logan nodded at Gabe. "I know a few veterans who wouldn't mind some temporary work with the grounds."

The boss snorted. "I'll keep them in mind. With luck, Donald will come to his senses and see the additional expense of opening early. In the meantime, let's get our day started."

Scenarios raced through Logan's thoughts. Short term, the change in plans might prove beneficial. His two veterans, Tank and Boomer, could provide extra eyes on Rachael Brookson. In addition, Monroe could have two more agents book a cabin as guests. As far as the lodge finances? With luck, Pam would uncover the reason behind Rachael's demand for breaking with tradition.

With the day's chores in hand, Logan and Wendell separated to work on the cabins. Most were in decent shape, but some had rain gutters busted by tree branches. Any cabins meeting one hundred percent on the checklist were relayed to Mrs. Sanchez. Housekeeping had their own checklist to ready the rooms for guests. Of course, if no one came running after the announcement of their new opening day, hurrying to prepare the cabins would turn into a total waste of time.

By the end of the day, Logan drove his cart toward the maintenance building with the wagon loaded with scrap metal from busted rain gutters. A dust cloud on Chaddy-Wonker Drive drew his gaze. Wendell's blue truck flew up the road like the forest was on fire. Knowing Wendell left provided Logan with the opportunity to talk to Gabe—provided the boss was still around.

Luckily, Gabe's black pickup truck was parked on the gravel parking area next to the building. Logan hurried to unhitch the cart's wagon near the growing pile of recyclable metal, then drove the cart into the garage to plug it in for the night. Taking a few seconds to brush the leaves and dirt from his clothes, he strolled into Gabe's office.

The older man had his head bent over a large map of the resort. He looked up. "Hey, heading home?"

"In a minute." Logan stuffed his hands into his front pockets. "I wanted to ask you about Maddie. You

149

didn't think she was unstable, but Wendell thinks otherwise. I have concerns about Midnight getting caught in the middle of a feud."

Sighing, Gabe leaned back in his chair and rocked. "I haven't seen Maddie for a while. Wendell could be right."

"That's not what your face told me earlier." He sat in the chair by the wall. "Tell me about her."

Gabe clamped his hands behind his head and stretched. After dropping his arms to the armrests, he gave a soft smile. "I've known Donald, Maddie, and Wendell since they were teenagers. When Donald inherited the resort from his grandparents, he met Rachael and fell in love. From the beginning, Maddie spoke ill of Rachael and even disrupted the wedding." He stopped rocking. "I was on vacation for my twenty-year anniversary when Maddie supposedly attacked Rachael."

Gabe didn't sound convinced about Maddie's behavior. Was his opinion a worthwhile clue? Logan narrowed his gaze. "What do you mean *supposedly*?"

"Just that. I have no idea what happened. Maddie hasn't been on the resort grounds since."

"Wendell sent her to a mental institution, right?"

Gabe waved a hand. "The place is one of those new facilities where patients come and go. Maddie could have kept her apartment and her job at the yoga studio and still receive counseling, but Wendell convinced her to save money by giving up both."

"That doesn't make sense. Why resign her job?"

Gabe shrugged. "Made no sense to me, either. Wendell signed her up for a room at the facility, kind of an all-inclusive deal complete with meals." He scratched his ear. "From what I know, that's expensive."

"Wendell foots the bill, then."

"I never asked. None of my business. As far as her being unstable because of Rachael's pregnancy, I can't help you. Doesn't sound like her, though. I couldn't believe she needed counseling, either."

"And what about her martial arts?"

Gabe shook his head. "News to me. Maddie's limber, I'll say that for her. She's been doing yoga for years, so I'm not surprised she embraced martial arts. She's probably good, too."

Ah, well. Logan hadn't learned anything earth-shattering. Digging up the dirt was Monroe's job. He said good night to Gabe and headed to the cabin. Despite Gabe stating he would not overwork his two men, the boss had kept them hopping. For lunch, Logan scarfed down the remainder of last night's chicken-and-mushroom casserole, along with two bottles of water. The food held him for like two hours, and he compensated by drinking more water. Now, his gut sounded like a cage full of lions. Nearing the cabin, he stopped short.

Well, this is a surprise. Pam O'Connor's yellow car sat parked next to his. For such a small size, the vehicle had a huge trunk, which Pam loved, especially when she traveled with her electronic equipment. No one told him she was coming, though. He entered the cabin. "Honey, I'm home!" He loved saying that. The words made their fake engagement feel real. He'd never tell Sky, of course, but on several occasions, he caught her staring at the ring on her finger. She always looked pensive or, maybe, the word was wistful. Frankly, he didn't know what the hell her expression meant.

Sky, followed by Pam, moseyed out of the spare bedroom.

As usual, his heart thumped at the sight of his woman. She had the power to drop a man to his knees.

Walking alongside her, Pam O'Connor couldn't be more different. A redhead with freckles and green eyes, she was small and petite and wore all kinds of colorful clothes. Today, she wore a bright pink T-shirt with *I'm the Best* printed on the front. She had a right to brag. As an MIT graduate at the top of her class, she was a brilliant IT tech. Pulling his damp shirt away from his chest, he smiled. "Hey, you two. What's going on?"

Sky approached him for a quick kiss. "Pam surprised me, too. If anyone asks, she's my cousin. She was in the area and stopped by."

"And I come bearing gifts." Pam threw a thumb over her shoulder. "Vicki cooked lasagna. I'll heat the dish while you take a shower." She headed for the kitchen.

His mouth watered. Vittoria Carbone, office manager and grandmother to all, was a legendary Italian cook. "How much time do you need?"

Pam glanced over her shoulder. "Probably twenty minutes."

"Great. But first—" While Pam's back was turned, he grabbed the front of Sky's T-shirt and hauled her against his chest. His mouth pressed onto hers for a real kiss. If he wasn't so hot and sweaty, he'd wrap her in a tight embrace. He released her and grinned. "Hi."

She patted his chest. "Hi to you, too." She scanned him from head to toe. "You're covered with dried leaves. Busy day?"

"Yeah, and I'll explain why during dinner. I'm starving. How was your day?"

She exaggerated a sigh. "Rachael went shopping…alone. She drove herself. I found out after the fact." She snorted. "So much for me being her driver."

Rachael Brookson's reluctance to have Sky in her house was a glaring red flag. What the hell was that woman's problem?

Chapter Sixteen

After washing away the grunge from a hard day replacing one too many rain gutters, Logan joined Sky and Pam already sitting at the table by the front window. The cabin smelled like an Italian kitchen, and knowing Vicki's culinary skills, the lasagna was loaded with cheese and meat—in his opinion, a man's meal. Pam even bought two baguettes—the super large size. No wine, though. Pam avoided alcohol in every shape and form. So, naturally, buying wine to complement dinner would be far from her mind. Sky, bless her, had a can of beer waiting by his plate.

Pam cut the lasagna into serving pieces and loaded each dish. Glancing his way, she smiled. "You look much better. All clean."

Dropping into his chair, he grunted. "You won't believe how many cobwebs I walked through."

Sky and Pam shared a look, then spoke simultaneously. "Eww."

He kept his mouth shut about the one-inch wood spiders he encountered. Man, they were bigger than his thumb. The women would have nightmares. Scanning the food on the table, he rubbed his hands together. Because he was thirsty as hell, he grabbed the beer can, popped the tab, and guzzled half the brew. The cold liquid felt like heaven on his parched throat. Heaving a satisfied sigh, he smacked his lips. The fluid gave him the fortitude to handle what was coming. He couldn't imagine why Pam drove so far when a phone call would do. "Okay, Pam, tell me why you're here."

After licking red sauce from her finger, she cocked her head and grinned. "Isn't it enough that I like you two, and I think you're such a cute couple?"

"No." After picking up his fork, he looked at Sky. "Did she tell you?"

Chuckling, she cut her portion into bite-size pieces. "Nope. She said she hates to repeat herself."

"That's right. So, let's eat, and I'll tell you." Pam shifted her chair closer to the table, grabbed one of the baguettes, and broke off a piece. Her cell phone sang a strange little tune. Slipping it from her rear pocket, she stood. "Excuse me. Personal call." She hurried from the room.

Ordinarily, Logan had no interest in someone's personal life, but he caught a tiny smile on Sky's lips. He narrowed his gaze. "What?"

"Nothing."

"Don't give me that. What made you smile?" He shoveled in a mouthful of lasagna. Damn, as expected, it was loaded with meat and mozzarella cheese—a perfect combo for a hungry man.

She glanced toward the spare bedroom. "She's probably talking to Boomer."

His lasagna almost went down whole. Hurriedly chewing, he swallowed with the help of his beer. "Boomer?" He shook himself. "Since when?"

"A couple of months. I don't think it's serious…yet." Catching his gaze, she chuckled. "Don't look so surprised. It's not a secret, but they're being discreet…like us."

And doing a hell of a job if he failed to catch on. He was a trained detective. How in the world did he miss the clues? He drummed his fingers on the table. "How long have you known?"

Breaking off a piece of bread, she shrugged. "About a month. I caught them sneaking a kiss over by the punching bags." She bit into her bread and chewed. "I don't know Boomer that well. He hasn't been on my mat, but I've seen him working the weights. How did he get his name?"

Logan swallowed his mouthful. "He's actually Boomer, Junior. Named after his dad who was a demolition derby competitor."

Brows high, she sat back. "I have no idea what you're talking about."

He waved his fork. "Years ago, there was a sport called the Demolition Derby. A bunch of ordinary street cars went into an arena and smashed their back ends into each other. The last car moving under its own power was declared the winner." He chuckled. "That was way before my time."

Mouth gaping, she blinked. "You're serious?"

"The competition was very popular, Sky. My granddad talked about it being on TV every weekend." He ate a large mouthful, chewed, then swallowed. "Cars back then were made of steel and capable of ramming into another without falling into pieces. Today, vehicles are constructed of aluminum or fiberglass and, of course, are way too expensive to crash. By the time Boomer, Junior, was of age to drive, the sport was pretty much dead, but the name stuck."

Pam returned and plopped onto her chair. "Okay, where was I? Oh, yeah, why I'm here." She picked up her fork. "As you know, Bob asked me to find out what I could on the resort's finances. I hacked into the reservation desk easily enough. The resort is booked from June first on—just as Brookson said. I even accessed the maintenance computer, but I could not access any computers in the lodge office. I assume Rachael uses one. In this day and age, keeping books by hand is tedious." She shifted her gaze between Logan and Sky. "Do either of you know how many computers they use?"

Before answering, Logan sipped his beer. "Sky and I aren't cleared to enter the main lodge."

Brows rising, Pam sat back. "Cleared?"

Sky swallowed her mouthful. "Yeah, cleared. It pertains to third floor access where the offices are."

"Oh." She frowned. "Okay. Then, I'll assume the office computers are taken offline whenever they are not in use." She used her bread to push lasagna onto her fork. "I'm here today because the resort offers free Wi-Fi for their guests. You know from my constant drilling that free equates to unsecured. On the off-chance Rachael or Donald access their computers, I want to be ready. If a good security program is in place, I need to work quickly before it cuts me off." She ate her forkful and hummed. "This is so good."

Logan stifled a laugh. "Don't get all orgasmic on us. Continue."

Grinning like a cartoon character, she broke off another piece of baguette before proceeding. "Not too many people turn off their computers these days. Those in the know realize how easily a hacker gets into the system on an open network. I set up my equipment in the spare bedroom to detect any computer on this property, and I'm here because I need time without technical interference before I'm so rudely disconnected." She stuffed half the bread into her mouth and chewed.

Logan helped himself to another large portion of lasagna. He glanced at Pam and Sky. "Anyone else want more?"

Both women shook their heads.

Yes! Their refusal meant more for him. He made sure every morsel fell off the spoon. "Was anything significant uncovered with anyone else?" He dug in.

Pam swallowed. "Madeline Harris popped up on my name search. About a month ago, she bought a used 2021 silver sedan and paid cash."

Logan shook his head. "I can't see how she can afford a car when the room and board at the institution must cost an arm and a leg. Someone had to give her the money."

"Like a brother?" Sky waggled a brow. "How much, Pam? Oh—wait!" She cringed. "You don't have to answer. I don't want you in trouble for breaking into a bank."

Sitting back, Pam laughed. "Don't worry. I have no need to break into an account when a statement is left wide open." She dabbed her mouth with a napkin. "Do you know how many people never sign out of their online accounts? The habit is especially dumb when they leave their computer on with all the tabs open. It makes for easy pickings for a hacker—like me." She grinned, then cleared her throat. "But in answer to your question, the car cost eighty-seven hundred. According to Wendell's bank records, the money didn't come from him."

Hmm. Logan stared at his plate. "We've got a real mystery here." He caught Pam's gaze. "Does Maddie have a bank account?"

"A small one. No deposits or withdrawals, either." She cut a portion with her fork. "Funny thing is I found the account open on Wendell's computer. I mentioned it to Bob. He said he'd check into it."

Sky wiped her mouth. "What about Maddie's institution? Even an open-door facility costs money. Who's paying for her care?"

Pam broke off another piece of baguette. "Sad to say, the institution was the easiest hack of all. If I was a criminal, I'd have a field day with all the available info. As for Madeline, a small percentage for her room and board came from her brother and—get this—the larger part from the Chadbury Lodge Resort. Rachael signed the checks. Strangely enough, the payments stopped four months ago."

Whoa. That was a surprising piece of news. Brow raised, Logan straightened in his seat. "Why would Rachael pay for a woman who attacked her?"

Pam waved her fork. "That, dear sir, is the million-dollar question. And I want to know why the payments stopped."

His cell phone rang. He reached into his rear pocket to check the screen. "It's Monroe." He hit the *Accept* button. "Hey!"

"I'm ten minutes away."

He opened his mouth, then snapped it shut. "You're coming here?"

"Didn't Pam tell you?"

He shot Pam a one-eyed glare. "She's too busy stuffing her face with Vicki's lasagna."

"Well, save me some. I can use a good home-cooked meal."

"Okay. We'll see you in a few." He disconnected.

Pam shrugged. "Bob's been busy."

"And you won't clue us in?"

"Nope. He'll explain."

A beeper chirped. Startled, Logan looked around the small cabin but had no idea where the sound originated.

Chuckling, Pam pulled a rectangular device from her back pocket. "Someone is on the network." She shoveled in the last bite on her plate, grabbed another piece of baguette and her water bottle, and hurried to the spare bedroom.

With her gaze following Pam, Sky released a heavy sigh. "That woman is amazing. She can uncover the most hidden information on the web. I have enough trouble looking up a phone number."

Logan toyed with his napkin. "I've a feeling this case is a lot more than what we signed up for."

She met his gaze. "I feel that way every time I approach Rachael." Grabbing her napkin, she wiped her mouth. "The woman isn't the least bit afraid of Maddie. She doesn't want the security guards or me. All she wants is Wendell to fix this or fix that. The grounds will never be ready for an early opening if she continues to distract him."

Brows coming together, Logan peered. "How did you hear about the change?"

Placing her napkin on the table, she shrugged. "What can I say? With Rachael out for the day, I was bored. So, I took a walk and met up with her security guard. Bill Coban is his name. He's the one who looks like a bulldog. Anyway, Rachael came right out and told him about his numbered days." She tapped the table. "And get this. The contract terminates on opening day. If the resort opens early, they're done."

Well, hell. Rachael's suggestion for an early season made sense. What better way to dismiss the guards than to go around a clause in a contract? Eyes wide, Logan sat back. "That's the dumbest thing I've ever heard. What kind of an outfit did Donald employ?"

"If you ask me, the company name of Guardem Guys doesn't instill a lot of confidence." She stood and grabbed the empty plates. "I hope Bob has a place to stay because he won't be too comfortable on the couch." She headed for the kitchen.

Logan finished the last of his beer and stood. "He owns a fishing cabin, remember? If he's staying overnight, he'll sleep there. I'm just surprised he's coming. He could have waited for our eight o'clock conference." He grabbed the nearly-empty lasagna dish and followed her. Stopping by the refrigerator, he stared at the contents, then heaved a sigh. "We'll give Bob the last of the lasagna."

Laughing, she grabbed the dish from his hand and covered it with foil before slipping it into the refrigerator.

Like Pam, for Monroe to drive three hours when a conference call would do triggered warning bells to sound. And damn, his itchy feeling increased ten-fold.

Chapter Seventeen

True to his word, Monroe arrived ten minutes later in a white pickup truck. At first glance through the front window, Skylar wasn't sure it was him. The truck surprised her. She never saw him drive anything other than a dark-gray sedan. Even more of a surprise, when he stepped out, he wore a flannel shirt and faded blue jeans. This wardrobe was a deviation from his standard attire of dark suit with white shirt. What the hell hit him?

Sky almost rubbed the window glass to make sure the rays of the setting sun weren't playing tricks with her eyes. Robert Monroe's big, brawny body already resembled a lumberjack. Now, he looked like one. The two details missing were the ax on his shoulder and a beard. After closing the drapes, she turned to open the door.

As he entered, he sucked in a deep breath. "Smells like Vicki's lasagna. Any left?"

She rolled her eyes. "Hello to you, too." Poor Logan. No leftovers for him. Laughing, Sky headed for the kitchen. "There's enough to fill a plate. I'll zap it in the microwave. You want beer or water?"

"Water's fine. Where's your bathroom?"

"That door." She pointed.

Logan walked from the spare bedroom. "Hey, Bob, you could have called. Why drive all the way here?"

"Because I don't like how this case is going, and my gut says the shit is about to hit the fan." Approaching, he slapped Logan on the shoulder. "My fishing cabin over in Bushkill Falls is waiting. I'll stay there while I do some preliminary research with the local police. I'll explain everything in a minute." He hurried into the bathroom.

Catching Logan's gaze, Sky raised both brows. "Is Bushkill Falls a real town?"

After stepping into the kitchen, Logan leaned against the counter and crossed his arms over his chest. "It's near the Delaware River on the Pennsylvania side. This entire area has a strong American Indian history. Shawnee, Analomink, and Minisink Hills are just a few towns I remember."

She knew nothing about the Delaware River, except the body of water separated New Jersey from Pennsylvania. The river flowed into the Atlantic Ocean, but how far north did it go? Was it still as wide? Maybe one day, she'd look at a map and see where the river ended—or maybe the better word was started. She filled a plate with the last of the lasagna and slipped the dish into the microwave. A two-minute cycle should be sufficient. She set the proper buttons and hit *Start*.

While staring at the empty lasagna tray, Logan pouted. "Vicki should have sent two."

Her lover boy gazed at the dish as if he stood in front of a coffin at a funeral home. If he attempted the sign of the cross, he might feel a hard pinch on his ass. She patted his cheek. "Sorry, honey. Bob needs to eat."

Huffing out an audible breath, he moved away from the counter and looked toward the front room. "This is the first time I see an advantage for our cabin being so far from everything. No prying eyes."

"Except for the woods off our one side. Anyone can hide in those thick trees. I closed the drapes, anyway."

"Yeah, smart move."

Sky opened the fridge and extracted a cold bottle of water. "No one told us we couldn't have company."

"True. Cousin Pam and Uncle Bob." He grinned.

Bob strolled into the kitchen. "Pam's barely got enough room in the bedroom for all her equipment. Good thing she always travels with an outlet strip."

The timer dinged.

While rubbing his hands, Bob scanned the small kitchen. "Where do you eat?"

"Living room table." Using a potholder, Sky removed the dish from the microwave. "Grab the fork and your water bottle from the counter. Napkins are already on the table. The dish is hot, so I'll carry it."

Leaving the men to talk about man topics—like hunting and fishing, Sky stayed in the kitchen to finish with cleanup. Knowing Bob, he would tell them the purpose of his visit when he was ready.

A few minutes later, Pam joined her. "Here's Bob's plate. The man ate like he was starving. Can I do anything?"

Turning from the sink, Sky took the plate and fork, washed them, then slipped them onto a dish holder to dry. She grabbed the towel to wipe her hands. "Nope, all done. You want coffee?" She looked toward the living room. "Bob, how about some coffee?"

"No, thanks."

Pam shook her head. "Me, neither. I'll never get to sleep."

Yeah, not too many people were like Skylar Dawson. The caffeine in coffee never interfered with her sleep.

Finished in the kitchen, she and Pam sat on the sofa and waited for the two men to end their discussion about deer hunting. *All right, already. Let's go.* She bounced her leg and shifted her butt. Normally, she was cool and calm, but this time, she sat on pins and needles. With any more delay, she might have to relieve her nervousness by running a lap around the cabin.

Pam yawned…loudly.

Catching Pam's gaping orifice, Bob smiled. "I can take a hint. Have a seat, Logan."

Logan, with jaw set and gaze bright, sat alongside Sky but leaned forward with elbows on his knees.

The boss settled in a side chair and whipped out his little notebook. After flipping through several pages, he crossed his legs. "As you know, I always do a preliminary investigation with every case before I involve any of my staff. I didn't have the luxury of time here. So, I sent you, Sky, and Logan, to protect Rachael."

"Who doesn't want protection," Sky mumbled. "Or a housekeeper, or anyone in her house."

"Precisely, which is why I had another talk with Donald Brookson. During the course of our conversation, I confirmed what I suspected. All the information pertaining to Madeline Harris came from one source—her brother, Wendell. Granted, Brookson had no reason to question his best friend. They've known each other for years, but when Wendell spoke to Logan, he gave the impression his sister escaped from a maximum security facility and was hell-bent on vengeance. We're into our third week since her supposed escape. Why hadn't she made her move?" He held up a finger. "I am now working with the assumption that everything we were told is a lie."

Oh, boy. This can't be good.

Logan bounced his leg. "Is it true Madeline assaulted Rachael?"

"Yes and no." Monroe met his gaze. "Madeline slapped Rachael, and Rachael pressed charges. The judge found Maddie guilty of a second-degree misdemeanor, ordered her to pay a fine, and receive counseling." Again, he held up a finger. "Counseling, not committed to an institution. I found no record of a restraining order." After uncrossing his legs, he readjusted his butt on the seat cushion. He caught Sky's gaze. "This chair's a little hard."

She almost laughed. "We're not in a five-star resort, Bob."

Grunting, he again squirmed. "I also questioned why Maddie quit her job and moved into the facility. The only reason that made sense was coercion, but by whom?" He tapped his notebook on his thigh. "Yesterday morning, after I presented my credentials and the reason for my visit, I had a nice conversation with Gloria Whitman, the administrator at Maddie's mental health center." He shifted his gaze between Sky and Logan. "As I suspected, Madeline Harris never needed to be in that place. She entered with the insistence of her brother. Also with Wendell's insistence, she stayed in the institution in a shared room. Once she accepted the yoga position, she got herself a small apartment about two blocks away so she could walk to work. This change occurred about four months ago."

Well, that fact explained why payments to the institution stopped. Frowning, Sky shook her head. "She doesn't sound like a woman on a vendetta."

"No, she doesn't. What's more—" Again, he shifted his gaze between Sky and Logan.

This time, he had a twinkle in his gray eyes. The look raised the hairs on Sky's scalp, and several scenarios flashed through her mind. One was Maddie sunning herself on a beach in Belize while sipping exotic drinks, and their services were no longer needed. *Wishful thinking*.

Straightening his back, Logan spread his arms wide. "Okay, Bob. Enough with the suspense. What else?"

A small smile touched the corner of Monroe's mouth. "Maddie has been living in Wendell's home for the past three weeks. Her apartment building is changing into condo units." He winked at Pam. "Our clever IT tech found Maddie's bank account open on Wendell's computer. That was my first clue something was amiss."

A bomb could have exploded in the middle of the living room. No one moved. Sky gaped like a guppy, then slapped her mouth shut. Even worse, Vicki's wonderful lasagna turned into lead. What the hell was going on here? Sky shook her head. "Weren't the police watching his place?"

"No. Small department, small staff, and no viable evidence of threat."

Logan cursed. "That son of a bitch lied—again, and Donald believed him. Didn't the damn man think to question his so-called friend?"

Sky raised a hand. "Pam said Maddie purchased a silver sedan. Surely, the police spotted the vehicle parked at Wendell's."

Monroe held up a finger. "When Pam found out about the car, she notified me. Then, I called Chief Snyder and asked if he'd send officers to check Wendell's house. Maddie was home, and there was no silver sedan. She said she doesn't own any car. Yet, the records clearly indicate otherwise. To get to work, Wendell drives her. Witnesses see her coming and going in Wendell's resort truck."

Logan fell back against the seat cushion. "Why doesn't Brookson know any of this? Why is Wendell being so secretive? And where the hell is the car?"

"That, Logan, is a question I can't answer." Bob looked at Pam. "Has your trip here paid off?"

"You bet!" Straightening in her seat, Pam cleared her throat. "A little while ago, an alert sounded to tell me a computer accessed the resort's Wi-Fi. It was Rachael. She transferred twenty-five hundred dollars from the resort's account to a New York City account with the name REB Enterprises."

Sky narrowed her gaze. "How did you know the user was Rachael?"

With a sheepish grin, Pam shrugged one shoulder. "I turned on her computer camera for a little look-see and found Rachael staring at the screen. I deactivated the camera before she noticed the light. Anyway, while the account was open, I downloaded a list of systematic transfers of the same amount done weekly for the past five months. That's over fifty grand."

Monroe recrossed his leg. "FYI, Rachael's middle name is Elaine."

Sky closed her eyes and groaned. "Rachael Elaine Brookson. REB. She's stiffing her own husband." Opening her eyes, she leaned forward. "Is Donald blind? Doesn't he look at the books?"

Pam waved a hand. "All this can be done online without making entries into the books. And that's not all. I also found a withdrawal of eighty-seven hundred in cash."

"The price of the silver sedan!" Sky arched a brow. "But did she give the money to Maddie or Wendell?"

"More likely Wendell." Logan hissed through tight teeth. "He buys a car, puts it in his sister's name, but never tells her." Cursing softly, he jumped to his feet and paced. "I'd like to know what the hell is going on here. Is Maddie after Rachael or not?"

Sighing, Monroe tugged on his left ear. "Truthfully, I can't answer that. My guess is Madeline Harris is completely innocent."

Sky spread her arms wide. "And what proof do we have about Maddie's MA skills? Could Wendell have lied about that, too?"

"You can take anything Wendell says with a grain of salt, Sky."

Logan stopped pacing. "Gabe said he wouldn't be surprised if Maddie took up martial arts. She was limber enough."

Frowning, Sky fell back against the cushions. "All this new information explains why Rachael doesn't want me around. She knows Maddie isn't a threat. Wendell probably told her where Maddie is. I'm willing to bet Rachael and Wendell are an item. I'm also willing to bet the baby is his."

Nodding, Monroe again tapped his notebook on his

thigh. "Plausible. And from all this intel, we can conclude?" Gaze sparkling, he lifted his brows and drifted his gaze from one face to the other.

Sky clenched her jaw. "That Donald Brookson is the target, and Madeline Harris is being set up to take the fall."

Chapter Eighteen

Skylar prayed she was wrong, but Monroe's news clicked a lot of pieces together—like why Rachael called Wendell to *fix things* and why a seven-month preggo refused protection. And the biggest fact of all was the way Wendell and Rachael worked together in a little scheme with the earrings. "What I don't understand, Bob, is why would Rachael and Wendell go through so much trouble? They could have easily killed Donald and framed Maddie without alerting Donald." She sat forward. "The resort isn't open. All day staff goes home at four. The compound would be deserted, if not for the two guards and me and Logan."

Still pacing the small living room, Logan stopped. "She's right, Bob. Instead of doing everything quietly, Wendell tells Donald, who goes to the police. Bodyguards are contracted, but Donald isn't satisfied with Rachael's two-guards-only demand. He hires us. I'm willing to bet that was the first kink in their plans."

Sky waggled a finger. "And since Rachael found the check to Monroe Security, she can take a pretty big guess we are both bodyguards."

Smiling, Monroe shifted his gaze between them. "I considered all this." He replaced his little notebook into his breast pocket. "When Donald told the police, he forced them to create a report that could be used as evidence against Madeline. Basically—and you know this, Logan—the police can't arrest someone because of a threat or rumor. Their hands are tied. Tomorrow, I'm having breakfast with the chief of police. I'll give him a heads-up on what we think might happen. He won't do anything without proof, and he's already admitted he doesn't have the personnel for a problem like this. Hell, even I don't have the personnel available. I'm running three separate security details, but I'll see who I can pull out to lend us a hand."

Sky bit her upper lip. "Do we tell Donald?"

Brows high, Monroe shot his gaze to Logan.

Logan gave a hard shake of his head. "He won't believe his best friend and wife are plotting to kill him."

"Logan's right." Pam tucked her legs under her butt. "If we tell him his life is in danger, then he might be dumb enough to confront Wendell or Rachael. They could kill him on the spot."

Monroe tugged on an ear, then dropped his hand and sighed. "I have to agree. The man must have complete faith in his wife to ignore the books." After pursing his lips, he connected to Logan's gaze. "Your call."

Logan stuffed his hands into his pockets. "We keep silent. I'll warn Brookson when the time is right. Otherwise, Sky and I will work to uncover the when and where everything will happen."

"Okay, then." Monroe slapped his knees and stood. "I'm beat. I should have stayed overnight in my cabin after yesterday's appointment with Gloria Whitman. This driving back and forth is a bitch." He suppressed a yawn. "Pam, what are your plans?"

Pam tucked a strand of hair behind her ear. "I'll do an overnight here and leave in the morning. I'm sure these two lovebirds won't mind for one night." With a wink, she grinned.

Sky rolled her eyes. "We're not that bad."

Chuckling, Monroe shook his head, but he sobered quickly. "My cabin is forty minutes away. For any emergencies, call my cell." He headed for the door. "Thanks for dinner." He paused with a hand on the knob and turned, his expression grave. "I don't have to tell you to keep alert. Let me know if something changes around here." He let himself out.

Logan ambled to the door and secured the lock.

As a former bartender, Sky listened to all kinds of stories about cheating spouses. Most people admitted to not having a clue what was going on. How could someone cheat and erode the trust of a mate? She glanced at Logan. No way, no how could she knowingly cheat on any man. If dissatisfaction came into the relationship, well, hell, time to move on, right? Fair play and all that.

Pam stood and stretched. "My equipment will stay connected to the resort's network until tomorrow. I'll try not to make too much noise, but right now, I'm turning in. See you two in the morning."

"Hold on, Pam." Logan approached Sky's side of the sofa. "We'll be taking our perimeter walk soon. We'll lock you in."

Sky waved toward the kitchen. "And help yourself to whatever you want in the fridge."

"Thanks." Hiding a yawn, she disappeared into the bedroom and closed the door.

After checking his watch, Logan flopped onto the sofa cushion and, without a second of hesitation, wrapped an arm around Sky's shoulders and tugged her close.

Sky loved quiet times like this, when she and Logan just talked about their day. Sometimes, they'd watch TV, but usually, he'd tilt up her chin and kiss her until a light peck progressed to a heavy make-out session. Tonight, though, with Pam in the spare room and with so much information swirling around in her brain, she lounged with her back to his chest and tucked under his arm. She hugged the thick arm draped across her chest. "This is a horrible turn of events."

He kissed the top of her head. "I've been surprised before. Look at our last case. You were supposed to stay behind the bar and observe. Because circumstances changed, you became an active participant. If Rachael and Wendell plan to kill Donald and set up Madeline to take the fall, they, more likely, will kill Maddie and claim self-defense. A dead suspect can't challenge their story. And with Donald's visit to the police, they'd be home free. One way or the other, Maddie will be toast."

"Along with Donald." Arching her head, she met his gaze. "What do we do?"

He puffed out a breath. "What we have is pure conjecture. All we can do is play along and keep an eye on Donald."

What possible proof could they get except to catch Rachael and Wendell in the act? The notion didn't sit well. What kind of brother framed his own sister? Even worse, killed her? The idea of such a double-cross made Sky appreciate being an only child.

Sky kissed his thick arm. "At least, I understand why Rachael and Wendell connived to get me arrested. I'm in the way." She nudged his arm. "I'm still in the way, Logan. Bob never told me to stop playing her housekeeper slash driver." When calculating the longest she stood inside the Brookson house, she amassed a grand total of twenty-five minutes. If she combined the whole four days together, the number might reach two hours. *Whoop-de-doo*!

In the morning, after her lover boy left for work, Sky joined Pam at the table by the front windows with a coffee mug in hand. She yawned.

Holding the mug close to her lips, Pam smiled. "Busy night?" She waggled her red eyebrows.

Sky rolled her eyes. "You know I'm not a morning person, but I pushed myself out of bed to see Logan off." She leaned forward. "And you."

"Aw, that's so sweet." She sipped. "I came out last night to grab a bottle of water. You took a walk kinda late, didn't you?"

"Actually, a longer walk than usual. We don't know how or where Brookson will meet his fate, but we studied every structure in the compound to be sure we recognized where we were in the dark. We can't do anything if he's killed inside his house. If outside, we can intervene." She rotated her mug and sighed. "There's a helpless feeling with all this."

"Well, what about the silver sedan? By now, Maddie knows the car is registered in her name." She sipped her coffee. "If she's smart, she'll question her brother."

"And he'll tell her something believable."

Pamela O'Connor was four years younger than Sky, but she and Sky clicked from the moment they'd met. Sky never understood why. They were as difference as night and day. Pam loved dance clubs, while Sky preferred to stay home and relax. Pam hated all forms of alcoholic beverages, while Sky enjoyed the taste of a good beer. A lot of what Pam uncovered for Monroe Security was inadmissible in court, but the info gave Monroe an edge over the constraints placed on law enforcement. The girl knew what she was doing and never used any of the gathered intel for her own personal gain.

Pam stifled a yawn. "I'll be heading out this morning. We know enough to understand the real purpose of your assignment."

"You mean, assuming we're right." To save Donald, Sky and Logan needed to uncover Rachael's plan. But how? Sky was never in Rachael's orbit long enough to discover anything. She tapped the table. "On the Atlantic City case, you hacked into the cell phone of our primary suspect. Why don't you do it now? You'd save us a lot of trouble."

With gaze averted and lips pursed, Pam slid a finger around the rim of her mug. "Bob hasn't given me the go-ahead." She met Sky's gaze. "I was tempted, but Bob trusts me to do what's right. When I return to Jersey, I'll call and ask." Lifting her cup, she sipped. "Wendell would be the likely candidate."

Sky chewed her inner lip. "I'm not so sure. I think Rachael is the brains behind their sinister plot." With a phone tap, Rachael could say something about a time and place. Having the information beforehand would definitely help. Of course, the way Wendell arrived every day to fix something, he and Rachael could easily plan in person. Then, what?

Pam shot a sideward glance at Sky. "I have a small favor to ask."

"Sure. Anything." She sipped her coffee.

"Teach me jive."

Sky almost spewed her coffee. Swallowing quickly, she stared. "Eh…what?"

She straightened in her seat. "Look, I heard you talking to one of your students. I caught up to him just before he left. He told me you spoke good jive. Teach me."

Wow. Sky didn't know what to say. She had learned the language in Chicago from a transplanted New Yorker. Her martial arts student was also from New York. He thought he was being smart by speaking in a language she couldn't possibly understand. She met Pam's pleading gaze. "I can teach you, but why?"

"The language is fascinating. It's English but not English, you know? We could make it a code language."

The young MIT grad was serious. Sky scratched her head. "Okay. We'll start when I get back."

Pam gave a fist pump. "Great. Thanks. It'll be fun." Gulping the last of her coffee, she stood. "I better get going."

After helping Pam load her gear, Sky gave her a hug and watched her drive away. With a glance toward the overcast sky, she shook her head. The dismal view matched her mood, but she headed for the Brookson house anyway—for what good she could do. This job had become the most boring and questionable assignment ever created. Not like she had a list of cases to compare. Her prior case with Logan involved closing down a murderous enterprise. With every second, she had to keep on her toes. Now, she fought to stay awake. *What wonderful scheme will Rachael try today*? She could hardly wait.

Instead of using the side gate to enter the property, Sky strolled to the front of the house, then headed around to the back deck. The extra distance killed a little more time. A quick glance at her watch showed twenty minutes past ten. *Oh, joy.*

As she neared the large deck, she slowed her steps. Something didn't look right. Buddy the Bulldog wasn't in his usual chair by the cottage or walking anywhere she could see. The two outdoor chairs were stacked and placed off to the side. What's more, the cottage door was wide open and propped with a maid's yellow carryall. *Uh-oh.* Fighting a wave of uncertainty, she hopped onto the deck and knocked on the kitchen's door.

Wearing her usual frown, Rachael swung the door wide. She shook her head. "Okay, you're here." She disappeared into the kitchen.

No hello. No come in and kiss my ass. Nothing. *Well, hello to you, too!* At least, Rachael didn't slam the door in Sky's face. She hadn't said go away, either. But geez, if the woman wasn't careful, she'd develop a permanent crease between her eyes. Sky had yet to see a smile...no, that was wrong. Rachael always smiled at Wendell. Sky stepped inside. "Where's your guards?"

"They're gone." She headed for the stove.

Sky raised her brows. "What do you mean *gone*? Aren't they supposed to watch you?"

"Not anymore." With a smug expression, she faced Sky. "They've been dismissed."

Stunned, Sky dropped her jaw, then quickly snapped it shut. *Wow.* The guards' dismissal eliminated any possibility of backup. She and Logan would be on their own, and her gut tightened. *Logan will not be*

178

pleased. Moving with a nonchalance she didn't feel, Sky stepped away from the door and unzipped her jacket. "What happened? Was Maddie caught?"

"I don't care what happens to that bitch." She grabbed the washcloth from the sink and wiped the stovetop. "I told Donny we had to cut expenses." She sneered over her shoulder. "You're next." She waved the cloth over her head. "Yes, I know. Donny will be the one to fire you. Unfortunately, to get his permission to dismiss the guards, I had to compromise and keep you."

"I'm flattered, but I'm not a bodyguard."

Gaze flashing, she whirled. "Well, I believe you are. I still don't want you here. I like my privacy."

Yeah, with Wendell. The little woman was a spitfire. Then again, if Rachael had plans to kill her husband, she wouldn't want someone in the way.

Rachael narrowed her gaze. "If Donny is worried about me being alone, I've taken care of that." She puffed out her chest. "That's why I'm sending you to the drugstore when Wendell comes to fix the washing machine."

Wendell again. Things sure broke a lot in this house. Was Donald totally blind to Wendell's constant visits? Didn't Brookson ever watch those reality shows where the best friend always screwed around with the spouse? Sky stuffed her hands into her jacket pockets. "I don't have any idea where your drugstore is, Mrs. Brookson." Naturally, Rachael discovered another way to push Sky out of the house. More likely, the drugstore was an hour drive one way.

"Don't worry. I'll give you directions." Rachael rinsed her washcloth and then dried her hands on a towel. She faced Sky and gave a closed-mouth smile. "My prenatal vitamins came in and also Donny's blood pressure medicine. After Wendell's done with the washer, he'll escort me to the office where I will stay until Donny and I come home together. See? I won't be alone." She folded the towel and placed it on the counter. "You can use my car."

Whoa! Every fiber in her being said the woman was setting her up—again. *Does she think I'm a moron*? Sky narrowed her gaze. "Why your car? Ten to one, you'll accuse me of stealing it." She folded her arms across her chest. "After the stunt you pulled the other day, you aren't very high on my trust list. In other words, I got your number, babe. So, no, thank you." Rachael could rig the vehicle to cause an inconvenience, like suddenly dying on a deserted stretch of highway, or maybe a flat tire with no spare in the trunk. Sky released a slow breath. "You know, Mrs. Brookson, I could drive you to the pharmacy. This would give you a chance to get out. Wendell can fix the washing machine while we're gone."

She waved a hand. "I'm fine. Besides, I have a lot of work waiting on my desk." Leaning against the counter, she rested her arms on top of her belly. "Did you know we're opening early?"

"Logan mentioned it. Do you think that's wise with Wendell's sister on the loose?"

"Pfff." Dropping her arms, she pushed away from the counter. "Maddie isn't a threat. Otherwise, she'd be here by now."

"But if Madeline's waiting for an opportunity, she'll see the guards gone, and sending me on an errand won't help your situation. I'm not trained to be a bodyguard, but my presence could be a deterrent."

"That's why I'll have Wendell by my side. Maddie won't hurt her own brother."

But her brother thought nothing of sacrificing his own sister. *Oh, what a tangled web we weave.*

Chapter Nineteen

While standing in the middle of Rachael's kitchen, Sky felt a wave of uselessness. Her being here was ridiculous. She wouldn't butt in on anyone who considered her in the way. Yet, Monroe said to make a nuisance of herself. She could take the initiative and clean something, but Rachael would have a stroke. The woman was downright meticulous with her house. Anyone could eat off the floor.

Sky slipped her arm from her jacket sleeve and paused. The last time she hung her jacket on a chair, she found earrings in her pocket. *Fool me once...* Replacing her arm into the sleeve, she straightened her shoulders and met Rachael's gaze. "What can I do until Wendell arrives?"

With a quick scan of her spotless kitchen, Rachael heaved a deep sigh. "I guess you can unload the dishwasher and put the stuff away. Wendell won't be long."

I'm sure he won't. Where are you, Donald Brookson?

The front doorbell chimed.

"Oh, good, he's here. Forget the dishes." Rachael hurried to the side counter and rummaged through her purse. "Here's the key fob for my car. It's in the garage." She slapped the fob into Sky's palm.

Anxious much? Small wonder the woman hadn't

pushed Sky straight out the back door. She stared at the fob in her hand. "I haven't agreed to take your car, ma'am."

"Nonsense. It's gassed and ready to go." She fussed with her hair. Pausing with her primping, she shot Sky a smirk. "I won't call the cops. You're doing me a big favor." She waved Sky to follow. "You can spend a nice afternoon out."

Tempting—if she wasn't supposed to guard the woman. She cleared her throat. "You didn't tell me where the drugstore is, Mrs. Brookson."

Rachael stopped short in the archway to the kitchen. "Oh…right. Let me open the door for Wendell first." She hurried out.

Oh, this can't be good. Yes, Sky smelled a setup, but this time, she had ample warning. After last night's conversation with Monroe, Sky understood why Rachael was bound and determined to get Sky out of the house. What she couldn't understand was Donald Brookson. If the man was so worried about protecting his wife, why wasn't he around more? Even more important, how could he let Rachael dismiss the guards? What the hell was wrong with the man?

Cheeks slightly flushed, Rachael strolled into the kitchen.

Wendell followed with a tool pouch over his shoulder.

Sky half-expected them to enter arm-in-arm. She often caught the subtle eye locks so prevalent with lovers, and she felt like an intruder—which she was.

After adjusting the pouch, Wendell smiled. "Hi, Midnight. Rachael tells me you're heading to the drugstore. That's nice."

Nothing nice about it. Rachael probably calculated to the second her alone time with Wendell. Gad, was Donald a dimwit or what? Clearing her throat, Sky forced a smile. "It's time to see outside the complex. Rachael's letting me use her car. I'll tell Logan where I'm going and have him take a good look at the make and model. I'll also stop by the main building and point out the vehicle to John at the front desk. The more people who know, the more I can't be accused of stealing her property." She glared pointedly at Rachael.

Rachael coughed, then turned to Wendell. "You know where the washing machine is."

"Right." After shooting a quick glance at Rachael, he headed to the laundry room off the kitchen.

Rachael walked to the far wall and hit a button. She faced Sky. "I opened the garage door. You shouldn't have any trouble backing out." She gestured for Sky to follow into the living room. "Go out to the main entrance and make a right. You'll drive about nine miles until you come to the first traffic light. Go down to the next light, and you'll see the shopping complex. It's not very big, but the drugstore is right next to the Pizza Palace. You can't miss it." She stopped by the already-opened front door and placed her hand on the knob. "I'll call ahead to make sure they don't give you any trouble and to charge the total to the resort account. Do you have your cell?"

"Sure. You want my number?"

"Yeah, just in case." She waggled her fingers, palm up.

Since Sky had orders never to let anyone handle her phone because of important contacts in the phone app, she waved her phone. "Give me your cell number.

I'll input into mine and send you a text."

Rachael rattled off her number. Ten seconds later, her phone dinged from the kitchen.

"There, done." Sky replaced her phone into her cargo pants. "I have to return to our cabin first. I don't have my wallet."

"No problem. Take the car with you. Oh, and Midnight, don't rush." She shot Sky a grin.

Yeah, she would say that. Even her grin looked a little sinister. *Oh, boy, what does she have planned now?* Sky stepped onto the front porch.

Once the door shut behind her, Sky stood on the porch and shook her head. Really, what more could she do? Refuse to go? Then, what? She glanced skyward for some divine strength, then headed down the steps.

As expected, the garage door was wide open. Wendell's blue pickup truck with the Chadbury emblem on the door sat to the side. Hands on hips, Sky stood at the garage opening and scanned the huge expanse.

She'd never seen a garage so...empty. Her dad's two-car garage was cluttered with boxes and tools with barely enough room for one car. After her father died, she and her mom spent the next three months going through all his so-called treasures. Here, though, no tools hung on the walls, no ladders, and no shelving. On the left, two carts were plugged into an electrical outlet ready to be used, and that was about the extent of clutter. The garage could easily house two large vehicles. Rachael's white SUV with Chadbury emblems on the back and side door took up half of the concrete slab. The vehicle was mid-sized and sparkled, like it came off the showroom floor.

Using the fob, Sky unlocked the car door and swung it wide. The smell of new leather hit her nose. *Nice.* The interior was spotless, and those prickly little doubts rose. Without question, giving Sky errands to run was another of Rachael's ploys to get her out of the house, but how could Rachael trust a stranger with her brand-new SUV? *Oh, yeah, she was definitely up to no good.*

As a precaution, when she arrived at the pharmacy, she'd tell the pharmacist to secure the package and take a picture. This way, Rachael couldn't accuse her of tampering with the drugs. After slipping onto the cushy seat, Sky took inventory of the controls on the steering wheel. The computer screen she'd ignore since it had no bearing on actual driving. Once she closed the door, she hit the *Start* button, backed out, and maneuvered around Wendell's blue truck. The driveway gate was already opened, so she turned left and headed for her cabin.

A minute later, she pulled in front of Logan's car and alighted. With the use of her card key, she opened the door to the cabin just as her cell phone rang. Pulling the device from her pants pocket, she glanced at the screen and arched a brow to see Rachael's name. *Hmm.* Entering the cabin, she closed the door before hitting the *Accept* button. "Mrs. Brookson, do you need something?"

"Are you still at your cabin?"

"I just arrived."

"Good. Would you mind stopping at Jonesy's Meat Market? It's not too far."

Oh, sure. Why not? Anything to keep Sky out longer. "No problem. Give me directions."

"It's—oh, hold on. Donny's calling."

With the phone plastered to her ear, Sky stared out the front windows. Being an errand girl was not advantageous to protecting someone. Sure, Wendell arrived to fix the washing machine, but he already knew his sister's whereabouts. Since the general consensus indicated Donald was the target, someone should be watching Donald. She sure as hell wasn't, and neither was Logan. With Rachael taking her good ole time, Sky placed the phone on speaker, then meandered into the kitchen and grabbed an apple. She took a big bite.

She was halfway through the fruit when Rachael returned. A quick glance at her watch told her twelve minutes had passed. *Bloody rude*. Ordinarily, she'd have disconnected a person who kept her on hold so long.

"Sorry about that. Donny gets a bit winded at times. Are you still in your cabin?"

An odd question. "Yes."

"Good. Now, where were we?"

Rachael sounded breathless. Did she and Wendell have a quickie on the washing machine? Shuddering at the visual, Sky held the phone closer to her mouth. "You were about to give me directions to the meat market." Finished with the apple, she tossed the core into the trash bin.

"Yes. It's farther down the road about a half mile. After the drugstore, turn right out of the parking lot. Go to the next intersection. On the left, you'll see the market sign by the road. I'll call in an order, and like the drugstore, they'll charge the purchase to Chadbury Lodge. Any questions?"

"Nope. Got it. I'll call you when I return. You'll

probably still be in the office."

"The office? Oh, yes—yes, call me. You can pick me up."

"Will do." She disconnected and stared at her phone. Not only would she ask the pharmacist to secure the package, she would tell the butcher to do the same. *Wouldn't want Rachael to accuse me of poisoning the meat.* She called Logan.

He answered on the second ring. "Honey? Is everything all right?"

At the concern in his voice, a flood of warmth filled her chest. She should confess how she fell head over heels in love with him. Every time she tried, she choked on the words. When had she turned into such a chickenshit? Even more important, why was it so hard? Fear? Of what, she wasn't sure.

"Sky?"

Oh, hell, she drifted into la-la land. She shook herself. "Rachael is sending me on a few errands. I'll be driving her white SUV."

"She's not going with you?"

"No. She's back at the house with Wendell."

He snickered. "What broke this time?"

"The washing machine. Next will be the garbage disposal." She leaned against the kitchen counter. "And by the way, the two guards have been dismissed."

Silence. "Are you shitting me?"

Well, Logan's analogy of Brookson not being the sharpest pencil in the box held true. He sounded just as surprised. "No joke, Logan. She compromised and told her husband she'd never be alone."

"But you're going out."

"Wendell's there. And she knows she's not in

danger."

"But Brookson doesn't. Why the hell did he allow her to dismiss the guards?"

"That's the million-dollar question." She pushed away from the counter and headed for the bedroom. "Someone should be watching Donald."

"Yeah, I'll call Monroe. Maybe he can find out why Donald listens to his wife all the time."

"Let me know what he says. In the meantime, I'll stop at the registration desk and let everyone within earshot hear me announce I'm going shopping for Mrs. Brookson and using her SUV. I'll shop for a few goodies for us, too."

"Great idea, but be careful, will you? After Rachael's stunt with the earrings, she might have something else up her sleeve." A short pause. "Maybe you should take my car."

"I considered that, but on the other hand, I'd like to play this through. As a precaution, I'll send you a photo of the SUV."

"I'll also track you on Pam's *You Can't Hide* app. I don't trust Rachael."

"Neither do I. But I'll be careful. I'll call when I return." She disconnected the call.

As a loner all her life, she appreciated him watching over her. Sure, she had martial arts skills and could handle a bad situation, but she didn't have the years of experience doing undercover work. Logan was the pro. He had the knowledge to foresee what lurked in the shadows. All she could do was be wary, and where Rachael was involved, be extremely cautious. Shaking herself from the thought, she refreshed herself in the bathroom, grabbed her wallet, and returned to the white

SUV. With photos taken and sent to Logan, she drove to the main lodge.

Under the pretense of being the resort errand girl, Sky entered the lodge and asked John at the registration desk if he needed anything from town. She also talked to the girl—Betty was her name—stocking the gift shop. On her way at last, Sky headed up Chaddy-Wonker Drive toward the main entrance and turned right.

The two-lane asphalt road cut through thick forests and gave her the feeling of driving through a tunnel. The sky overhead still cast an eerie gray and made the ride a tad gloomy. Still, the idea of doing something other than sitting around the cabin lifted her spirits. Although, she shouldn't let the freedom go to her head. After all, she drove Rachael's new SUV, and she definitely didn't want to crash into something and get slapped with a huge bill. Out of spite, Rachael would make Sky's life miserable. *Pay for this, pay for that, yada yada.* Not like she encountered a lot of traffic to worry about an accident. Basically, the road was deserted with an occasional car coming in the opposite direction.

For the life of her, she couldn't call the area a honeymoon paradise. Where was the romance and fun activities for a young couple to enjoy? To be fair, she'd only seen one unimpressive resort, but to be surrounded by so many trees caused her skin to crawl. Granted, she passed a dirt driveway here and there and, occasionally, a chalet, but in her mind, she entered a kind of twilight zone. The area had nice smooth roads, though. Between the overcast sky and the shadows from the forest, the ride was a little too dark. Headlights would help, but she'd have to stop to figure out where and how to turn them on.

Funny how, within the past two years, her life took a one-eighty degree turn. Big-city living meant a million-plus population, everyday crime, and the constant wail of police and fire sirens. Her inheritance forced her to relocate to a small South Jersey community with a little over four thousand people. For her, quiet was a foreign word, but out here, amongst all this nature, she felt stone-deaf. She had no experience with nature and probably couldn't start a fire to save her life. By her definition, nature meant riding a motorcycle to feel the wind in her hair. Even *that* was a joke. She always wore a helmet.

She glanced into the rearview mirror. *Well, what do ya know?* A car! The vehicle was still far away, but wow, she wasn't alone on the road anymore. *Another human being. Imagine that.* Considering how deserted the road, the driver would soon pass. Another glance in the mirror confirmed her assumption. The car sped closer…and closer. She eased on the gas pedal to allow the driver to go around.

Wham!

Holy crap! The left-side air bag exploded from the impact. With her heart jumping straight into her throat, Sky struggled to keep the car on the road. She glanced left, but the now-deflated air bag blocked her field of view. She could barely see the hood of a light-colored sedan pushing against her side. Was the driver drunk or in the midst of a medical emergency?

Wham!

The second impact pushed the SUV onto a gravel shoulder. Gripping the steering wheel tight enough to cramp her fingers, Sky slammed on the brakes. The loose gravel made traction impossible. And the damn driver still pushed! What the hell was wrong with the guy? At this point, she didn't give a damn if the driver was choking on a wishbone. She couldn't hold the road. The car skidded straight into a ditch and rolled.

Chapter Twenty

With her heart beating a mile a minute, Sky stared sideways out the cracked windshield, breathing hard. Still with a death grip on the steering wheel, she checked her surroundings. The car had only rolled onto its passenger side—thank God. Her body felt jarred and shaken but, for the most part, uninjured. The air bags had deployed and done their job.

I'll kill that son of a bitch. This was no ordinary accident. The driver purposely pushed her car off the road. Cursing through tight teeth, Sky struggled to disconnect her seat belt. The damn latch was jammed and probably because she was hanging sideways with all her weight pressed against the release mechanism. Defeated, she stared out the front windshield to see a silver sedan drive away.

Silver sedan! And it smashed into Rachael's SUV. Sky gasped. Was Rachel the target after all?

The car shook.

Startled, she shot her gaze toward the front and side windows. She wasn't going anywhere. The SUV was perfectly wedged in the ditch with the passenger side buried in dirt.

The vehicle shook again. Thumping followed.

"Hey, lady! You okay?" An old guy with a scruffy beard peered through her driver-side window.

Relief flooded her. But how could one answer such

a question? No, she wasn't okay. She was shook-up and mad as hell. Biting back a scream of frustration, she met the concerned gaze of her good Samaritan. "I'm okay. But my seat belt's jammed."

He tugged on the door handle. "Unlock the car. I'll see what I can do."

She pressed the Unlock button on the door's armrest, and her heart lifted to hear the click. "Try now."

Since the driver's side of the SUV was smashed from the intentional sideswipes, Sky hadn't a whole lot of faith on him getting the door open. Using one hand to grab onto the steering wheel, she again lifted her body weight from the seat belt latch and pressed the release. *Nope.* The damn thing just wouldn't disengage.

The car vibrated, a little violently.

"I still can't get the door open."

And she couldn't unlatch her belt. *Great.* Now, what?

"Hold on, honey. I'll be right back."

Hopefully, he went to call an emergency squad. Her phone was zippered into her right hip pocket and squished between her hip and a very tight safety device. Even if she got the phone out, how could she explain where she was? She hadn't seen a road sign since turning out of the resort.

The old guy returned carrying a crowbar.

Oh, good. He could pry—

"Cover your eyes."

Shit! "Wait!"

He struck the side window with several hard whacks.

Releasing a cry, Sky raised her arms to cover her

face. The glass shattered and flew everywhere, including all over her.

"Hold tight, honey."

Like I'm going anywhere.

The man reached in and tugged on the seat belt draped across her hips.

Oh, holy hell, no! She caught the glint of a monstrous knife. *Dear Lord*! He was— "Wait! You can't...aagh!"

The belt sprung free and slapped her face with a smack that stung. She dropped with a thud into the passenger side of the car.

The man would kill her before anyone else came to her rescue. Damn good thing the car wasn't dangling on the side of a cliff. From the way he jostled the car, he'd have pushed her over the edge.

Dazed, she stared up, and her spirits lifted at the sound of another voice. Someone else came to help the old guy. *Thank God.* If he attempted to right the car on his own, he'd surely die of a heart attack. Obviously, rescue shows weren't part of his nighttime viewing on TV, because he did everything wrong.

The car rocked. Within seconds, someone yanked on the driver's door and forced it open with a series of metal grinding against metal.

Tank Davenport stuck his bald head through the opening. "You okay?"

She blinked at a man she never expected to see. Tank was another Monroe operative. He epitomized the big, black, and beautiful description. At six-foot-four, the man could lift three hundred pounds with one arm. She truly expected him to yank the door off its hinges. She gaped. "What are you doing here?"

"I'll explain later. Look, I've got the old gent calling 9-1-1. Are you hurt?"

"I wasn't until he cut my belt, and I dropped like a stone." She shifted her butt. "I'm sitting on glass." *Ouch.* Nothing like glass pieces cutting up a derriere.

"Don't move, okay? Let the emergency people check you out."

"Where did the old man come from?"

"I assume from across the road. That's where he headed to make the phone call."

Sirens echoed through the trees.

"Tank, did you see what happened?"

"Afraid not. I came after the fact. I was tailing Donald Brookson." The big man glanced over his shoulder. "I see flashing lights." He turned back. "I'll call Logan and Bob. We'll meet at the hospital."

"I don't need a hospital."

He gave her a stern expression. "You're going. Monroe will insist. No argument, hear?"

"Yes, sir." Sighing, she forced a smile. "Thank you, Tank."

He was tailing Brookson? Then Donald passed her in the ditch. Even though a million white SUVs drove on the road, he couldn't miss the Chadbury Lodge emblem on the rear of his wife's car. So, the big question, why wouldn't Donald Brookson stop?

****

Skylar popped open one eye to see an unfamiliar room. *All right, where am I?* She opened the other eye. Handrails on the bed? But not really a bed. No, more like a stretcher. *Oh...yeah.* Judging from the medical equipment against the wall, she was still on the gurney in the hospital. But where were the curtains? She swore they enclosed her behind privacy drapes. And this room had a door. She shifted onto her back.

Ouch. Everything hurt—her arms from the struggle to control the vehicle and her back and butt from falling like a rock onto the passenger door. But her face— *eoww*—it stung like crazy where the seat belt slapped. The old guy was nice enough to help, but he should research what *not* to do. Stifling a yawn, she looked around.

The room resembled a large storage closet. Portable monitors, blood-pressure machines, and oxygen tanks crowded one wall. To the right of her stretcher, plastic containers with attached rubber tubing filled a counter, and on the ceiling above, metal tracks with hooks dangling indicated what was once a place for curtains. When had they rolled her in here?

The door opened.

Logan strolled inside. Catching her gaze, he smiled and approached the bedside. Leaning over, he used one finger to tilt her chin and gave her a light kiss. "Have a nice nap?"

Mouth like a guppy, she blinked. "Nap? You mean I wasn't unconscious?"

"I hope not." He shot her a one-eyed glare. "Don't you remember?"

"Oh—right." The nurse gave her a mild muscle relaxant because of the bruises covering her body. In her groggy state, she overheard Monroe request someplace private, and she was rolled into this closet-like room. All this medical equipment gave her the creeps. It reminded her of a horror movie where some crazed weirdo stomped around with a large needle in his hand, ready to stick it into some poor soul's eye.

"Can you raise the head of my bed?"

Frowning, he stood back and scanned the gurney. "I'm not sure I know how...ah, here we go. It has grooves on the head part. Tell me when."

Three clicks later, she gave him a thumbs-up. Now that she could see better, she glanced toward the windows and stared at a brick wall. From the shadows, the time was either dusk or dawn. She couldn't tell which. She stared at her watch. For all she knew, the time could be a.m. or p.m. She rubbed her eyes. "What time is it?"

Logan checked his watch. "Nearly three...in the afternoon. The overcast sky makes it look later, but you've only been here a couple hours." He leaned on the bed rail. "We moved you to this out-of-the-way room to avoid eavesdroppers. Now that we're alone, what happened?"

Did she have another memory lapse? She stared at her handsome partner. "I told you everything."

"Maybe and maybe not. You know what a debriefing is like. Consider it more practice. You told me it was a silver sedan. Did you see the driver?"

"No. All the windows were tinted. Besides, I was too busy hanging on to dear life—and barely succeeding. Do you think it was Madeline?"

"That's the consensus. You were driving Rachael's car."

"Then, our theory Donald as the target flew right out the window."

"So, it seems. We've returned to square one."

Yeah, whoopee. Sky lifted the bedsheet to adjust the sling holding her left arm. A brace covered her left wrist. On her right foot, the same type of brace immobilized her foot and ankle. She wiggled her fingers and toes. Everything moved. "These braces will be an inconvenience."

He patted her shoulder. "Not for long."

Too long, in her opinion. She hated the disadvantage of not using her limbs to defend herself. She traced her fingers along the gauze pad plastered to her forehead. "And this patch on my head?"

He shifted his gaze from one side of her face to the other. "Looks good to me."

She rolled her eyes. "That's not what I mean, and you know it."

"Glass cut your forehead."

It did? Shouldn't she have felt blood trickling down her face?

A knock sounded on the door.

Without waiting for a reply, Monroe walked inside. Tank Davenport followed.

Well, gee, the gang was all here. *Hoorah, hoorah*! Three big men standing around her stretcher made her feel tiny. Even worse, she wore this stupid hospital gown meant for a three-hundred-pound patient. Despite the ties behind her neck, the material kept slipping off her shoulder. Sexy, it was not. She straightened on the gurney and caught Tank's gaze. "Thank you for stopping. Obviously, Brookson hadn't noticed his wife's car in the ditch." She shifted her gaze to Monroe. "Is Tank in trouble for not following Brookson?"

Monroe held up a finger. "My staff takes priority, Sky. He did the right thing."

Tank passed a hand over his bald head. "I'd been watching the road for several hours before you pulled out in the SUV. Brookson came out ten minutes later."

Gaze steady, Logan crossed his arms over his chest. "Do you think he was following Sky?"

Tank shook his head. "I can't say for sure, but if you want to tail someone, you don't wait ten minutes."

Well, that was true enough.

Monroe leaned back against the counter and crossed his arms over his chest. "Before coming here, I inspected the accident site while the car was still in the ditch. The SUV's tail end was up in the air with the resort emblem in full view. The fact Brookson hadn't stopped when his wife's car looked all beat to hell raises quite a few questions."

"He does seem oblivious at times," Sky said. "Like his wife always calling Wendell to fix things. The man's blind." Sky shifted her gaze between Monroe and Logan. "Do you think we're wrong about him being the target?"

Frowning, Monroe tugged on an ear. "At this point, I don't know what to think." He met Sky's gaze. "You said the silver sedan drove away. Was a wheel wobbling?"

"Not that I noticed. Although, the damage to the passenger side of the car was extensive. Obviously, not enough to disable the car."

Sighing, Monroe pushed away from the counter. "I contacted Brookson and told him what happened. He sounded surprised he passed by. I'm not sure I believe him." He checked his watch. "He and Rachael are on their way to see you, Sky. With this new development, I'm heading to the local police station to have another chat with the chief." He turned to Tank. "You better head out. I don't want them to see you."

"Right." Tank gave a two finger salute and hurried

out the door.

Monroe turned to Sky. "I need to leave, too. If you two think of anything, call me. I don't like where this case is going, and I can't help feeling we're approaching a climax. Be careful, will you?"

"Hold on." Logan dropped his arms and clamped onto Sky's bed rail. "Is Tank still watching Brookson?"

Pausing by the door, Monroe frowned. "I'll reevaluate all this new information and make a decision whether he should continue. In the meantime, Tank will stay at my cabin until I come up with another game plan. More importantly, I want to know how Brookson passed his wife's car when anyone could see the emblem so clearly." He shifted his gaze between his two agents. "I hate like hell having you two do this alone, but my last option is to put people in the woods." Frowning, he shook his head. "Let me think about this for a while. I'll be in touch." He hurried out the door.

Sky shifted her butt on the gurney. How long did the nurses keep a patient on this uncomfortable slab of a mattress? Damn good thing she didn't have a bony butt. She patted Logan's hand resting on the bed rail. "Men usually notice things that are action-oriented. A car accident would definitely make most men slow down or stop. Brookson doesn't have the excuse of emergency vehicles blocking his view. What are your thoughts?"

Logan had been staring into space but, at her words, focused on her face. "I honestly have no clue, Sky. It's possible he was preoccupied, like on his cell phone. But you're right. Most men will see an accident and look for blood and guts all over the road. That's how we're built."

True. She watched many a movie with blood

squirting all over the scene, limbs flying, and heads coming off. She'd cover her eyes. Logan, of course, cheered and told her she was missing the best part. Shaking her head, she searched her surroundings. "I'd like to disappear before Rachael and Donald arrive. Where are my clothes?"

A knock sounded on the door.

Aw, damn. Too late.

Rachael stuck her head through the opening. "Good. You're awake." She hurried into the room. "Is it true? Was it Maddie?"

Well, no *how ya doing or are you gonna die soon*? This damn woman irritated Sky in so many different ways.

Donald followed his wife. After scanning the length of the gurney, he nodded. "Glad to see you're okay."

She forced a smile. "Yes, all arms and limbs are still attached if, however, damaged." She looked at Rachael. "To answer your question, I never saw the driver. The car windows were tinted dark." She fussed with her gown. "I'm sorry about your car, but I'm glad you refused to ride along."

Standing behind his wife, Donald rested his hands on her shoulders. "Don't think twice about the car. It's Maddie we should concentrate on." He jerked his chin at Logan. "What's the plan? Are you leaving?"

Logan shook his head. "I'll keep working, but as you can see, Midnight will be out of commission for a while. Those braces stay on for at least two weeks."

"Well, that's a shame." Rachael pouted, but her gaze danced.

Oh, yeah, Rachael sounds all heartbroken. As soon

as the preggo left the hospital, she'd do a happy little jig. Sky resisted the urge to roll her eyes.

Rachael rested a hand on her belly. "How long do you have to stay here?"

"I can answer that." Logan passed a hand over Sky's mussed hair. "She's being discharged as we speak."

Mouth stretching into a smile, she met his gaze. "That's nice to hear."

"Good." Rachael latched onto her husband's arm. "We'll leave you two. If you need anything, let me know. I'll send Mrs. Sanchez to your cabin."

"No, I'll be fine. Logan can help me hobble around." As if Mrs. Sanchez would be thrilled to assist a woman who refused to fall under her thumb. *Get real.*

Alone once more, she frowned at the closed door. "I hope Brookson realizes you're the only one available to protect his wife." Resting her head on the gurney, she turned to look at Logan. "Maybe he'll rehire the guards."

While staring at the closed door, Logan shook his head. "Hard to say what he'll do. He wasn't overly concerned with someone targeting his wife's car."

She passed a hand through her already mussed hair. "I'm confused."

"You're not the only one, sweetheart." He winked. "Sit tight for a minute. Let me see if I can catch Brookson alone." He ran out the door.

Sky sighed. Sit tight, indeed. What else could she do?

Chapter Twenty-One

Logan didn't put too much stock into finding Donald Brookson alone. Knowing Rachael, she'd want to hurry home to her beautiful house and Wendell, but he took a chance. Hurrying through the automatic doors to the emergency room, he spotted the man standing off to the side on the concrete loading platform while smoking a cigarette. Rachael was nowhere in sight, but she could appear at any second. Before approaching, Logan activated the record mode on his phone, then crossed the platform. "Hey, Mr. Brookson, where's the wife?"

Donald released a long puff of smoke. "Bathroom."

"Then, let's talk quickly." Scanning the area for any eavesdroppers and finding none, he faced him. "I want to know why you drove by your wife's car. You had to see it."

The man took another long drag from his cigarette and blew the smoke into the air. "Yeah, I saw it." Shooting Logan a sideward glance, he lifted one shoulder in a shrug. "I didn't want to stop. I actually hoped Rachael went out alone again."

Wow. That was a cold comment. "But the baby—"

"I'm ninety-five percent convinced the baby isn't mine, Logan." Brookson held up a palm. He flicked cigarette ashes into the air. "She probably thinks I'm stupid, like I don't see how often Wendell comes around while I'm at the office or away from the resort. I demanded a DNA test. She refused. Legally, at this time, I can't force her, but I will request one after birth—which is my legal right." He flicked more ashes into the wind.

Well, Sky was right. Wendell and Rachael were an item. But to have such a callous view of the baby she carried... Logan inwardly cringed. *Bloody hell.* Who was he to judge? If in the man's shoes, he might feel the same. Rather than fanning away the smoke blowing directly toward him, he shifted to be more upwind. "The baby could still be yours."

Brookson shook his head. "I doubt it." He meandered to a cigarette disposal can, crushed the hot tip, and dropped what remained into the opening.

"You told us you gave up smoking."

Turning back, Donald snorted. "I did it for the baby. I don't give a damn now." After glancing at the double-door entrance, he faced Logan. "A few days ago, I visited my lawyer to change my will. If anything happens to me, I don't want Rachael to inherit the resort. When I finished, I stopped into a coffee shop, and you wouldn't believe who I ran into."

With such a mocking tone, Logan already knew the answer. He grimaced. "Madeline?"

Smiling, he tapped his nose. "She just came from a yoga class at the institution. She told me she'd been living with Wendell for the past three weeks. The bastard outright lied. Maddie is no more a threat to Rachael than the man on the moon."

"This is important information, Brookson. When were you planning to tell us?"

With hands in his pockets, he stared out at the

emergency room parking lot. "Wendell's betrayal hit hard. I was more upset with him than Rachael. Truthfully, I didn't know what to do."

"Telling Monroe would be a start." The damn man was an idiot. Not to mention, he endangered Sky's life. All for what? He gritted his teeth. "When did this revelation hit about the baby not being yours?"

"After I signed on with Monroe. I almost canceled the contract."

"And you never told your wife about the new will?"

He released a snort. "Of course, not."

Yeah, no love left in this man. "So, since Maddie isn't a threat to Rachael, you dismissed the guards."

"Yes."

Squaring his shoulders, he crossed his arms over his chest. "Why not us?"

"Because I believe Rachael and Wendell plan to kill me."

Well, Donald figured it out. The guy wasn't as clueless as believed. Logan hissed through his teeth. "Do you know that for sure?"

"Only a gut feeling. That's why I don't want her to get the resort." He locked onto Logan's gaze. "You and Midnight are still here because I need backup when the time comes. But now, Midnight is out of commission."

"Right. That leaves me—unless you rehire the guards, but Rachael will wonder why you changed your mind." He rubbed his forehead. Sighing, he dropped his hand. "No offense, Mr. Brookson, but you could have left the guards in place, especially if you guessed Rachael's real intentions. You've got me at a big disadvantage." Clenching his jaw, he stared at the automatic doors for signs of Rachael. He wanted to slap the man around a little to knock some sense into his pea brain. "Look, I'll call Monroe and see if he can send someone pronto." He wouldn't tell Donald about Tank being in the vicinity—not yet, anyway. Something still didn't feel right, and damned if Logan could put a finger on what it was.

****

Looking around the room for something to catch her interest and finding nothing, Sky sighed. Logan left without lowering her bed rails or searching for her clothes. She had no way to call a nurse, either. What if she was dying back here? Would anyone hear her croak? She was half-tempted to crawl out the foot-end of the gurney.

The door opened.

Logan walked in with a scowl covering his face. He glanced up. "Okay, gorgeous. Time to leave." Approaching the gurney, he searched for the latch to lower the bed rail. Successful, he helped her swing her legs over the side.

Funny how he could call her gorgeous and still look as if he wanted to punch something. With a finger, she tipped up his chin. "Your facial expression tells me you either missed Brookson, or the news was bad."

He grabbed her hand and kissed her finger. "It's bad, all right. He knows everything we know. I'll let you listen to the recording on our way to the resort."

Brookson knows everything? She found that surprising. The man always acted so clueless. She looked around. "Where are my clothes?" Placing her free hand behind her back, she arched her spine to relieve the stiffness.

"Here they are." He reached under the gurney, then handed her a large plastic bag full of her belongings. "Make sure you shake each garment first. You might find a lingering piece of glass."

Yeah, thanks to her Good Samaritan. She lifted her injured arm. "Can I take the braces off to get dressed?"

Heading to the door, he stopped and turned with a smirk. "No, you cannot. I'll let the nurse know you're ready for your discharge instructions. Then, I'll send the recording to Monroe." He grabbed the door handle.

"Wait a minute." She held her T-shirt at arm's length. "Can't you help me?"

Gaze turning dark, he released the knob and stomped back. Latching onto her head with both hands, he gave her a hard kiss.

The man could kiss. Even after all this time together, he still caused her body to go limp. If she wasn't sitting on the gurney, she'd have melted onto the floor.

Lifting his head, he stared into her eyes. "You know what will happen if I see your body all bruised. I'll want to kill whoever did this." Gaze softening, he stroked his thumbs across her cheeks. "When I heard you had an accident, I almost lost it. I love you so much, Sky." After a quick kiss, he released her head and left the room while closing the door softly behind him.

I blew it again. She had the perfect chance to open her mouth and say the words he wanted to hear, but as usual, she was stunned into silence. He had a habit of turning her brain into mush. One of these days...

Cursing herself for another lost opportunity, Sky stripped off the sling and hospital gown to put on her bra and T-shirt. Since the wrist brace allowed her fingers to move, fastening her bra wasn't a problem. Her pants were another matter. She lifted her braced foot up and down to feel the weight. The thing was shaped more like an open-toed boot that secured her ankle. An elastic bandage was wrapped from the arch of her foot to midway up her thigh. Frowning, she glared at the nylon straps securing the boot when the door opened.

An older, female nurse walked in with a clipboard in hand. "You look like you're contemplating world peace." She flashed a set of bright, white teeth.

Sky lifted her booted foot. "I don't know how to undo this contraption to slip on my pants."

"Oh, it's nothing, honey. I'll show you. I'm Connie, by the way." She placed the clipboard onto the stretcher. Connie proceeded to undo the straps and widened the fabric sides so Sky could slip out her foot.

With the nurse's assistance, Sky was dressed in no time, her boot straps refastened, and her foot again secured. She listened to Connie's detailed instructions on aches and pains common with a car accident and the warning signs of a brain concussion from being jostled around.

In all her years with martial arts, Sky never once sustained a head injury. Her ninja speed saved her time and again. Yet, two years ago, while investigating the murders at the manor, she suffered her first concussion from a push down the stairs. She totally blew it that day and hadn't sensed the person behind her. She was damn lucky.

A half hour later, she sat beside Logan in his black sports car. While en route, she listened to the recorded conversation between Logan and Donald Brookson. Finished, she placed his phone onto the center console. "So, Brookson isn't such a dimwit, after all. I'm glad."

He glanced her way. "Why are you glad? This complicates everything. With him releasing the guards, he willingly signed his own death certificate. That was a shit-ass move."

"Watch the road. I don't want another accident." She shifted her butt. His car seats were comfortable, but her bruises cried out for more cushioning. "Donald never mentioned who would inherit the resort." Staring straight ahead, she puffed out her cheeks. "Rachael could contest the will—especially with a newborn in her arms. If she kills Donald before the DNA test, she'll probably win."

"Then, we need to find proof she plans to murder her husband." He glanced her way. "That would be akin to searching for a needle in a haystack."

So true. Sky adjusted the sling on her left shoulder. "We have another possibility. If Donald tells Rachael about the change in the will, then she could incapacitate him in some way so that he turns into a vegetable. Legally, she'd have control of the resort."

"That's a good point, Sky." With a hand clenching the steering wheel, Logan hissed. "We have no idea if the resort plays into her plans to eliminate her husband. For all we know, she and Wendell could go riding off into the sunset with all the money she already transferred."

"Geez, it's only fifty grand. In this day and age, that isn't much."

He held up a finger. "Rachael might have transferred more than what Pam uncovered."

Well, hell, yeah. Sky shifted her butt. "Then, she should divorce Donald, not kill him. She's taking a big risk." Frowning, she waggled a finger. "You know, Rachael insinuated Maddie was driving the silver sedan, but we both know that can't be true."

"Agreed." After pressing his lips into a thin line, he shot her a glance. "Wendell, then."

"Had to be." She stifled a yawn. "When I returned to the cabin for my wallet, I got a call from Rachael. She put me on hold for quite a while. After she gave me directions to the meat market, I called you, then stopped at the lodge. From the time I left the Brookson house with her vehicle to the time I actually left the resort, I wasted forty-five minutes. The time span gave Wendell sufficient opportunity to pick up the silver sedan and lay in wait." She turned slightly to face him and felt a twinge in her back, right around the area where she slammed into the armrest on the passenger door. *Ouch.* "That car came from a side road or driveway because I hadn't passed any intersections. And with the resort emblems on the vehicle, Rachael's white SUV stuck out like a neon sign."

He slammed a fist onto the steering wheel. "Dammit, Sky! You *were* the intended target." He cursed under his breath. "That woman sacrificed her own vehicle to remove you from the picture."

Not a nice thought to be on a hit list. She shuddered. "With me out of commission, and the two guards dismissed, all Rachael has to worry about is you." Another horrible thought. She'd hate like hell to see Logan hurt, and her gut tightened. She stared out the windshield. "Since Donald knows what's going on, he might create an elaborate scheme to get rid of his wife and best friend. Kind of a payback plan."

"If that were the case, Donald would have sent us home."

She plunked her head onto the headrest and closed her eyes. "All these potential outcomes are boggling my mind." Popping her eyes open, she turned her head toward him. "Does this happen when you go undercover?"

"Not often. Most of my cases are straightforward." He shot her a grin. "Our last one certainly wasn't."

Their last assignment involved multiple plan changes to trap the culprits. This case had one plan shift from protecting Rachael to protecting Donald. Somehow, she had the strange feeling another shift was about to happen. But what, she wasn't sure. She turned her head to look out the side window. Like earlier, nothing but trees. She'd rather look at Logan. Her lover boy had a nice profile—strong jaw, cute ears, and thick neck to go with broad shoulders. "I'll take a wild guess and say whatever is to happen will be tonight." She blurted the statement without thought. Would something happen tonight? *In her view, yes*. Was she sure? *Hell, no. See?* She wasn't cut out to be some secret agent. She adjusted the sling strap around her neck. The damn thing scratched like sandpaper.

While shifting his grip on the steering wheel, Logan worked his jaw. After a minute, he met her gaze. "What makes you believe it's tonight?"

How could she explain a gut feeling? She wasn't clairvoyant or empathic or any of those other weird words. He'd think she was nuts. She rubbed her forehead. "I'm pulling straws out of the hat, Logan." She stifled another yawn. "The guards are gone. I'm out of the picture. As they say in the movies, the coast is clear. Why would Rachael wait?"

Brows furrowed, he remained silent.

Sky couldn't blame him. No matter what scenario came to mind, nothing was concrete. She and Logan had no evidence. What they had was a big guessing game. *Who will be the winner*? As if selecting the right door would reveal the grand prize. She hated to admit it, but she was curious as hell—and a little jittery. Donald's life was in danger. Somehow, they needed to prevent his death from happening.

Twenty minutes later, Logan pulled into the resort.

Dusk had settled over the complex. The pole lamps along Chaddy-Wonker Drive hadn't activated yet. They were on a timer that turned them on an hour after darkness fell. "To save money," Brookson had said. The practice made sense when no one was around, but geez, shouldn't he up the wattage for his own safety? On her nightly strolls with Logan, she fought like mad not to whip out her phone to use the flashlight app. Not like she had any fear of the dark but…well, wild animals and all.

Guiding the car into the parking spot alongside the cabin, Logan shifted the gear into Park and killed the engine.

Skylar breathed a heavy sigh. Coming to a complete stop felt wonderful. On the drive home, every bump radiated pain through her body. She didn't have any broken bones—thank God—but her bruises complained. Overall, she considered herself lucky. The accident could have been devastating.

Logan opened her car door and leaned in. "Make this look good, Sky. Eyes could be watching."

Straightening, he extended a hand. "Wait a sec." He reached behind her car seat and came out with her right boot. "Okay. Up you go." He, again, extended a hand.

A little playacting wasn't necessary. Her body turned into a stiff board. She would need to do some serious stretching tonight. But with his help, she hobbled like she couldn't put weight on her foot. Even with Logan's arm wrapped around her waist, she still shuffled like she had one too many at the bar. "This feels so weird."

Logan squeezed her waist. "I'd carry you, but this looks better. Just lean against me."

Oh, leaning against him was never a problem. She loved the feel of his strong arm around her and the way he always tugged her close to his side. Snickering, she nudged his hip with her own. "You're the expert at hobbling around."

While on assignment to find the killer at Ginger's Manor, Logan impersonated a disabled gardener, complete with a forearm crutch. He fooled everyone, herself included.

Once she entered the cabin, she flopped onto the sofa and waited for the all-clear.

Two minutes later, Logan returned from the bedrooms. "All drapes are closed."

"Yay!" She whipped off the sling and wrist brace. Next came the boot on her foot and the elastic bandage. The last was the gauze on her forehead. She sustained small cuts from the shattered glass but not enough to warrant a covering. Other than feeling a little used and abused, she survived her ordeal okay, but she'd rather not repeat the experience. She fell back against the sofa cushions and puffed out a breath. "How in the world did Monroe get the doctor to agree to fake injuries?"

Smiling, Logan lowered alongside. "Bob has his ways. When you think about it, it's a great idea. With you out of the picture, you can do covert surveillance." Reaching into his rear pocket, he whipped out his cell phone. "I'll call Monroe and let him know we're at the cabin. I'll also mention your theory about what might happen tonight."

Oh, dear. Covert surveillance didn't sound at all appealing. Alone and in the dark? Logan was out of his mind. She hoped like hell Monroe came up with a better plan.

Chapter Twenty-Two

Thirty minutes later and feeling clean and refreshed from a hot shower, Sky joined Logan in the kitchen. The aroma of Fay's turkey casserole filled the air. The woman should bottle the scent and earn herself a fortune. "What did Monroe say?"

Using a pair of worn-out oven mitts, Logan slipped the casserole from the oven and placed the dish on the counter. "Want a beer?"

"Sure." His evasion of her question hadn't gone unnoticed. Either the news wasn't good, or the man was starving. Probably both.

"Grab a few beers, will ya?" He carried the casserole to the table by the front windows where he had already placed plates and utensils.

Beers in hand plus napkins—since men never think of wiping their mouth—Sky followed.

Logan gave her a cursory scan. "How do you feel?"

"Pretty good. After my shower, I did a few stretches and hardly felt any resistance. The hot water helped." If she couldn't move, she wouldn't be of much use tonight. And she sure as hell would not allow him to go out alone. After popping the tabs on the beer cans and slapping down a napkin next to his plate, Sky took a seat on the chair to his left.

That feeling of wedded bliss flashed through

her…again. She and Logan had eaten together many times and not once had she pictured a walk down the aisle. She glanced at the engagement ring on her finger. This damn piece of jewelry was the problem. The diamond acted like some sort of mind control. So what if they ate meals together and shared the same bed? Marriage had never entered her mind…well, until now. Not that she would say anything to Logan. Like any man, he thrived on freedom, and freedom meant being available for whatever assignment Monroe needed. As for her, she lived her life with the philosophy of her martial arts—peace and harmony with mind, body, and spirit. Simple rules. While she and Logan got along great, would their different personalities create conflict down the road?

The thought was something to consider. And what about children? No, she was getting way too far ahead of herself. Maybe, while inside the cabin, she should take off the damn ring.

Logan dished out a large portion of the casserole and plopped the slab onto her plate. He took two large portions for himself and picked up his fork. "Pam ate all the bread."

"Yes, I know. I'll have to ask where she bought it." She forked a mouthful of casserole and savored the taste of turkey with tiny peas and carrots in a thick, creamy white sauce. She chewed and swallowed. "So, Monroe?"

Holding up a finger, he swallowed what was in his mouth. "He found our reasoning sound and agrees with tonight being a possibility."

She poised her fork midway. "And?"

"He'll get back to me." He shoveled in another

mouthful.

Wonderful. What she'd like was for Monroe to call out the army and get the complex surrounded. But even she recognized the futile cost of a *possibility*. Sky sipped her cold-as-ice beer. "I have one big question, Logan. Where is Wendell hiding the sedan? The passenger side should have extensive damage. If Maddie is to be framed as we suspect, the car needs to be found, right?"

Grabbing his napkin, he swiped it across his mouth. "He could hide a car anywhere, Sky, but rest assured, when the time comes, Wendell will make sure the cops find it." His phone chirped with a text message. Lifting the device from his rear pocket, he read, then nodded. "Tank will take a position on the road outside of the complex and wait for Maddie to appear."

"That's something, at least." Staring at her plate, she pushed the food around with her fork.

Reaching, he squeezed her arm. "Look at me, Sky." When he had her attention, he raised his brows. "We will be very careful, got it?"

She'd rather be in Jersey, watching some stupid reality show. She touched his cheek. "Careful is my middle name." Waiting around for something to happen must be the most boring part of an assignment, like watching grass grow. A total yawn.

"Eat. You'll need energy."

Those words were a prerequisite for a little planned activity in the bedroom, but he was talking about an all-nighter patrolling the complex. Really, did it have to be all night? Would they sit and stare at the Brookson house until dawn? *Oh, joy.* Internally shaking her head, she dug into her casserole and ate with gusto. If Logan expected her to last the night, waiting for whatever to occur, she needed sustenance. About halfway through, she stopped to take a breath and wiped her lips with a napkin. She looked up into his wide gaze. "What? You said eat."

Squinting, he pointed to her plate. "You're supposed to taste your food, not wolf it like a starving Neanderthal."

She waggled a finger. "I don't think the term applies to women."

"Whatever." He made a face. "Just don't choke to death. My Heimlich maneuver might be rusty."

"All right, sorry. I didn't realize I was starving. I've had a stressful day." She pointed to her plate. "I still have half left." To force herself to slow down, she used her fork to cut the rest into small portions. "I've been thinking. If Rachael and Wendell plan to kill Donald, they won't do the deed in the house. Rachael keeps the rooms spotless. She'll have a fit if Donald bleeds all over the place."

Sitting back, Logan laughed. "I can't argue with a woman's logic." Leaning forward again, he helped himself to another large portion.

She stopped chewing. "Do you think they'll use a gun?"

After returning the spoon to the casserole dish, he picked up his fork. "Hard to say. You and I are the only two people in the complex. If a shot is fired outside, we will hear the blast, and the surrounding forest will echo the sound and make any nearby neighbors curious." Pausing, he pursed his lips. "I'm going with Wendell using a bat or some other heavy object. It's quiet but messy." He chewed with a gaze focused on his plate. "Guns are a normal part of living in the mountains. To protect his guests, Donald would have a few choice weapons at his disposal." He lifted his gaze to meet hers. "Ten to one, he will carry a gun and take care of both of them."

"Dear Lord, I hope not." She cringed at the visual. "His attitude toward the baby is all wrong. The child could still be his. If he kills Rachael—"

Logan waved his fork. "First off, we need to stop them before anyone gets hurt. At the same time, we need to see or hear their intent to kill."

"And Maddie?"

"Somehow, Wendell will lure his sister to the resort. Your job will be to stop her at the entrance. At that point, Tank will see her drive in and join you."

"She won't have a car."

He stopped mid-chew and stared. "You're right. Wendell can't leave his truck for her to drive because she'll wonder how he got to the resort." Frowning, he rotated his beer can, then met her gaze and hissed. "Dammit, Sky. He'd have to kill Maddie first."

Holy moly, he's right.

Sky lost her appetite. Killing Maddie before the fact would be something she or Logan could not prevent, and a helpless feeling swamped her. Dropping her fork onto the plate, she pushed the dish to the side. "I don't like where this is going. If Wendell kills his sister at home, there's no way in hell we can save her. Maybe Tank should go to Wendell's."

"We're still not sure if anything will happen tonight, Sky, but I will send a quick message to Monroe." Again, he whipped out his phone from his pocket and typed.

The phone immediately chirped with a return message.

He read. "Monroe agrees. He will go himself to Wendell's place and keep us advised. Tank will still maintain his position outside the complex." Slipping the phone onto the table, he stared at the screen. Looking up, he gave a curt nod. "Tell you what. You take a walk around the complex. Keep an eye out for anything unusual. I'll maintain a position near the Brookson house. Stay in the shadows as much as possible. Remember. You're supposed to be incapacitated."

She rolled her eyes. "Hiding in the shadows won't be hard. Brookson doesn't have all the pole lamps lit yet."

With a quick check at his watch, Logan stood and grabbed their dinner plates. "We should get ready. We might have a long night. Dress accordingly. I don't have to tell you to wear all black, do I?" He waggled his brows.

Smart ass. She shot him a one-eyed glare. Then, gathering what was left on the table plus the casserole dish, she followed him to the kitchen.

His cell phone rang. Hurriedly placing the plates into the sink, he rushed to the table for his phone. After glancing at the screen, he raised his brows. "It's Brookson." He hit the *Accept* button. "Yes, sir, what can I do for you?" He changed the phone to Speaker.

"Rachael wants to go for a nighttime stroll. What should I do?"

Sky flicked her gaze to meet Logan's. Brookson was whispering. *Not good.*

"Where are you?"

"In the bathroom. I told her a walk at this time of night is too dangerous. Rachael doesn't care. I need some help here."

"Tell her *no*. Make up an excuse. Tell her you're tired."

"I tried that. She still insists."

Her gut quivered. Of course, Rachael insisted. Tonight was the night, and the deed would be done outdoors to prevent messing Rachael's spotless home. *Egads, what a cold-blooded woman.*

While rubbing a hand down his face, Logan shifted on his feet. "Look, Mr. Brookson, give me ten minutes to get Midnight situated. I'll tail you and Rachael. Keep your eyes open, and don't look for me, okay?"

"Will do."

Logan disconnected and ran straight for the bedroom. Returning a minute later, he held two objects in his right palm. "Here, take these. We'll use them to communicate. Put the small piece in your ear. It's wireless."

Sky stared at what he placed in her hand. One looked like a black watch with a digital face, but it wasn't a watch. A tiny antenna protruded from one of the corners. The second object reminded her of a hearing aid. She plugged the latter into her left ear. It tickled.

Lifting his left wrist to his mouth, he pointed to his ear. "Can you hear me?"

Brows high, she cleared her throat. "Oh, wow, yes, loud and clear." *Cool.*

"Speak into the watch, Sky, and always keep your voice low."

Since she wore her diamond-studded watch on her

left wrist, she strapped the device to her right wrist and lifted it to her lips. "Testing, one, two, three."

He gave her a thumbs-up. "Here, keep this handy." He shoved a small penlight into her hand. "This is a red light. Red helps you see without spoiling your night vision."

She stared at the little light and toyed with the switch. Shouldn't he have introduced her to this stuff earlier, like before rushing off to follow Brookson? She would never understand men.

"Safety first, Sky. Don't talk if you don't have to. Same with the light. Put your cell phone on silent and turn on voice record." He lifted his right foot onto the chair and adjusted the ankle holster beneath his pant leg. "I'll go out the front door. You use the rear. Look for Wendell's truck. Check it out. If you find Maddie, get Tank in here. Also, contact Monroe. Tell him what's happening, but tell them both not to come in unless we give the go-ahead. If you can't find Maddie or Wendell's truck, let me know. It's possible Rachael and Donald are really only out for a stroll." He headed for the front door.

"Wait a minute. Shouldn't we turn out the lights first? Anybody can see you." Not that the resort was loaded with guests. *Can't be too careful.*

"Good idea. We need to hurry. Brookson isn't giving me a whole lot of time." He headed for the bedroom.

She turned off the lights in the living area but left the oven light on in the kitchen. The glow was a dull yellow, but it gave enough light to see.

Logan returned quickly. "I kept the small nightstand lamp on in the bedroom where you're

223

supposed to be laid up."

Hurrying toward him, she grabbed the front of his sweatshirt and pulled him close. She gave him a hard kiss. After lifting her head, she stared into his copper-colored eyes. "Please, be careful."

He winked. "You, too. I love you." He hurried for the front door.

Oh, God. She faced a now-or-never time. *Don't be such a damn coward*. She sucked in a breath. "Logan."

He stopped, hand on the knob, and turned his head.

Swallowing hard, she locked onto his gaze. "I love you, too."

****

She loves me! If his heart could sing any louder, the entire compound would hear. For so long, he wanted to hear those three little words. He knew how she felt. Every touch and every kiss conveyed her love, as did the glow from her beautiful eyes, but she never verbalized her feelings. He couldn't understand why she found the words so difficult. Men were notorious about hiding their emotions, not women.

Had something occurred in her childhood to create all this caution? Or how about a man who broke her heart? Her past was still a mystery, but he sure as hell saw her future. Turning away from the door, he took two steps toward her and wrapped her into a tight embrace. He plastered his lips onto hers for another firm kiss.

She went limp in his arms. Skylar Dawson, a three-time black belt martial arts expert, yielded, as she had done so many times in the past. Lifting his head, he met her stunned gaze and smiled. "I love you so much." But because time was against him, he dropped his arms and held her at arm's length. "Move away from the door…just in case."

While biting her lower lip, she stepped toward the dark corner of the living room.

Pausing with his hand on the knob, he glanced over his shoulder. "Be careful." He opened the door and stepped out.

Never in his life had he fought the urge to turn around and say to hell with the job. He'd rather be with Sky, in bed, naked. But could he let a murder take place because he wanted to celebrate? *A resounding no*. He was a professional, and despite her timing, he had a job to do.

As he stood outside the cabin door to let his eyes adjust to the darkness, he couldn't ignore the sense of dread sweeping through him. Preventing a murder, when the entire plan was one big guessing game, might take an act of divine intervention. Being in the far corner of the complex didn't help. He was too far away to get into position.

Unable to wait any longer for his vision to adjust, he stepped toward Chaddy-Wonker Drive and scanned his surroundings, then glanced skyward. If a moon hovered overhead, the overcast skies obscured the glow. He took off at a steady trot toward the Brookson house. Since his heavy boots clomping on asphalt would make too much noise, he stayed on the grass. As hard as he tried, he could not run silently. His height and weight worked against him. He'd never be like Skylar Dawson. She had this nimble way of floating across the floor. She moved with the grace of a dancer, and in bed…*oh, hell. Focus, man, focus*.

He cursed Brookson. The damn fool listened to his

wife and allowed her to release the bodyguards. Right now, Logan sure as hell could use their help. Whether Maddie had martial arts skills or not didn't matter anymore. Maddie was being set up by her own brother, and Sky's expertise was unnecessary. Hell, Tank could have stayed in the spare bedroom. Then again, Logan wouldn't have the pleasure of Sky's company every night. He slowed his pace as the dark Flipper and Oar Store came into view.

Without having any idea of Rachael and Donald's direction, he had to be careful. Rachael would guide Donald to wherever Wendell waited in ambush. Would they throw Donald into the lake? No, that scenario wouldn't do, not if they wanted to frame Maddie. Would Donald grab a weapon to carry in his pocket? *Probably*. With his life in danger, any normal man would take a weapon—unless Rachael stopped him, but what excuse could she give?

Pausing just past the store, Logan listened. Rachael and Donald had no need for silence, but he heard nothing. Had they headed in the opposite direction, like toward the main entrance? Since the pole lamps were spaced at least five hundred feet apart, and every other one was lit, the darkness between them left the perfect opportunity for a predator to strike. The main lodge, maintenance building, and store had exterior lights, but they wouldn't be activated until opening day. He resumed his trot toward the house.

If he paused to think this through, he should have told Brookson to give him fifteen minutes instead of ten. The added time would have allowed him to reach the house and follow the pair. If they strolled along the drive toward the lodge, then Logan was too damn far.

He quickened his pace.

Voices stopped him. He crouched behind a bush and listened. Definitely male and female in a normal conversation. Craning his neck, he couldn't see anyone. But knowing how voices carried with the breeze, he had to be careful. He looked again and spotted the swing of a flashlight beam somewhere along Chaddy-Wonker Drive. At a guess, they headed in the direction of the maintenance building. Not what Logan would call a romantic stroll—

Whack!

Excruciating pain from the back of his head created bolts of light to shoot out both eyes. The surrounding trees whirled, and he dropped to the ground with a thud.

Chapter Twenty-Three

Skylar should give herself a swift kick in the butt. What impeccable timing! Why in the world had she said those three little words when Logan had one foot out the door to face who knew what? If her admission distracted him, she would never forgive herself. But God forbid, if something happened, and he got hurt, he needed to know. No matter what, she would be by his side. She loved him, and high time she put her heart on the table.

Before she did anything else, she slid off the engagement ring and placed it on the kitchen counter. If her confrontation with either Wendell or Rachael came to blows, she would hate to see the diamond take a flying leap into oblivion. On second thought, she also removed her wristwatch. Her father's gift was even more precious than the ring. After a quick text to Monroe—for which she had no time to wait for an answer—Sky hit the voice record app, then silenced her phone and slipped it into her pants pocket. Mentally running through her checklist and feeling satisfied, she threw on her black jacket and opened the sliding glass door to the back deck.

The night was eerily quiet. The overcast sky hid any moon or stars, and even the lake resembled a black void. The weather was too cool for any bug sounds, but she caught the hoot of an owl somewhere in the trees.

Since the darkness inside the cabin helped her eyes adjust, she had no trouble seeing her surroundings. Stepping off the small deck, she rounded the corner and crept to the front of the cabin. Pausing, she glanced both ways.

The overhead pole lamps barely gave enough illumination to light the asphalt drive. If Donald Brookson had a brain inside his skull, he would have activated all the lamps to brighten his walk with his pregnant wife. But if Rachael had her way, she'd convince her husband lights weren't necessary. After all, she wouldn't want him to see Wendell pop from a bush with a bat or whatever weapon in his hands. Sighing, she stayed on the grass to prevent her heavy boots from clomping on the asphalt. With a steady pace, she searched for Wendell's truck.

With cabin number eight being the farthest from the main entrance, Sky followed the road leading away from the Brookson house. Over the years, she developed excellent night vision and not because she enjoyed eating carrots. As a bartender in Chicago, she worked until two in the morning and often closed the bar. In order to survive, she honed all her senses.

This assignment was no different. Her body was on full alert. But one thing bothered her. She should be with Logan as his backup, not wandering around the complex. Logan was doing the more dangerous job of preventing a murder. Anything could…*where the hell am I?* She slowed her pace.

Her surroundings were so dark she could barely make out the numbers on the cabin doors. She rounded a bend about a hundred yards back. So, the main entrance was about eight or nine cabins away. Her nightly strolls with Logan helped orient her to what was where, but since she had no idea where Rachael would guide Donald, she had to be careful not to call attention to herself. After all, she was supposed to be injured and laid up in bed.

Something on the left caught her eye. With a glance in all directions, she stopped. What could it be? A flash? No, a better word might be a reflection of some sort. From an overhead lamp? Or how about the glow in an animal's eye? Hell, she wasn't used to dark forests. Fear said to ignore the sighting as insignificant and keep moving. Instincts said to investigate, and that tiny little voice served her well throughout her life. Besides, Logan had instructed her to check for anything unusual.

Sky retraced her steps. The reflection came from behind one of the cabins. Clicking into ninja mode, she crept between cabins number seventeen and eighteen until reaching the rear. She shivered. These cabins were entirely too close to the forest. Getting a grip on her nerves, she glanced left, then right. *Well, I'll be damned.* A sedan sat nestled between two trees. Even in the dark, she could see the damage to the passenger side. *So, this is where Wendell hid the car.* She clenched her jaw.

Within the thick trees, a snap broke the silence.

Sky jerked her gaze toward the sound, half-expecting to see someone—or something— approach. But nothing moved. Being this close to so many trees put her on edge. Crowds and city noise calmed her, not all this ungodly quiet. The snap probably meant an animal foraging for food, and she better not be on the menu. Gad, what if the sound came from Bigfoot?

Controlling a shudder, she concentrated on the vehicle and frowned. Could Madeline be in the car, already dead? Slipping the penlight from her jacket pocket, she clicked on the switch, and the area glowed a dull red. Swinging the beam inside the vehicle, she checked front and rear seats. Empty. Not wishing for anyone to see the light, she clicked the switch off and replaced the small device into her pocket. Maddie could still be stuffed into the trunk, but if some of the car's damage involved the rear side panel, she'd make too much noise raising the lid. Besides, what if the car had an alarm system? Grabbing the door handles could set off an ear-splitting wail. So, no. She would wait to inspect the trunk.

She stepped away from the car and returned to the front of the cabin.

Should she call Logan? She really had no clue what would be important, but he said no unnecessary communication. Logically, she should continue her search for Wendell's truck, then break radio silence. She resumed her pace along Chaddy-Wonker Drive.

She stopped. Something else caught her eye—this time, on her right. Another reflection? At this rate, she'd never accomplish anything, but the first reflection turned into something important. This second one could prove the same. Unable to ignore what might be another clue, Sky crossed Chaddy-Wonker Drive and traversed the long stretch of open grass leading to the main lodge.

The shape of a pickup truck came into view. The vehicle was parked on the side of the building. Even in darkness, the truck could still be distinguished from the dark structure because of the difference in shadows. She slowed. Now, that was odd. The front asphalt parking lot didn't extend around to the side. So, the vehicle had to be on grass.

Her gut twisted. She'd bet any amount of money the truck was blue with a resort emblem on the door. After glancing in all directions, she approached the vehicle. Without a doubt, the truck belonged to Wendell. Again, she took out her little light and inspected the interior. Empty. As was the truck bed. *Shit, shit, shit*! Now, what? Both the truck and sedan were here. Maddie had to be on the premises, probably dead and hidden in some bushes. Regardless, Logan needed to know. She raised the communication watch to her lips and kept her voice low. "Logan."

No answer. She checked the device. Was it on? Shouldn't he have given her a few quick lessons before slapping the watch into her hand? He might get a kick out of playing with new technology, but she had enough trouble with the TV remote. She tried again. "Logan." She pressed on the earpiece inside her ear. Nothing.

Was he okay or too busy to answer? She wasn't used to analyzing scenarios, and she needed some expert advice here. Should she look for Maddie? The woman could be anywhere within the compound, and searching in the dark wasn't a feasible option. What in the world should she do?

"Well, hello, Skylar Dawson."

Tensing at the use of her real name, Sky whirled.

A shadow advanced from behind a clump of bushes.

With her heart jumping straight into her throat, Sky stiffened. The voice was deep and unmistakably female, and she addressed Sky by name. Only a student of martial arts would know Sky's true identity. Raising her chin, Sky straightened her shoulders and stepped away from the truck. "Hello, Maddie."

The shadow stopped. Then, a tall, slim figure with a long ponytail emerged from the darkness into the scant light provided by the pole lamps. She was dressed entirely in black and strolled toward Sky like she had all the time in the world. In her right hand, she gripped a pair of nunchucks, the martial arts weapon consisting of two sticks connected by a chain or leather strap. For Maddie to carry such a weapon told Sky her skills in martial arts could be comparable to her own. Nunchucks were a dangerous weapon and, when used properly, often deadly.

Confusion flooded her. What was Maddie doing here with a weapon? She was supposed to be the innocent victim of her brother's scheme. Could Sky and Logan be wrong? After all this time, was Wendell telling the truth about Maddie being after Rachael?

No, dammit. She and Logan didn't get it wrong. Rachael and Wendell planned to kill Donald. Since Maddie and Donald had a conversation at a coffee shop, they could have devised their own plan. But if that were the case, why hadn't Brookson dismissed Monroe Security? She internally screamed. All this back and forth shit boggled her mind.

"So, we know each other's names." Maddie took a few more steps and, again, stopped.

"So, it seems." Something in Maddie's voice put Sky on alert. The tone was not quite menacing but not friendly, either. Maddie had narrowed the distance from Sky to about twelve feet but still out of range for an effective nunchucks attack.

Sky gave a quick scan of her surroundings. The

openness allowed plenty of room for a martial arts confrontation. She took a few more steps away from the truck.

"Who came up with the idea to fake your injuries?"

Maddie's question jerked Sky from her perimeter assessment. "My idea." A bold lie, but hey, Monroe wouldn't mind. "Someone wanted to eliminate me from the picture. I suspected Wendell, not you. How did you know I was driving Rachael's car?"

The woman furrowed her brows. "Wendell drove you off the road, hon. Since the sedan is in my name, naturally, I'd be blamed."

Well, Sky was right. Rachael intentionally delayed Sky's departure so Wendell could ambush her. He probably left the house right after Sky, and since everything was planned, the vehicle had to be parked close by. "Weren't you suspicious when the cops came to ask about your car?"

Squaring her shoulders, Maddie jerked her chin upward. "Of course, and I questioned Wendell when he came home. He gave me some cockamamie story about the sedan being a surprise birthday present, and he was having some front-end work done. The pieces fell into place when I ran into Donald at the coffee shop. He answered quite a few of my questions. We are both being set up." She took a step toward the left.

"You and Donald planned a countermove, didn't you? If that's the case, why are you here? Shouldn't you be with Donald to, you know, give him some support?"

She harrumphed. "We have to let Wendell believe he can still frame me. We don't want him to change his plans."

Why did Sky have a nagging feeling something wasn't right? And how much had Donald revealed? *Think, Skylar.* How in the world should she play this? Monroe always told her she had a good brain in her head, but thanks to the confusion surrounding this case, her mind was a jumbled mess. She lifted her chin. "Okay, what now?"

Madeline slipped her left hand into her pants pocket. "Our plan is a solid one—except for you and your fiancé. You are witnesses to our grand scheme. With you supposedly incapacitated, that left your other half to remove from the picture. But sadly, I now have to do something about you."

Remove? Like spots on clothing? Sky pursed her lips. "Who are *we*, Maddie? You and Donald?"

The woman grinned. "Maybe."

Yeah, maybe. A nothing answer. She pointed to the weapon in Maddie's hand. "Those nunchucks will hurt someone."

Maddie turned them this way and that. "They *are* an effective weapon."

Too effective. "Look, Maddie. Wendell explained to my fiancé about how you're after Rachael."

Face pinched, she narrowed her gaze. "Don't try to deny it, honey. Donald told me you and your fiancé are agents from Monroe Security."

Ah, well. The dimwit struck again. "Mr. Brookson should have kept quiet."

"How could he? The poor guy practically poured his heart out at the coffee shop. It's what we did when we were kids...before Rachael entered the picture. He had to talk to somebody." She shifted her feet. "Funny thing, though, meeting Donny was an opportunity I couldn't pass up. He played right into our hands."

Our—what? Sky shifted on her feet. "Whose hands are you talking about?"

Maddie shot her a twisted grin. "Rachael and me, of course."

Well, damn. She hadn't seen that coming. This bit of news turned the entire case on its axis. Sky hissed. "All right, let me get this straight. Rachael and Wendell plan to kill Donald. But Donald already knows what's coming and is prepared to what? Kill Wendell and Rachael? Again, why are you here with me when you should be helping Rachael?"

Maddie waved the comment aside. "Rach is in no danger, hon. Donald thinks I'm in the background ready to pounce. He'll be carrying one of his guns, but Rach had Wendell remove the firing pins in his two pistols."

Wow, what a heartless woman. And Logan needed to be warned. Sky rubbed her forehead. With a heavy sigh, she looked at Maddie. "You left Donald defenseless."

"Well, we wouldn't want him to kill the baby, you know." She took a few steps to the side. "Rach talked Donny into letting Guardem Guys go, and Donny was more than willing after he uncovered Rachael's plans. Our big problem was you and your fiancé. I can't tell you how surprised and thrilled I was to discover Skylar Dawson—aka Midnight Sky—was on the premises." Maddie chuckled softly. "I studied every one of your videos. At first, I couldn't believe it was really you." She tilted her head. "I also can't believe you became a security agent."

Sky rolled her eyes. "Not by choice, I assure you."

Maddie took a step closer. "Doesn't matter. I

finally have a chance to put my martial arts skills to use."

Aw, hell. No argument now. If Maddie sought the opportunity to fight Skylar Dawson, she must have comparable skills. Most students of martial arts backed away from someone of her expertise. On the other hand, cocky students soon learned a hard lesson. Regardless, Sky had a big problem brewing. Maddie stood within striking distance with her nunchucks. Her yoga limberness combined with some obvious martial arts skills would give her speed and agility. But the discipline required to master such an ancient weapon took years of practice. The recoil alone could easily cause self-injury.

If Sky's masters drilled anything into her brain, she learned never to underestimate an opponent. Even more important, Maddie had yet to remove her left hand from her pocket. What was she hiding? A ninja star, perhaps? Regardless, Sky never backed away from an opponent. She took her own step closer to Maddie and scanned her from head to toe. She pointed to the weapon in Maddie's hand. "Is that why you hold the nunchucks, to give yourself an advantage?"

Grinning, Maddie nodded. "I've trained a long time with these. So, yeah. I know how fast you are. But you don't have any idea how fast I am."

Yup. Cocky bitch. That particular attitude had no place in martial arts. Sky shook her head. "You might as well tell me why you're doing this. I assume you intend to kill Donald."

"Of course."

"What about Wendell? How can you kill your own brother?"

Maddie shrugged. "Easy. He wanted to sacrifice me, so we might as well give him payback." She stepped a little more to the right. "Wendell has been in love with Rachael for years. So, after he found out she carried his child, he happily went along with her plans to eliminate Donald. What surprised us was how easily he set me up to take the fall. He made Donny think I was in a locked facility, and my mental state was questionable. How can I possibly let him live after all that?" She pressed her lips into a thin line.

"I don't have a brother, but I understand betrayal." She shifted her stance. "Is all this worth a prison term?"

"Ha! We have no intention of getting caught. All we have to do is eliminate the witnesses." With a tilt of her head, she narrowed her gaze. "And don't expect your fiancé to come to the rescue."

The hairs on Sky's scalp stood on end. Tensing, she met and held Maddie's cold-as-ice stare. No wonder Logan didn't answer. The bitch got to him first!

Chapter Twenty-Four

With his head throbbing like crazy, Logan pried his eyelids apart. Blinking to clear his vision, he started. *Well, shit.* He was tied to a tree. Tape covered his mouth. Rope circled his body and legs like he was a cartoon character being sacrificed on a railroad track. He puffed out his chest to test the give. *Yup. Tight as a drum.*

His damn skull hurt like hell. Someone had slammed him from behind. He hadn't even heard footsteps or seen the weapon swing toward his head. Yes, all right, the night was black as coal, but he should have sensed something. *What the hell kind of agent am I?* No one should have snuck up on him. He had excellent hearing and peripheral vision. And now, he was about as effective as a...what? Hell, his brain was scrambled, too. Cussing to himself, he ignored the pain of moving his head and took a good look around.

The darkness of the forest hid him. Thanks to Wendell sending him all over the complex, he recognized the rear of cabin number five, the one closest to the Brookson house and the woods behind it. Part of the beach stretched before him, along with the lake. No one would think to follow the path into the forest to find him.

A breeze blew against his left shoulder and hit the dampness covering his sweatshirt. Blood from the wound on his head? *Son of a bitch.* Whatever hit him probably cracked his skull. Maybe half his brain was hanging out. Small wonder he hadn't bled to death. Even more of a wonder was how he could still be alive. How much time had he lost? Was Sky all right?

Tramping down the fear of Sky being equally taken by surprise, he struggled against his tight restraints and cursed. Whoever tied him used an entire cord of rope. Wendell always carried several in the bed of his truck, so this had to be his handiwork. He shifted his butt. *Ouch*! A tree root jabbed his ass. Lifting one butt cheek after the other did nothing since he could barely move. All he got for his efforts was more of a headache, but dammit, he had to loosen these ropes…somehow. Since his ankles were bound, in all probability, his attacker found his gun. He didn't feel the earpiece either. He cursed under his breath.

All right, time to bite the bullet. He'd been bound on prior cases, and he learned to carry a small penknife in his right front pocket. Not every case had him wrapped like a sausage, so this was a first. With luck, he had enough room to slip his hand into his jeans pocket—*if* his attacker didn't clean out his pockets. But in order to reach the small weapon, he had to somehow move his right hand. The rope had his extremity plastered to the side of his hip, and he could barely wiggle his fingers.

Time passed. The effort to free his hand increased the painful throb in his head, but with Sky on his mind, he didn't give a damn if he popped an artery. He worked up a good sweat, though, and somehow wiggled the ropes enough to flex his wrist. Bending his hand into the pocket slot, he palpated for the little device. His jeans were tight as hell. Within minutes, the denim material cut off the circulation to his fingers, but he found the knife and inched it up with two fingers holding on tight. He should learn to wear cargo pants—like Sky. Loose pants gave her maneuverability to kick her feet into someone's face.

Stopping to close his eyes against the painful throb in his head, he sucked in large amounts of air through his nose. Nausea threatened to expel the contents in his stomach, but with tape over his mouth, that shit would come out his nose. He sucked in more breaths to calm his stomach, and after several minutes, the nausea passed. *Time to put the tiny blade to work.*

The small knife wasn't designed to cut easily through three-quarter inch rope, but it was better than nothing. Carefully, with two fingers and a thumb, he exposed the sharp metal and began the tedious job of cutting. Once the first loop snapped free, he slithered the rest up and off. Praying he didn't rip off his lips, he removed the tape covering his mouth and immediately sucked in a large breath of air. *God, that felt good.* He took a second large breath before tackling his bound ankles. As suspected, the ankle holster was empty. His communication watch, earpiece, and damn, his phone were gone. With his hands and feet free, he palpated the back of his head. His hand returned sticky. One sniff of the faint metallic smell told him the fluid was blood. He replaced his little knife into his pocket.

Using the tree for support, he edged up the trunk and onto wobbly legs. A wave of dizziness hit, and he closed his eyes. A lot of damn help he'd be if he passed out again. Considering he had no idea how much time passed, he could already be too late. Feeling a little steadier, he opened his eyes.

A thumping sound echoed through the trees. *Well, that noise isn't normal.* Someone chopping wood? At this hour and in the dark? *Not likely.* Gritting his teeth to control another wave of nausea, he headed toward the sound—more like staggered since he couldn't run in a straight line.

The thumping stopped.

Logan stopped. The maintenance building loomed in the darkness. He silently cursed. Brookson was a cheap bastard. Even with his life in danger, he refused to activate the lights. What kind of moron was he? Logan crept toward the building.

Voices drew him into a crouch, and he stayed close to the rear of the building, thankful for the support for his dizziness. Reaching the corner, he peeked. He had barely enough light from a nearby pole to see three people standing in a triangular pattern. His chest tightened. He wasn't too late, but damn, the situation wasn't good.

His gaze like slits, Donald Brookson aimed a pistol at Wendell.

Off to the side, Rachael stood with one hand over her mouth and the other on her belly.

To complete the triangle, Wendell held a bat in his hand and thumped it onto a nearby log. "The gun will do you no good, Donny. I took out the firing pin." He stepped toward Brookson while pounding the bat into his opposite palm.

Hissing, Brookson took aim and fired. Nothing but clicks. "Damn you." He threw the gun at Wendell, then shot his gaze to Rachael. "Damn to both of you."

Laughing, Wendell raised the bat into a striking

position.

Fighting another wave of dizziness, Logan clenched his teeth but charged after Wendell. Out of the corner of his eye, he caught movement.

Rachael had whipped something from her jacket pocket and extended her arm.

Holy hell, no!

****

"Give me your phone."

How in the world had Maddie incapacitated a trained undercover agent? She must have taken Logan by surprise and…Sky gasped. *The nunchucks*!

A surge of anger swelled within her chest, and her hands furled into tight fists. Anger combined with guilt flooded her heart. Hell, she just admitted she loved Logan. *Oh, God*! Did her words distract him? In hindsight, she should have waited, but then, if something happened to him—which it did—she'd never forgive herself.

"Yo! Where'd you go?"

Sky snapped her gaze to Maddie. "What?"

The woman waggled her fingers. "I said give me your phone. I can't take a chance of you recording our pleasant conversation."

Oh, damn. All the evidence collected thus far would be lost. Sky lifted her chin. "No."

Maddie sharpened her gaze. "Fine." She slipped her left hand from her pocket and pointed a thirty-eight snub-nosed pistol at Sky's chest. "Now, give me the phone."

Ah, well. Since she asked so nicely. Sky huffed out a breath. Her chest felt a little too tight, and the feeling probably stemmed from the gun pointed her way. She might have ninja speed, but a bullet was faster. So, a phone wasn't worth losing a life. Sky slipped the device from her pants pocket and held it out.

"Toss it to the ground. And I want that watch and the earpiece."

How did she know about…oh, right. Logan. She debated aiming the objects at Maddie's head, then take her down with a few swift blows. But one gnawing question would not go away. "Why are you doing this, Maddie?"

"No questions until you give me the phone." She waved the gun and grinned. "I really don't want to shoot Skylar Dawson."

All right, I'll play this through. Sky flung the phone toward Maddie's feet, followed by the watch and earpiece.

Maddie promptly stomped on the device several times until the plastic shattered. She did the same to the watch. "There. That's better. Now, to answer your question, we're doing it for money, of course." She pointed the nunchucks toward the lodge. "FYI, with Donny heading for the great beyond, all rights to this property passes to Rachael."

Oh, my. Maddie didn't know. Should Sky tell her? *Well, hell, yeah.* Only for a chance to spare Donald's life. While releasing a slow breath, Sky passed a hand through her hair. By all appearances, she might look as if her gaze left Maddie, but in truth, she watched the woman like a hawk. "It's a logical assumption—being married and all." She dropped her hand. "But Donald changed his will. That's why he was in town and met you at the coffee shop. He just came from his lawyer's office."

Maddie narrowed her gaze into thin slits. "You're lying."

"Nope." She shrugged a shoulder. "Sorry."

The woman growled. "That bastard never said a word, and I doubt Rachael knows. Did he say who was to inherit?"

"No, but it's none of my business."

Maddie shook her head. "That stupid jackass. All along, he's been a thorn in Rachael's side. She received offers to sell Chadbury Lodge, but Donny won't even discuss the subject. Her highest offer to date is twenty-four mil. Donny's a fool to dismiss an amount that would make him and Rachael comfortable. He'd rather keep Chadbury Lodge as a second-rate destination." She cursed under her breath. "This complicates matters." Tapping the nunchucks against her leg, Maddie pursed her lips and frowned. After a minute, she released a heavy sigh. "Well, too late to change our plans. By now, the man should be dead. Rachael has enough money socked away to keep us comfortable for a while." She shot Sky a glare. "Looks like I'll have to take care of you first."

A gunshot echoed through the trees.

Logan! Skylar snapped her head in the direction of the sound, and her gut rolled. Her firearms education hadn't progressed to the point where she recognized one shot from another. For all she knew, the sound could be from a small cannon.

Madeline snickered. "Relax, honey. That was the lovely sound of Rachael finishing the job. Oh, and don't worry. She didn't use your fiancé's gun. I have his weapon right here." She waved the gun in her hand.

She has Logan's gun? *Well, yes, of course, she*

does. Even as a well-trained agent, Logan couldn't avoid the nunchucks.

Sky studied Maddie in the dim glow of the pole lamps. An opponent holding a pair of nunchucks need not be close to their victim for a powerful blow. Maddie could have hidden behind a bush and, as Logan passed, swung the weapon. She cringed at the thought. *All right, focus.* She closed her eyes for a brief second before concentrating her attention on Maddie and the gun pointing at her chest. Sky sucked in a controlling breath. "Did you kill Logan?"

With a soft laugh, Maddie shrugged. "He could be dead. I might have hit him a little too hard with these." She raised the hand holding the nunchucks, then met Skylar's gaze. "You and your fiancé have created a bit of a dilemma." Gaze steady, she pursed her lips. "I suppose your boss is on the way?"

"Yes, he's on his way." She wasn't about to deny it. What would be the use? The game was up. Madeline could easily kill Sky, Logan, and whoever else created an obstacle, but where would she go? Sky pointed a finger at Maddie. "You could give up. You know, stop before the bodies pile into a heap."

With a cutting gaze, Maddie sneered. "Oh, you are so funny. Shut up, and let me think." She chewed on her lower lip. "Another gunshot will raise questions and go contrary to our plans."

That was good news. Sky could handle the nunchucks far better than a bullet. Across the compound, movement near cabin number two caught her eye, but the building was so far she could be seeing an animal out for a late-night stroll. She shifted her attention back to Maddie.

Frowning, Maddie eyed Sky with a steady gaze. "I could kill you and worry about the gunshot later."

A chill shot up Sky's spine, not from fear but from the coldness in Maddie's voice. Given the opportunity, the woman could turn into a serial killer. But Sky wasn't about to stand here and waste time. She needed to investigate the gunshot, find Logan, and see if he was all right.

"You might be fast, Skylar Dawson, but you're not faster than a bullet." Smiling, she released one of the nunchucks and dangled it by her side.

Well, this was indeed a dilemma. Nunchucks, Sky could handle. Add a gun? *Oh, boy*. And it looked as if Maddie intended to use both. But killing Skylar Dawson with a gun would not satisfy Maddie, not when the woman studied all the videos. Taking a step to the side to get her feet in position to swing, Sky unfurled her fists. "Really, Maddie, you said you didn't want to shoot me. I took that as your challenge to show off your MA skills."

Maddie pursed her lips. "Maybe."

"No maybe about it. You have nunchucks to give yourself an edge." Of one fact Sky was certain. No way in hell could Maddie control two weapons at once. One or the other had to go.

Grinning, Maddie twirled the heavy stick.

The woman was a fool. She could easily hurt herself, but judging from the glint in her gaze, Maddie had the confidence to use the weapon properly. Whether her confidence was justified remained to be seen. "How long have you studied martial arts?"

Maddie twirled the stick faster. "Long enough."

Unlikely. Maddie's arrogance showed. She was

undisciplined. Sky shifted several steps to the right.

"Don't try to run, hon. I'd hate like hell to shoot you in the back." Still twirling her weapon, Maddie shifted closer to Sky. "How could you become an agent for Monroe Security?"

"I'm their martial arts instructor. My boss dragged me off the mat because your brother told Brookson about your skills, and Donald had a pregnant wife to protect. He was scared."

Snickering, she shook her head. "How thoughtful of him."

"FYI, Skylar Dawson does not run." Sky pointed at the gun. "Two weapons against none. You can shoot me, but you don't get bragging rights by using a gun. If, however, you kill me with the nunchucks, you can brag all you want." Of course, Maddie would be charged with murder, but Sky wouldn't mention that little tidbit. She pursed her lips. "What if I don't want to play?" *My, my*. Even in the darkness, Sky caught the flash shoot from Maddie's gaze. "Look, Maddie, if you watched all my videos, then you know what I'm capable of doing. Why don't you surrender?"

"Don't make me laugh. Truth is I know who I'm up against. You do not." Gun held steady in her left hand, Maddie again twirled the nunchuck with her right. She took a slow step toward Sky and swung the stick.

A tease, for sure. Maddie could have easily reached. But holy moly, her gaze glinted with pure evil.

Another swing. Another miss.

That one came a little closer. Her next swing would be for impact. But the harder the swing, the better chance of uncontrolled recoil. Maddie should know this.

Laughing, Maddie slipped the gun into her pants pocket and took a stance worthy of a nunchucks attack with knees bent and body facing forward.

Putting away the gun was a surprise move, but Sky took the advantage given her. If Maddie was cocky enough to challenge a three-time black belt expert, then she practiced…a lot. Caution was required.

Twirling her weapon, Maddie swung.

Sky ducked. The whoosh of the nunchuck close to her head confirmed a miss by mere inches.

Still laughing, Maddie stepped forward and swung again.

Using the speed that earned her reputation, Sky caught the stick with her left hand, whirled, then threw her right elbow into Maddie's face. She connected solidly with her opponent's temple.

Maddie staggered, but her grip stayed firm on the other stick. She pulled Sky forward and lifted a knee.

In a split second, Sky turned, caught Maddie's upraised knee, and flipped the woman.

With a gasp, Maddie released her grip on the nunchucks and hit the ground with a loud *oomph*. Doing a flip worthy of a yoga instructor, she jumped to her feet and swung a leg at Sky's face, missing by inches. Another swing. Then, another.

Sky avoided all three with a simple tilt of her head. The damn woman was becoming an irritating pest. Brave, too—or crazy. Now that Sky held the nunchucks, she could easily demonstrate their proper use, but she didn't want to kill Maddie—yet.

"Fight me, dammit!"

The woman was a glutton for punishment. "I don't

want to hurt you, Maddie. But I am impressed by your skills."

Growling, Maddie withdrew the gun from her pocket.

Aw, hell. Now, that isn't nice. Before the woman could take aim and fire, Sky whirled and connected her left boot to the side of Maddie's head.

Maddie hit the ground with a thud and stayed.

Smirking, Sky leaned over the unconscious body. "Never challenge an expert."

Chapter Twenty-Five

Lifting Maddie's hair out of the way, Sky checked the woman's carotid artery for a pulse. Relief shot through her to feel the steady beat against her fingers. Since her kicks were capable of breaking someone's neck, Sky had to be very careful to hold back a little. Maddie almost received the full force of her boot because—well, dammit—she hurt Logan, and Sky was equally tempted to hurt her. The woman should consider herself lucky to be breathing.

Sirens echoed through the forest—lots of sirens. Sky snapped her gaze toward the sound. Within seconds, flashing lights brightened Chaddy-Wonker Drive and lit the resort grounds like a Christmas tree as one car after another sped down the drive. Two ambulances followed.

Briefly closing her eyes at such a wonderful sight, she said a silent prayer of thanks. But who called the police? Logan? Or how about Tank? Could he be the movement she saw near cabin two? Really, though, she'd take help any way it came.

Since she had nothing to secure Maddie and couldn't leave weapons within easy reach, Sky took the gun from where it fell alongside the unconscious woman. Then, she patted Maddie's pockets in search of a car or truck fob. Finding none, she double-checked for the safety lock on the pistol, then slipped the gun

251

and nunchucks into her cargo pants pockets. Next, with the intention of restraining Maddie, Sky hurried to Wendell's truck and scanned the bed for rope. She found only gardening tools. Swinging open the driver's door, she dug through a multitude of trash in the back seat. The entire truck resembled one big trash bin— nothing but fast-food wrappers, crushed plastic bottles, and crumbled takeout bags. *Yuk.*

If she couldn't secure Maddie, then she'd make damn sure the woman couldn't drive away. Switching to the front of the cab, Sky slid her hands over the bench seat in search of the key fob, lowered the sun visor, then checked under the floor mat. Nothing. If the fob was anywhere within the truck, it would send a signal to the computer. She pressed the *Start* button. Nothing happened. Satisfied that Maddie couldn't drive off into the night, Sky closed the truck door and ran toward the Brookson house.

Oh...wait! All the flashing lights illuminated the maintenance building. She detoured through the trees, past the tennis courts and pool, until rounding the side of the building where all the activity congregated.

Spotlights from the emergency vehicles turned night into day.

Two paramedics worked on someone on the ground, while a third medic rolled a stretcher toward them.

Her heart lurched. Was the victim Logan? Biting her lip, she edged closer, then stopped. Donald Brookson! The man was alive and looked as if he'd been shot in the left rear shoulder. What the hell happened here?

Cops struggled to restrain a wild Wendell who

cursed up a storm.

Rachael was handcuffed and being eased into the rear seat of a police car.

Ignoring the tightness in her chest, Sky searched the scene for Logan and spotted Tank standing off to the side. He was a sight for sore eyes, and she released a long breath.

Tank nodded and pointed toward the left.

Sky followed his direction and spotted Logan on a stretcher by an ambulance. With her heart taking a flying leap, she ran over.

"That's far enough, ma'am."

Almost plowing into a police officer in full SWAT gear, she skidded to a halt.

"Let her be."

At the sound of the familiar voice, she nearly jumped into his arms.

Robert Monroe approached and wrapped her in a hug. After a gentle squeeze, he held her at arm's length and studied her face. "Are you okay?"

She nodded, too full of emotion to speak. Forcing in a deep breath, she swallowed. "Logan?"

"He'll be okay. Maddie?" He raised a brow.

Cringing, she threw a thumb over her shoulder. "She's on the far side of the lodge, in a clearing beyond a large clump of bushes. She was still unconscious when I left. I had no restraints, Bob. She might have regained consciousness and run off on foot. I found no car keys in any of her pockets. And yes, she is part of this elaborate murder plot. I'll explain later—after I see Logan."

Suppressing a smile, he twitched his lips before turning to the officer in full SWAT gear. He relayed her information.

Raising a hand, Sky stopped the officer. "She has decent martial arts skills. Please, watch yourself." She turned to Monroe. "Can I see Logan now?" She didn't wait for an answer. She ran to the stretcher, ready to push aside any more interruptions. Nearing him, she stopped, and her breath froze.

Oh, my God! Blood covered the left side of his head and had saturated the shoulder of his black sweatshirt. His eyes were closed, and his face pale, but he grimaced as a medic wiped off some of the blood on his face. She almost burst into tears and had no clue why. Because she loved him? Well, yeah, that plus Maddie could have killed him. She bit her lip. "Logan?"

Eyes popping open, Logan peered around the paramedic. He released a long breath. "Thank God, you're all right."

Too choked up to respond, she approached the right side of the stretcher, grabbed his hand, and squeezed. She wanted to kiss him, but hey, the paramedic wouldn't think too kindly of being shoved to the side.

Monroe walked up behind her. "Sky, Logan, this is Chief Tom Snyder."

The chief was a short, rotund man with gray hair at the temples and a kind face. His body shape reminded her of a nursery rhyme about the egg falling off the wall.

The chief stepped forward. "Tell us what happened, Mr. Greene."

Logan cringed as the medic pressed a gauze pad to the back of his head. "I didn't get far after I left our cabin. Someone struck me from behind, and I woke up tied to a tree."

Sky stroked his hand. "Madeline hit you with nunchucks, Logan."

Raising his brows, he winced. "Maddie? I blamed Wendell...hey!" He pulled away from the medic and shot him a glare.

"I'm sorry, sir, but I need to wrap this wound."

"Yeah, okay, sorry." Wincing again, he focused his gaze on Sky. "Nunchucks? No wonder my head is killing me. It feels like it's split wide open."

The paramedic, a young man with black hair, leaned over. "It *is* split open, sir." He continued wrapping Logan's head.

Logan closed his eyes for a few seconds, then opened them again. "Once I freed myself from the restraints, I stumbled over to the maintenance building to see all three suspects in a standoff. Brookson had a gun, but Wendell had removed the firing pin. Wendell went after Donald with the bat, and you know, I didn't think Donald had it in him, but he wrestled Harris to the ground like a pro."

Monroe chuckled. "Donald Brookson holds several college wrestling records. He was actually a contender for the Olympics."

Sky glanced toward the medics working on Donald. They were loading him onto a stretcher. The teddy bear could handle himself, after all.

Logan coughed and flinched. "Next thing I know, Rachael pulls out a gun and shoots Brookson in the back. I couldn't get to her fast enough, but Tank sprinted onto the scene and disarmed her." He glanced at Monroe. "My gun's missing."

Sky released his hand. "No, I have it. I took it from Maddie." Sky slipped the gun from her pocket and practically shoved the weapon at Monroe. Everyone at the firm knew how she detested guns. *See? Not agent material.* She also dug into her pocket for the nunchucks and handed them over. "Maddie hit Logan with these."

Taking the gun and double-checking the safety, Monroe sniffed the barrel. "No gunpowder smell, so it hasn't been fired." Handling the nunchucks by the chain, he slipped them into a plastic bag and handed the bag and Logan's gun to the chief. Turning back to Sky, he smiled. "Pam called and said she lost Logan's signal. I contacted Tank and told him to get inside the complex. Then, Pam called a second time to tell me she lost *your* signal. That's when I notified Chief Snyder and told him to meet me here."

The medic finished another blood pressure check on Logan, then unclipped a small oxygen reader from his finger. "You need an X-ray and stitches, sir." He turned to Chief Snyder. "Any objections?"

Sky shot her gaze from one man to the other. "Can I go with him?"

Chief Snyder stepped forward and jammed his fists onto round hips. "We'll need statements from both of you. Mr. Monroe and I will follow the ambulance to the hospital."

Once Logan and the stretcher were loaded, Sky hopped inside and immediately bent to kiss him. She gazed into his tired eyes. "I was afraid Maddie killed you." She lowered onto the bench seat alongside the stretcher. "Maddie and Rachael had everything planned and a twenty-four million dollar incentive to carry it through. It's a wild story, but Donald never told Rachael about changing his will." God, he looked so tired and pale. She wanted to kiss him again, but the medic was fussing with the blood pressure cuff on his arm. *Oh, what the hell.* She snuck in a kiss anyway.

****

While Sky waited for Logan to return from a CT scan of his skull, she stepped outside the emergency room doors with Monroe and Chief Snyder to pass on the details of her encounter with Madeline Harris. "She destroyed my phone, Bob. It had proof of what she said. Otherwise, it's her word against mine."

Monroe looked at Chief Snyder. "With your permission, I'll have my man search for her phone and let my IT tech salvage what she can."

While scratching the back of his neck, the chief nodded.

Monroe immediately dialed Tank and gave his instructions. Finished with the call, he faced the chief. "Tank told me your men found the phone and bagged it as evidence."

With a half-smile, Snyder took out his phone and hit a few buttons. He spoke to a detective and relayed his instructions to hand the phone over to Tank Davenport. After replacing his phone to his pocket, he sighed. "I'd have to send something like that to our state police, then wait a month or better for results." Frowning, he, again, rubbed the back of his neck. "Mrs. Brookson claims she shot her husband by accident and that she actually aimed for Wendell Harris. She also swears Wendell took the firing pin out of Donald's gun without her knowledge. In other words, she's sending him up the river."

Wow. No loyalty on Rachael's part. "And, of course, she so happened to have a gun that worked perfectly. What did Donald say?"

"He contradicted his wife at every turn." He scratched his nearly bald head. "If all we have is conflicting statements, this case will be a tough one to prove. A recording would be a tremendous help." Chief Snyder turned to Sky. "Did you discover who ran you off the road?"

"Yes, it was Wendell. Rachael delayed me long enough for him to get into position for an ambush." She covered her mouth to hide a yawn, then glanced at the ER doors. "Do you think he's back yet?" She hoped like hell Logan wasn't badly hurt. Would he have to stay the night? If necessary, she'd sleep here—if the doctors allowed her.

Monroe placed his large hand on her shoulder and squeezed. "You did very well...again. I'm proud of you, Sky." Before dropping his hand, he patted her shoulder. "We still need statements from you and Logan, but it's getting late. If the chief has no objections, then we can do the paperwork tomorrow."

Chief Snyder shrugged. "No objections. I have enough to hold our three perpetrators." He checked his watch. "I suspect you'll be here for quite a while, Ms. Dawson. Let's meet in my office around one."

"Early afternoon is perfect." She glanced between Monroe and the chief. "If the hospital doesn't keep Logan, we'll need a ride to the resort."

Snyder waved a hand. "I'll have an officer waiting outside to escort you." He faced Monroe. "If you're ready, we'll head back to the resort."

Nodding, Monroe turned to Sky. "I'll pick you up a

little after noon time and drive over together. Sound good?"

"I won't have a phone to tell you if we made it back to the cabin. The best I can do is call before we leave the hospital." She hoped they wouldn't keep Logan, but without knowing the severity of his injury, her entire night was up in the air. After waving goodbye to Monroe and Snyder, Sky re-entered the hospital and found her way to Logan's bay.

An orderly had just pulled the curtains. Smiling, he held open the slit.

Thanking him, she stepped toward Logan's gurney. His eyes were closed, and his face pale. A big white patch covered his injured area. With his bloodied sweatshirt in the trash, he now wore a hospital scrub top that was one size too small. Her heart ached to see him hurt, and she silently cursed the woman who damaged him. Taking his hand in hers, she kissed his knuckle.

He popped open one eye and grinned. "I didn't think a nurse would get so personal. Give me a proper kiss." He puckered his lips.

She almost cried at his intact sense of humor, and every muscle in her body released its pent-up tension. She actually felt her knees go weak. Leaning over the rail, she obliged without hesitation.

Chapter Twenty-Six

Sky spent three more hours in the ER with Logan. X-rays showed a significant crack in his skull with the inevitable concussion and minor bleed under the bone, which the doctor assured her should heal on its own. After the doctor shaved a large section of his hair, Logan received twenty-eight stitches. An adhesive patch was placed over the area, which would allow him the freedom to shower. Otherwise, the dressing was to stay in place for ten days. *Miracles could happen.* Knowing Logan, he'd rip off the adhesive before that time. The hospital released him into her care with explicit instructions, and around two in the morning, thanks to a young police officer from Chief Snyder's department, she and Logan arrived at the cabin.

After a shower to wash the blood from his hair and body, Logan slipped into bed, grumbling.

She hid a smile. "What's the matter?" She had urged him into the shower first and was still fully dressed. She adjusted his bedsheets.

"I look ridiculous. I'll need a hat."

"You never wear a hat. Do you own any?"

He grunted in answer.

"Yeah, I thought so. Here, while you were in the shower, I put together a snack." A simple grilled cheese with a tall glass of iced tea should tide him over until morning. "I also threw your clothes into the washer. If you're okay, I'll run into the shower."

"I don't need a nursemaid."

"Well, you got one for a while. So, deal with it." She headed for the bathroom.

The last time Skylar played nursemaid was during her mother's cancer illness. Bathing and feeding a woman wasting away wasn't something she cared to repeat. Until the end, her mom's mind was sharp, and for that, Sky was grateful. Over the months, they created some precious memories that would stay with her forever. Even more important, she had a chance to say goodbye to her mom—unlike her father. He dropped dead at work, and even with CPR being initiated by coworkers, he never came back. She missed both her parents terribly.

By noon of the next day, en route to Chief Snyder's office, Sky sat squished between Logan and Monroe in the front bench seat of Bob's pickup truck. Along the way, she borrowed Monroe's phone to text Fay of their plans to return home. Knowing Fay, the woman would stock her fridge with food. Sky wouldn't know what to do without her.

When all statements were typed and signed, Monroe delivered them back to the cabin. "I ordered new phones for you two. Both will be shipped to your house, Sky." He leaned forward and shot a glance at Logan. "I'm making sure you stay with Sky for a while."

Logan harrumphed.

Once they were alone, she had a hell of a time keeping Logan from helping her pack their belongings. Really, what did it take to shove clothes into a suitcase? The stuff in the fridge went straight into a cooler. But the hardest part? She had to fight to drive *his* car. Just because she rode a motorcycle didn't mean she couldn't handle a vehicle. With the threat to sedate him, she finally got a hold of the key fob and drove them back to her New Jersey rancher.

Naturally, he protested and requested she drive straight to his apartment. Since he was being so difficult, he almost won. But she reminded him of the new cell phones to arrive in a few days. *That* shut him up for a while.

Thankfully, her nursemaid duties amounted to keeping the man still. Once she arrived home and had him propped with pillows on the sofa in a semi-darkened living room, she checked the freezer for one of Fay's wonderful casseroles. She wasn't disappointed. The freezer was loaded. She chose another shepherd's pie casserole and popped the dish into the oven.

Alone in her bedroom, Sky removed the engagement ring from her finger. For some reason, staring at the small piece of jewelry stirred up a slew of emotions. She didn't understand any of them. Sadness, maybe? Why? Did she really want to be engaged to Logan? Engagement meant marriage, and she wasn't sure she was ready for such a step. Before she searched for answers that weren't available, she opened the little black box and slipped the ring into its slot. Snapping the lid shut, she tucked the box into her underwear drawer.

After unpacking, Sky returned to the living room to hear a heavy sigh coming from the sofa. Smiling, she shook her head. "What's the matter now?"

Logan growled. "I don't like sitting around." He stretched for the TV remote on the coffee table.

Quick as a flash, she flew across the room and whipped the remote from his hand. "You heard the doctor. No eyestrain for at least three days. That means no TV, no computer, and no reading. After three days, you start gradually and see how you feel."

"What am I supposed to do in the meantime?"

"Rest. Listen to music. You're lucky the hospital didn't strap you to the bed and keep you."

He furrowed his brows. "I'd have walked out."

"Yes, we know. That's why you were discharged under my care. You can relax here, sit outside on the lounge, or chat with the guys on the manor's front porch."

He mumbled under his breath.

She almost laughed. He was like a little boy being punished. "Think you can eat?"

Gaping, he slapped a hand to his chest. "Of course, I can eat. I'm starving."

"Well, stay put. I'll serve you."

"I can walk to the kitchen. I'm not crippled." He swung one leg off the sofa.

She grabbed hold of his shoulder and gave as stern a look as she could muster. "Stay right there, buddy. No exertion for forty-eight hours." Shooting him a one-eyed glare, she waited for him to lift his leg onto the sofa, then placed her hands onto her hips. "You still have your headache, right?"

He crossed his arms over his chest. "Yeah."

"And you're still dizzy, right?"

Avoiding eye contact, he snorted.

"That's what I thought. We'll eat in here."

The timer for the oven dinged.

And not a moment too soon. Turning to hide the

smile stretching onto her lips, she headed for the kitchen. Over the years, she'd heard many women complain how men made the worse patients. Judging from Logan's steady pout, she had to agree. But he was cute. With luck, he wouldn't annoy the hell out of her over the next two weeks.

Reaching for a couple of dishes from the overhead cabinet, she took the casserole from the oven and loaded his plate with a hefty portion. With her plate, she served half the amount, but the aroma of beef and mashed potatoes whet her appetite. She added a little more to her dish and took a nice big sniff.

Taking Logan's plate and a tall glass of iced tea, she carried them to the living room. After handing over his dish, she dragged the coffee table closer to the sofa and placed his glass onto a coaster. Returning a minute later with her own dinner and drink, she sat on a side chair, facing him.

He waved his fork. "No, Sky, sit on the sofa with me." He bent his long legs. "I'll make room."

She'd never refuse. She liked being near him and especially enjoyed the subtle tingles his touch created. She settled in the opposite corner with his stocking feet resting against her thigh.

"I can't believe Maddie snuck up on me like that." He grumbled the words around a mouthful of food.

He had said the same exact statement twenty times already. Sighing, Sky smashed her casserole to allow the steam to escape. "Maddie had some impressive martial arts skills, Logan. Combine that with her yoga, and she could sneak up on anyone."

"She didn't sneak up on you."

After chewing her mouthful, she swallowed "In a

way, she did. The only reason she hadn't struck me with the nunchucks was because she wanted a confrontation. She told me she watched all my videos. In her mind, because she held a weapon, she assumed she had me at a disadvantage." She forked in another mouthful. Damn, Fay could cook. The red sauce alone was to die for.

"Well, Maddie can teach yoga in a women's prison." He chewed. "You were right about the baby being Wendell's. Rachael played him big time."

"Yeah, big deal. She'll go to prison, and the baby will go into foster care—that's assuming Pam can retrieve my conversation with Maddie." She lifted her tea glass from the table and took a big gulp. Sky usually brewed her own iced tea, but Fay saved her the trouble. The tea was nice and cold. She replaced the glass to the coaster. "I can't believe Rachael claims she shot Donald by accident."

"Yeah, well, her actions could be interpreted as protecting her husband. All she needs is a good defense lawyer." He ate several mouthfuls. After washing the food down with the tea, he sighed. "When did Monroe say we would get our new phones?"

"Within a few days." Amazing how lost she felt without one. Not like she frequented social media sites, but the device was useful for checking news and weather. She narrowed her gaze. "You will not be touching your phone for a while." She pointed her fork to emphasize her words. "And I don't want you to lie and say you're feeling fine."

He harrumphed.

With a heavy sigh, she pushed her food around on the plate. "You know, Logan, we nearly failed our mission. How do you handle something like that?"

"The guilt, you mean?" Shrugging, he lowered his dish to his lap. "Technically, we were hired to protect Rachael but were blindsided by a cleverly-crafted plan. Really, Sky, if Maddie had lain low, Rachael would have succeeded with a viable defense. From what I gathered, Wendell was to beat Donald with the bat. Then, Rachael would use her gun to shoot Wendell. But Donald spoiled their plan." He shoveled in another mouthful. "This stuff is good." He finished the last of his dinner and slipped the plate onto the coffee table. With his sock-covered foot, he nudged her leg. "Now, about us. Did you mean what you said?"

She finished the last of her dinner and placed the dish on top of his. This conversation was coming. She'd spent the last forty-eight hours with a chest far too tight to breathe. Why had she expressed her feelings just before he walked out the door? He wouldn't have been distracted to the point of nearly getting killed. Standing, she nudged him to move his butt closer to the sofa backrest, and she sat alongside while facing him. She touched the stiff stubbles along his unshaven jaw and gazed into his copper-colored eyes. "I meant every word, Logan. I'm sorry I took so long to tell you, and I'm also sorry I told you before you left the cabin. My confession distracted you, didn't it?"

He took her hand and kissed her wrist. "When I walked out the door, I was a happy man, but I'd hardly call myself a professional if I couldn't focus on my job. Did your declaration distract me?" He gave her a soft smile. "Truthfully, Sky, maybe a little, but Maddie came out of nowhere."

"If she swung harder, she would have killed you."

Again, she stroked his unshaven jaw and smiled. "I'm glad you have a hard head."

Gaze bright, he clamped onto the back of her neck and drew her close. His lips met hers, and he suckled. With his hand still behind her neck, he gazed into her eyes. "Now that we know how we feel toward each other, what should we do?" He released her.

With absolutely no desire to move away, she remained close, with her hip against his thigh and her face only inches from his. The tightness in her chest had eased, but now, a strange fluttery feeling filled her stomach. She bit her lower lip. "I'm not sure. I've never been this intimate with a man before."

He cocked his head. "We could move in together."

Oh, boy. Was she ready for that next step? Really, what the hell was she waiting for? They practically lived together now. "We could."

"We could also go into the bedroom and celebrate." Grinning, he waggled his eyebrows.

Giving him another one-eyed glare, she tapped his nose. "No sex for a week, buster. Doctor's orders. All our hot heat will raise your blood pressure."

He mumbled under his breath, then met her gaze. "What would you suggest?"

"How about a nice, slow walk around the property? We can stop in the gazebo and make out."

"That will *not* help my blood pressure, woman." He tapped a finger against her chin. "You are avoiding my original question."

Yeah, she was good at avoidance. Using her fingers, she lifted some of the loose hair off his forehead, then shrugged a shoulder. She kept her gaze locked onto his. "I don't know what we should do,

Logan. Can we just get you better and then discuss it?"

With the slightest smile, he stroked a finger along her jaw. "I can take you to meet my parents. They're still traveling in their RV but will be home in a couple of weeks."

The gentle tingles from his touch didn't do a damn thing to stop the panic tightening her throat. This was serious, right? Dear Lord, she couldn't even swallow. She had never in her life had a relationship progress this far. Pulling back ever so slightly, she raised her brows. "You want me to meet your family?"

He patted her hand and smiled. "They'll love you."

Oh, my. Shouldn't they try living together first? Yes, all right, she loved the guy, but meeting the parents was a very big step. "Logan—"

"Shhh." He pressed a finger against her lips. "Just think about it, okay? We can talk more over the next few days."

Her throat tightness disappeared and not because he offered a reprieve. She loved this guy too much to refuse. One way or the other, she had to pull up her big-girl pants and be brave. She swallowed hard. "All right, you're moving in."

He stretched his brows halfway into his hairline. "Really? When?"

"Starting now." They could discuss his parents another day. *Small steps.*

A word about the author…

Writing a cross between Romantic Suspense and Cozy Mystery, Jane Drager follows one cardinal rule—weakness is not an option. Her heroines are strong-willed, independent, and comfortable in their own skin. Throw them into a mystery, add a man to get hormones jumping, and watch the fireworks fly. Jane likes to keep the sex scenes to a minimum, focusing instead on the mystery that draws the two main characters together. Every novel has a happily-ever-after or a happy-for-now ending because—let's face it—the world is full of stress, and books are a great way to relax.
Visit janedrager.com

Other Titles by Jane Drager
All Chocolate, Extra Cherries
Ask Nothing in Return
Counting on Midnight, Midnight Sky series #2
Ice Cream Dreams, anthology
Infinite Choices
Memories for a Lifetime
No Plans for Tomorrow
Secrets and Assumptions
Secrets by Necessity
Testing Midnight, Midnight Sky series #1
The Riddle Key
Until We Say Goodbye

Thank you for purchasing
this publication of The Wild Rose Press, Inc.

For questions or more information
contact us at
info@thewildrosepress.com.

The Wild Rose Press, Inc.
www.thewildrosepress.com